*This special*
*signed edition*
*is limited to*
*750 numbered copies.*

*This is copy*

_110_.

# Plots and Misadventures

# Plots and Misadventures

## Stephen Gallagher

Subterranean Press 2007

**First Edition**

**ISBN**
978-1-59606-114-9

Subterranean Press
PO Box 190106
Burton, MI 48519

**www.subterraneanpress.com**

*Little Dead Girl Singing: Weird Tales*, ed. George H Scithers and Darrell Schweitzer, Spring 2002 (issue number 327)

*The Back of His Hand: Night Visions 8*, Dark Harvest 1990

*Restraint: Postscripts* magazine, ed. Peter Crowther, Issue 1, June 2004

*The Plot: Subterranean Magazine,*
ed. William Schafer, issue number 5, 2006

*Doctor Hood: The Dark* (Anthology, TOR Books), ed. Ellen Datlow, 2003

*Jailbird for Jesus: The Best British Mysteries* (Allison and Busby), ed. Maxim Jakubowski, November 2003

*Hunter, Killer: Night Visions 8*, Dark Harvest 1990

*My Repeater : The Magazine of Fantasy and Science Fiction,*
ed. Gordon Van Gelder, January 2001

*The Wishing Ball: Winter Chills 2*
ed. Peter Coleborn, BFS Publications 1987

*Like Clockwork: The Magazine of Fantasy and Science Fiction,*
ed. Edward L Ferman, March 1987

*The Blackwood Oak*: Original to this collection

*Tailpiece: Nine Horrors and a Dream: Horror: 100 Best Books,*
ed. Stephen Jones and Kim Newman, Xanadu 1988

# Table of Contents

*"A heartfelt thanks to all the editors and anthologists who have encouraged, supported and—importantly—laid out money over the years in which these stories were written.* And thanks to Professor Carole G Silver, author of Strange and Secret Peoples: Fairies and Victorian Consciousness, *for permission to use her elegant description of Paracelsus' Elementals in* The Blackwood Oak.*"*

# Little Dead Girl Singing

$\oint$ HERE'S one you won't have heard before.

If you're a parent with a musical child then you'll know the festival circuit. I don't mean anything that's big business or in any way high-profile. I'm talking about those little local festivals run on dedication and postage stamps, where the venue's a school theatre or a draughty church hall and the top prize is nothing more than pennies in an envelope. I'm talking about cold Saturday mornings, small audiences made up of singing teachers and edgy parents, judges whose quality varies depending on how their judgements accord with your own, and shaky little juvenile voices cracking with nerves.

As you might have guessed, I have been there.

Never as an entrant, of course. Even the dog leaves the house when I sing. But every young singer needs an adult support team rather like a racing driver needs a pit crew, to provide transport and encouragement and to steer them through the day's schedule. That's where the parents come in. Some children turn out with their entire extended families in tow, decamping with them from class to class like a mobile claque.

But not us. By the time Victoria was twelve we'd reached the point where she wanted as little fuss or pressure as possible. The thought of one of those three-generation cheer squads would have filled her with horror.

"One of you can come," she'd say. "And you're not to sit right at the front. I don't want to be able to see you."

This was last year. She liked to sing and she sang well, but she didn't like to make a big deal of it. So on the Saturday of the festival just she and I made the hour's drive to this tiny little town you've never heard of, way out in the middle of the flat country between home and the coast, with her entry slips and her piano copies and a bottle of mineral water.

They'd been running an annual festival here since nineteen forty-eight, and we'd done it twice before. This year Vicky's singing teacher had entered her for four different competition classes, spread throughout the day. The room where the earliest would take place was the one we liked least, the village hall with its high ceiling and tiny stage and no acoustic to speak of. Well, you could speak of it, but you'd have to shout to be heard at the back. And it was always so cold in there that at this time of year you could see your breath.

We sat outside in the car for a few minutes.

"All right?" I said. "Anything else you need?"

She shook her head. She didn't seem keen. I knew she'd had a bad throat for a few days and wasn't feeling entirely at her best, but in we went.

They'd already started and so we waited for an interval between competitors to find a seat. When the opportunity came, we dodged around empty chairs and a photographer's tripod and made our way down the hall.

The judge had her table out in the middle, while the spot for the singers was by an upright piano before the stage. The stage had a home-made backcloth for *The Wizard of Oz*. The judge was a woman in her late 'fifties, straight-backed, powdered, a little severe. None of which meant anything. I'd found you could never really get the measure of them until you heard what they had to say.

Vicky's name came halfway down the programme, so we settled in. The class was *Songs from the Shows* and the age group was the youngest. There was low winter sun coming in through the windows at the back of the hall and it was making the singers squint.

Early morning voices, little kids singing. Some in tune, most not, every one of them the apple of someone's eye.

Andrew Lloyd Webber was getting a real hammering. In the space of half an hour we had three *Whistle Down the Winds* relieved only by a couple of *I'm Just a Girl Who Can't Say Nos*. I recognised a few of the entrants from previous years. Only two young boys got up to sing and, bless 'em, you could tell that this was not their chosen element.

Vicky got up and did her piece. As she sat down beside me again she said, "That was rubbish."

It wasn't, but I knew that it wasn't a patch on what she could do at her best. But I also had that sneaking feeling that I'm sure I shared with every parent in the room, that out of this bunch I had the only real singer and the rest of them might just as well give up and go home.

We had a song from *Annie* and a song from *Les Miserables* and then another *Whistle Down the Wind*, and then the judge did some scribbling and called the next name.

She mispronounced it the first time and I looked at my programme to check... Cantle? But the name was Chantal, exotic enough amongst the Emmas and the Jennies. There was movement over on the other side of the room and I craned to see what a Lancashire Chantal might look like.

Up stood this little girl in a cardigan, with a bow in her top-knot and a dress that looked like funeral parlour curtains. She was tiny, and I reckoned she couldn't have been more than eight or nine years old.

She stood by the piano and waited for the judge's nod and then the accompanist started up, and then little Chantal sang a perfect piping rendition of *Don't Cry for Me, Argentina*.

Let me qualify that. It was perfect, but it was also horrible in a way that I still can't quite put my finger on. Her diction was clear and her intonation was bright. She hit all the notes dead-on, and she even acted the whole thing out.

But to see this eight-year-old doing such a precise imitation of mature emotion was like watching a wind-up doll simulating sex. She'd been drilled to a frightening degree. On one line her hand moved to her heart, on the next she gestured to the crowd. When the lines were repeated later in the song, she did exactly the same movements again in exactly the same way. There was a slightly American intonation there, as if she'd learned the words by listening to the movie soundtrack so many times that it rang in her head like tinnitus.

I looked for her mother. Sure enough, there she was. She had a little boy of about five or six beside her. The little boy was ordinary, fidgeting, eyes wandering, all his little-boy energies struggling against the imposed stillness like cats in a heavy sack.

The mother, though… she was as much of a study, in her way, as the little girl.

She wasn't old, or even middle-aged. But her youth was only there in traces, as if it had been harried out of her too soon. Her hair was a dirty-blonde froth of curls, cut short and pushed up high on her head above her ears. She was staring at her daughter as she sang, her lips twitching along. She wasn't mouthing the words as some of the mothers do, vicariously living the performance or, even worse, trying to conduct it from the side-lines. To me it seemed that she was just rapt, quite literally lost in the song, as the tenderest of souls might be overwhelmed by the greatest of artists.

I reckon you could have wheeled out Madonna herself and the London Symphony Orchestra, but you couldn't have given her a performance that could affect her half so much. And my cynical heart softened then, because whatever form it comes in, however it's expressed, it's hard to be critical of such uncompromising love.

The song ended. There was the standard scattering of applause, and the little girl's smile switched on like a bulb. Two seconds later it switched off again and she walked back to her seat as the next singer went up to take her place. Her mother bent over to whisper something but I was distracted then by a metallic bang from the back of the room, and I looked around to see a nondescript man noisily folding up his camera tripod.

The father, I assumed. My heart promptly hardened up again. I don't like it when people make it so obvious that they've no interest in the efforts of any other child than their own. It may be a universal truth, but I think we've all got a responsibility at least to pretend otherwise. Yet still you see them at school shows and concerts, not looking at the stage, flicking through the programme book, sometimes not even bothering to join in the applause. They're here to see the Third Wise Man triumph, and to them all the rest is just noise.

We've got a camera of our own, but I'd stopped taking it along. I'd started to find that if you make a big thing out of recording the moment, what you lose is the moment itself.

They stuck it out for one more song, which was about as long as it took for him to pack the video gear away, and then in the gap between entrants the four of them got up and left. The girl went out in front and her brother got dragged along behind, bobbing around in his family's wake like a rag-doll caught up on a motorboat.

We slipped out ourselves about ten minutes after that. Done quietly, it was no breach of etiquette. The class was running late and we had another one to get to, so for this one we'd check the results and pick up the judgement slip later in the day. That was how it worked; young singers and their minders in constant motion from one hired room to another, getting nervous, doing their best, hoping for praise, fearing the worst.

We planned to get some lunch after the English Folk Song. They always set up a tearoom in the church but, being no lover of grated cheese and pickle sandwiches, I had other ideas. On our way to the car, we stopped to pick up the slip from that earlier class and to check on the list of prizewinners.

Strange little Chantal had taken the first prize. Second and third places went to performances that I couldn't remember.

Well, what can you do? You note it and move on.

We got into the car and drove out toward the coast, which was only another three or four miles. I thought a change of scene would be a good idea. I could sense that Vicky was unhappy; not peevishly so, just unhappy with her own performance, unhappy with the way she felt, unhappy with the day ahead and the sense of a course to be run that had no great promise of satisfaction in it.

After being quiet for a few minutes she said, "I don't think I want to go back."

"No?"

"I just want to go home. There's no point."

I said, "If that's what you want, then fine. I'm not going to force you to stay. But be sure in your own mind that you're not throwing it in for the wrong reasons. All right?"

"Mmm." She was looking out of the window.

We found a cafeteria over an Edwardian parade and, wouldn't you know it, they'd run out of ham for the sandwiches but had no shortage of grated cheese and pickle to offer.

Over lunch, we talked about the morning. Specifically, about Chantal's win.

"I can't say she didn't deserve it," I said. "Technically she's very impressive and in two or three years' time there's a chance she'll be really good. Right now I'd say she's been drilled too much. She's very mechanical and over-controlled. But I'd also have to say she's got an obvious natural gift. From here it'll depend upon how naturally it's allowed to develop, as opposed to being forced."

Vicky sat there sucking her Coke through a straw, not over-happy but not disagreeing, either. She needed a straw to keep the ice from bobbing against the metal of her brace.

I said, "And of course, we know for a fact that the room's got a curse on it and the judges are always peculiar."

I said it as a joke, but felt there was a grain of truth in it. This was the third time we'd had the same experience. It was a catch-all class that started the day, with the age range heavily weighted towards the very young. The prizes had always gone to shrill little girls who maybe didn't get the notes but did a lot of eye-rolling and arm-waving. The judges marked high on smiling and gestures, and some of the teachers played to that. A real singer probably flew right above the radar.

Well, it got her laughing when I said it was no insult to miss out on a prize in a freak show. And as we were walking to the car she said, "I think I *will* go back."

So instead of going home, we went back.

I was glad, because later in the day was when the big girls came in and the musicianship got more serious. Vicky was caught somewhere in between the moppets and the teenagers but when she sang amongst the best, she sounded as if she belonged there. Even if she didn't get a prize, it would be good for her to see it through. Prizes are nice. But what really matters is who your peers are. The quality of the people amongst whom you clearly belong.

We were laughing about something else in the car when it came to me. The little girl had stuck in my mind and had been troubling me for some reason, and I suddenly realised why.

I found myself recalling an image from a TV documentary that I'd once seen. It was about the second world war, the London Blitz. I don't know how old I'd been when I saw it, but it was an early and shocking memory. Outside a bombed-out house, this family had been laid on the pavement. One was a baby, clearly dead, but not in repose. Its mouth was open, as if caught in mid-chortle.

The image was in my mind now because it shared something with the face of the girl I'd seen that morning. I'd hate to say what. But if I close my eyes I can still see her now, eyes hooded with dark rings under them, her downturned mouth hanging slightly open, her tiny teeth like points.

I saw her again, about half an hour later.

We'd moved over into the church, which was a big improvement. Inside the church there were several large informal rooms as well as the wood-panelled nave, and they were decently heated. In the nave was the best acoustic of them all, and the best piano to go with it.

I slipped out while we were waiting for Vicky's turn in the British Composer set piece. She was complaining that her throat was dry and the water bottle was empty. She stayed behind in the hall.

The tea room was in the middle of the building and had no windows. Metal-legged tables and plastic chairs had been set up amongst the pillars, and service was through a hatchway from a kitchen staffed by volunteers. There were some uncleared plates and crumbs on the tables but otherwise the seating area was empty apart from me and Chantal.

I recognised her easily, even from the back. That topknot, that cardigan. Just like a dressed-up doll. She was drawing something aimless in spilled sugar on one of the tables, and she was making a singsong whispering sound as she did.

"Hello, there," I said.

She jumped. Not literally, but you could see her start. She turned around.

I said, "I heard you this morning. Congratulations. You sang really well."

I was sorry I'd started this. She seemed panicked. I'd spoken to her and she didn't know what to do or how to respond. Her eyes were looking at me but her eyes were empty.

I didn't know what I could say now.

"Chantal," I heard from behind me.

It was her mother. I glanced back and saw her. She didn't meet my eyes but her gaze kind of slid around me to her daughter, as if she knew I was there and she ought to acknowledge me... and she *was* acknowledging me in her own way, but her own way was not direct.

She muttered something about being late and the two of them went off together, with me stepping aside to let them by. I don't know if she'd been speaking to me or to her daughter. I felt like an idiot, to be honest, and I wished I'd kept my mouth shut.

More than feeling stupid, I felt a little bit spooked. That was one creepy family. Chantal's eyes had been empty until her mother spoke. But I can't say for sure what I'd seen in them then.

The rest of the afternoon passed by. Other classes came and went and the voices got better and better. We heard some thrilling sopranos and one beanpole of a teenaged boy who ran in late and sang Handel like a spotty angel.

Our final session was in the nave of the church. Vicky was more or less resigned to the fact that this wasn't her best day, and she was taking something of a gonzo attitude to it all now... by which I mean that she wasn't worrying about placing or prizes, but was just getting in there and doing it. Which I've always liked better. Do a thing for its own sake, and let anything else that comes along be a surprising bonus. That's how to be an original. That way you can't lose.

So there we were. The first thing that I noticed on entering the church, up on the empty balcony above our heads, was the nondescript man with his tripod and camera. Once we were in our seats, I looked around for the other three.

And there *they* were. The boy was in the middle. Slumped, glowering. He was the one I felt sorry for. He looked like the normal one in the family and I could imagine his patience being tested to near-destruction by a day like this. It must have been Boy Hell, having to get scrubbed-up and endure hours of boredom and sitting still in the company of grown-ups, and all for your sister in the spotlight.

Vicky was up third. She sang her piece, and sang it well. The throat problem hadn't gone and she was up against her limit by the ends of some of the lines, but in contrast to the morning she was warmed-up and relaxed, and it was a great room to sing in. The atmosphere was completely different. The piping-little-kid factor was almost completely absent, but then I had to remind myself that all these mature and impressive young singers had probably been piping little kids once.

While Vicky was singing, there was a sharp noise from one of the rows. It didn't throw her—in fact she told me afterwards that she hadn't even noticed it—but it made me look back.

Chantal's brother had dropped something, I guessed. Probably a hymn book from the rail in front of him. His mother was giving him a kind of gritted-teeth, staring-eyes silent scolding. I looked past him to Chantal. She was completely slack, as if she'd been switched off.

That was when I started thinking of her as a little dead girl, in her funeral home curtain dress. In fact I fantasised about the whole family of them living above the funeral parlour, and climbing into the boxes to sleep at night.

But not for long. My kid was still singing.

Even the applause sounded better in here. She sat down flushed, and I could see that she was pleased with herself.

Chantal was the youngest entrant in this class. She went up about twenty minutes later.

If anything, her performance was more extreme than the one I'd seen that morning. Her diction was so sharp that it was unpleasant to the ear. Every *r* was rolled, every *t* was a gunshot. Whatever had served her well before, she was doing more of it now. The lightbulb smile was a bizarre facepull.

I nudged Vicky and she followed my glance over at the mother. The mother was doing it again, her mouth unconsciously making the shapes of the words, living the song with her daughter. I couldn't see the balcony from my seat but I knew for sure that Cecil B would be up there, capturing it all on tape for endless home replay.

It was only the youngest member of the family who seemed to have used up all his reserves of team spirit. He wasn't paying his sister any attention at all. To be fair to him, he'd probably sat through this a hundred times at home. He squirmed in his seat and stuck an arm up in the air, stretching. His mother quickly pulled it down so he stuck it up again, instantly computing that he'd found a way to annoy her. She pulled it down almost violently now and he tried it a third time, but by then the damage was done. The movement must have caught the little girl's eye and distracted her for a second. She'd stumbled on her words. I'd only been half-listening but when she went wrong, I knew it at once.

So did her mother. God, now *there* was a look. Medusa would have asked for lessons.

When it came time for the judge to give his results, Chantal got a kind mention along with everybody else but Vicky got a very respectable second prize. It was all the more welcome for being unexpected, and she was only one point behind the sixteen-year-old who took the first. I'd have been happy at the fact that she'd held her own so well amongst such a high class of singers. But what the hell, it was nice to get an envelope as well.

"I bet you're not sorry you stayed," I said to her as everybody was gathering up their papers and their coats, and she made a face that could have meant anything.

Outside the church, the sky was mostly dark and streaked with red but there was just enough light to see by. Some of the sessions would go on into the evening, but quite a few of us were dispersing to our cars.

This was never my favourite kind of countryside. Far too flat and featureless. I imagine it had all been under the sea at one time, and the best thing you could say about it was that the views were uninterrupted.

Looking out now, across the road and the fields beyond, I realised that I could see all the way to the far horizon. On the horizon sat the disappearing rim of the sun, on a strip of ocean that was like a ribbon of fire.

In a minute or less, the sun would have dropped and the effect would be gone. I wasn't the only one to have my attention caught by it.

I could see Chantal about halfway across the parking area. She was out where there were few cars and she was alone. She was little more than a shadow-silhouette in the fading light but, as before, she was immediately recognisable.

I saw this little ghost take a faltering step, and then another. And then I saw her break into a run.

I don't know why. But it was as if she'd seen a doorway open up between the sun and the sea, and she'd set her mind to reach it before it closed.

Whatever was in her mind, she was running straight for the road.

I wasn't near enough to reach her. I looked around for her parents and saw them, loading their stuff into a brown Allegro. I'll swear to what happened then, because I saw it. I don't think anyone else did.

Her mother looked back over her shoulder. That's all she did. She didn't call out and she didn't even change her expression. Just looked at the running child, and the running child stopped about a dozen yards short of the road.

A couple of cars zipped by. Then the child turned and started back.

She climbed into the brown car without a word and they all drove off together.

As I said, that was last year.

This year, we went again.

Vicky had picked up a first prize in one of the classes in the city festival a few months later, and it had raised her enthusiasm enough for her to want another crack at this one. When the time came around, we sent in the forms. We skipped that perverse morning session, finally giving in to the lesson of experience, and went straight for the afternoon.

I remembered little Chantal, and when we got there I looked for her name in the programme. I felt a slight disappointment when I didn't see it. I was curious to see how she might have developed—at that age, a year can make a lot of difference in one way or another—but it seemed that I wasn't to find out.

Well, it was only curiosity.

But here's the odd thing. Chantal wasn't there, but her family was.

I knew it as soon as I saw Cecil B up in the gallery with his camera. Of course I immediately looked around the pews, and saw the mother with the boy. But no little dead girl.

The boy was in short pants and a clean shirt with a little bow tie. He was behaving himself. Or was he? By the look of him, you'd think he'd been drugged. He certainly wasn't the squirming livewire I remembered from the year before. In fact he had the same kind of slack, dead-eyed expression that I'd seen on his sister.

So if they were here, where was she? Could she have changed so much that I'd passed her outside and hadn't recognised her? I looked towards the doorway, expecting her to walk in and join them, but the stewards were closing up the room ready to begin.

The competition started, and the boy just sat there.

Until a name was called, and with a nudge from his mother he got to his feet.

Surprised, I watched him move to the piano. He took short steps. If body language could show a stammer, I reckon that walk is what you'd see. When he reached the piano, he turned to face the audience. And when the accompanist hit the first note, he switched on his smile.

The woman leaned forward in the crowd, her gaze intent, her lips already beginning to shape the first of the words. Upstairs, the man rolled the tape.

I looked at Vicky, and Vicky looked at me.

And down by the piano, when the moment came, the boy placed his hand over his heart, opened his mouth, and sang like a clockwork nightingale. ❧

# The Back of His Hand

§ BILLY had done a lot of walking and pacing that morning, mainly to keep himself warm. He'd marked out a stretch of the pavement across the road from the tattoo parlour, and by now he knew it like... well, like the back of his hand. As long as he kept to this same piece of ground, he'd know the minute that anybody came along and went inside. He'd tried the door several times already.

But it was still early.

There was a greasy spoon café almost opposite the parlour. It opened at eight, and Billy was on the doorstep when the proprietor came down and drew back the bolts. The proprietor was a stocky man, dark-haired and not so tall, and he seemed to be in sole charge with no help. He made no comment as Billy shouldered past him, leading with his well-stuffed kitbag. The café interior didn't look much, but it was clean. The warmth of the place folded itself around him like a blanket. He let himself relax a little, almost as if he'd been wound up tight by the cold.

He picked out a table that was close to the café's paraffin heater but which also was near to the window. The window was already beginning to mist up on the inside. He could still see the tattoo parlour from here.

When the man came over to take his order, Billy kept his gloves on and his hands under the table. The man seemed not to notice. Billy ordered the full breakfast with nothing spared.

Though Billy had his problems, lack of money wasn't one of them.

The man went around into the back, where he had a radio playing, and Billy could hear kitchenware being moved around on a range. It was a reassuring, almost homely combination of sounds. He yawned, and stretched his back. He'd been hitching all through the night, and had landed here in this seaside town at some utterly godforsaken hour of darkness. He'd zigzagged the country, leaving a trail that he was pretty sure would be hard to follow, and he'd kept his gloves on all of the time apart from when he'd needed to pee, and that he'd done only in locked cubicles on motorway service areas. Two gloves weren't necessary, but one glove would have looked odd. It might have attracted attention to him.

And attention was the last thing that Billy needed right now.

He'd never been here before. But the name of the place had stuck in his mind from just a couple of years ago when about a thousand bikers had descended on the place and settled in for a long Bank Holiday weekend. The bikers had been able to protest to the TV cameras about how misunderstood they were, the police had picked up plenty of overtime and had the chance to wear all their spiffy new Darth Vader riot gear, and the local traders had made a mint out of everybody; in fact, just about everyone had gone home happy although not one of them would ever have wanted to admit as much.

The town looked different now. The dawn sea battered at an empty promenade, and the wind howled through the deserted spaces of the new shopping centre. Most of the guest houses had hung out their *No Vacancy* signs and roped off the two-car parking spaces that had once been their front gardens. He might find a place here tonight where he could go to ground for a while, but it might be better to move on. It depended on whether he could face another night in transit. He'd never thought of himself as a soft case, but the last few hours had been the most miserable of his life. He'd waited out the time before daylight in the town's bus station, sitting with his bag and drinking weak piss-flavoured tea from a machine and trying to look like a legitimate traveller between destinations. A soldier on his way home, maybe; he reckoned that he could look the part and he carried a genuine forces kitbag as well, bought from Mac's Army Surplus Store. He'd watched a total of three buses come and go, all almost empty. In the phone booth he'd found a Yellow Pages with most of its yellow pages ripped away (there was no paper in the squalid toilet, and it didn't take a genius to put two and two together) but there had been enough of the directory left to tell him what he wanted to know.

He looked out through the fogging window again. No action across on the far side of the road. According to the listing, the tattoo parlour was the only place of its kind in town. The whole biker scene had led him to expect more but, what the hell, one was all that he'd need as long as it was the right kind of a place.

It looked like the right kind of a place.

There was no shop window. The entire facade apart from the entrance had been boarded up and painted white, and this had become a background for a riot of hand-drawn lettering by someone who clearly had an eye for colour and design, but who equally clearly wasn't a trained signwriter. The style fell somewhere between 'sixties psychedelia and freehand baroque; across the top it read STEVE, 'PROFESSIONAL' TATTOO ARTIST, and the rest of it crowded out the frontage completely. From here, it was almost as if the building itself had been extensively tattooed, as an example of the owner's craft. It was the inverted commas around 'PROFESSIONAL' that had impressed Billy the most. That showed an education.

Breakfast came.

Billy realised almost too late that he'd pulled his gloves off without thinking, and his hands were on the table. He quickly drew them back and slid them underneath as the proprietor set a huge plate before him. 'It's hot,' he said, and the stuff on the plate was still sizzling.

Billy waited until he'd walked away, and then he rearranged the sauce bottle and the cruet set and propped up the plastic menu wallet so that it would screen his hands from the counter.

He kept an eye on the parlour as he ate. It was his first genuine meal in more than twenty-four hours, not counting grabbed snacks and chocolate bars along the way. A couple of transport drivers came into the café shortly after he'd started, but they didn't sit close. On the pavement opposite a few people walked by the parlour, but no-one went in.

He'd finished. He ordered something else. It was starting to feel as if this was an open-ended situation that could last indefinitely. His attention began to wander, so that after a while he only belatedly realised that he was actually watching someone over at the door who had stopped and seemed to be about to enter.

He sat up, and paid attention.

It was a man. A youngish man, tall and skinny, with an unkempt thatch of hair and some kind of a beard. He wore thrift shop clothing and carried a plastic Sainsburys bag. Billy didn't get the chance to see much more because then the man was inside, the darkness of whatever lay beyond swallowing him up as the door swung shut to keep out the rest of the world.

He finished, and went over to the counter to pay. He held the canvas handles of the kitbag with his gloved hand and paid with the other, so that nothing looked suspicious.

Then he crossed the street to the tattoo parlour.

There had been a padlock on the door, now there was none. The hasp and staple, both new-looking, hung open; the hasp had been crookedly fitted and secured, not with screws, but with nails. One of them had been bent over and hammered flat—either the work of an amateur, or the world's least 'PROFESSIONAL' carpenter. As before, there was nothing in the frosted glass of the door to say whether the place was open for business, or what its hours were, or anything. Billy pushed, and it opened. He went inside.

There were no lights on downstairs, but a door stood open to the daylight of a grimy kitchen beyond the main room in which he stood. Billy could hear somebody moving up above.

"Hey," he called out. "Anyone around?" and he heard the movement stop. A moment later there was the sound of a hurried tread on an uncarpeted stairway, coming down. As Billy waited, he looked about him in the gloom. The walls showed the signs of bad plaster under too many layers of cheap redecoration, none of them recent. There were signs in the same flamboyant, spidery lettering as the frontage outside (*Strictly over 18s only—proof of age may be required*, and, somewhat less tactfully, *Not having a tattoo? Then Fuck Off*) and then poster after poster showing about a hundred different designs. He saw cats, dragons, jaguars, skulls, women, swords, daggers, scrolls…

"What is it?"

The man stood in the kitchen doorway. Seen from closer-to, he had the look of an aged juvenile. His eyes were of a blue so pale that he would probably always seem to stare no matter what he might actually be thinking, and his hair had a coarse, faded texture like curtains left hanging for too long in the sunlight. He seemed a sensitive type.

Unlike Billy.

"Look," Billy said, "before anything else, I'm talking five hundred quid and no questions asked. If that interests you, then we'll take it from there. If it doesn't, then I'm walking out now and I don't want to be followed. Is that understood?"

And the man said, "Five hundred quid? For real?"

"I can show it to you if you don't want to believe me."

"I'm interested," the man said.

And Billy, looking at him, thought Yeah, I reckon you are… because he knew a Junkie when he saw one, and this starved-looking specimen had to be one of the classic examples. So then he looked around and said, 'Well then, how about some light?' And the Junkie, suddenly spurred into nervous action as if being jerked out of a trance, turned around and seemed confused for a moment as if he was so overcome by the idea that he'd forgotten where the switches were.

The overhead tubes flashed once or twice, and then one of them came on. The other just glowed orange at both ends, as if in resentment of its brighter neighbour.

The room didn't look any better. Quite the opposite. There were old grey vinyl tiles on the floor, the self-stick kind that often don't. A few of these had lifted and shifted, exposing the grimy wood flooring underneath. There were four straight-backed chairs over against the wall, and in the middle of the room a single padded chair with a headrest that was somewhere between the kind that you'd find in a hairdresser's and the kind that you'd find in a dentist's. The dentistry image was continued in the form of the hanging tattooist's needle on the end of its balanced and jointed support arm, with a system of long rubber drivebelts and gearwheels running all the way back to the motor at its base. On the table alongside the chair were a rack of needles, some dyes, and a bottle of Savlon antiseptic.

Billy said, "Show me your hands."

The man frowned, puzzled.

Billy said, "If I'm going to pay you that kind of money, I want to see steady hands first."

"I've got steadier hands than you," the Junkie said, offended, and held them out; they weren't exactly rock steady, but they weren't unusually shaky either.

Billy said, "You shoot up already this morning?"

And the Junkie said, "That's none of your damned business. Now show me the money."

Billy put the kitbag on the padded chair, and unzipped it a little of the way. It was enough to show some of the bundles of used notes, most of them still in cashiers' paper bands, that were inside. The man stared.

Billy said, "You haven't even asked me what I want you to do, yet."

And the man shrugged.

"For five hundred, who gives a shit?"

This was going to work out.

So Billy zipped up the kitbag again and then removed his glove and rolled back his sleeve and he held out his clenched fist, knuckles upward to show the dragon tattoo.

"I want this taken off," he said.

The man looked at it. Billy guessed that he had to be casting a professional eye over the design. It had cost Billy a lot of money, some ten years before; his friends at the time had told him that the man they were taking him to was the best in Europe. He'd been a big fat slob who hadn't looked like the best anything of anywhere, but Billy had been interested enough in the designs he'd been shown. They made the ones on the walls around here look like fingerpaintings.

The Junkie looked up at him. "Taken off?" he said.

"Completely off," Billy said. "You can do that? I mean, you can do it here and I don't have to go into a hospital or anything?"

"I can do anything you want," the man said. "But am I allowed to ask why?"

"No, you aren't," Billy said. "Lock the door, and let's get down to it."

The man looked again, and shook his head in disbelief. And then he made a little shrugging gesture as if to say *Well, it's your tattoo and it's your five hundred, so what does it matter to me?*

And he went to bolt the door from the inside.

Billy looked at the chair. It had a padded arm support at right angles to the seat, and the armrest had worn right away to the dirty-grey foam at its end. He felt his heart sink. Much as he knew he needed this, he hadn't been looking forward to it. Billy hated physical discomfort, not least his own. That ten years before he'd almost fainted when, after much more than an hour with his eyes screwed shut and his teeth gritted and his insides scrunched up tighter than a washleather, he'd finally looked at the new pattern on the back of his inflamed hand and seen the tiny beads of blood that had been welling up from every needle strike. This was why he'd only had the one hand tattooed, instead of the matching pair that he'd intended. Much as he'd wanted the dragon design in the first place, he'd never been able to bring himself to go through the experience again.

And now he was sorry that he'd ever had it done at all... now that it was *that* close to landing him in jail.

"Shall I sit here?" Billy said as the Junkie turned from the door.

"Wherever you like," the Junkie said.

"Will it take long?"

"I shouldn't think so."

Billy took off his coat and climbed into the chair, and laid his arm on the rest. It was at right angles to his body, and raised as if to fend off a blow. As he was doing this the Junkie was scratching at his beard, looking down at the tattoo needles and other implements on the table.

"Is this going to hurt?" Billy said.

"Oh, definitely," the Junkie said, nodding absently.

"What about blood?"

"Lots of it," the Junkie said. "You don't make an omelette without breaking eggs."

"Oh, shit," said Billy, and turned his face away.

The Junkie said, "If it was me sitting there, I'd take something for it. Painkiller. You know what I mean?"

Billy turned his head back again and looked at him suspiciously. "You mean smack," he said.

"Not necessarily. There's other things you've never heard of. You wouldn't feel a thing and, even if you did, you wouldn't much care."

"These other things. Do they have to go in through a needle?"

"For something like this, yeah."

"Oh, shit," said Billy, "I hate needles."

"It's okay," said the Junkie. "I think I've got a clean one."

"Oh, shit," said Billy.

So the junkie asked for another fifty and Billy offered another ten, and they finally settled on the fifty because Billy hadn't got a clue how much the stuff was really worth and, besides, a hard light seemed to come into the Junkie's eyes which suggested that he'd conducted this kind of negotiation a thousand times before.

And, besides, Billy was getting scared.

"Wait here," the Junkie said finally, and disappeared upstairs.

Billy slumped back in the chair with a feeling of miserable resignation. He wished that he didn't have to do this. He liked his dragon tattoo, and would be sorry to see it go; he'd had it for so long that it was like a part of him, and he was hardly even conscious of it for most of the time. That, in a way, had been his downfall. When he'd been standing there at the Building Society counter with the replica Luger and the open shopping bag and the ski mask (courtesy of Mac's, once again), the last thing on his mind had been the chance of his tattoo being picked up by the cameras. He'd been wearing his gloves, but the glove had ridden down the back of his hand and uncovered almost all of the design.

And then two nights ago there he'd been, sitting at home with a few cans of Draught Guinness in front of the TV while his mother pottered around upstairs, when up had come one of those *Crimewatch* shows where they asked for help with real-life cases and all the TV people who wished they were working in movies got the chance to ham it up doing crime reconstructions. He'd been watching it all with a sense of professional interest when, in a segment that they called *Rogues' Gallery*, he'd found himself looking at his own last job from an unexpected angle. He hadn't recognised himself straight away, but then he'd felt an inner leap of joy at the realisation that here he was, making the big time at last.

But then the joy had turned to ice as they'd taken a part of the picture and blown it right up and there was his one-of-a-kind tattoo, filling the screen from side to side and clear enough to be recognisable.

He'd packed his kitbag and been out of the house without any explanation that same night, almost within the hour. They were saying that the police had linked him with a string of other jobs. There was even a reward. Some of the people that Billy knew, they'd have sold their own parents for medical experiments if there was a drink in it for them. And the worst of it was that the people whom Billy knew, also knew Billy.

Millions of people watched that show. Those who made it crowed about their successes every week, and Billy sure as hell didn't want to become one of those. Even if his own friends didn't turn him in for the reward money, he'd inadvertently given the police a gift that they couldn't ignore. Small-time though he was they'd stay after him, like a man scratching around in his own behind until he dug out the peanut.

Somewhere upstairs, coming down to him through the ceiling, there was the sound of a floorboard being lifted.

Less than a minute later the Junkie was coming back down the stairs, and when he appeared in the doorway he was holding the same supermarket carrier bag that he'd had in his hand when Billy had first spotted him. In his other hand, he held an ordinary kitchen plate. On the plate lay a hypodermic syringe, an unlit candle, and a soot-marked spoon.

"Oh, shit," said Billy, and looked away again.

"I told you, it's clean," the Junkie insisted, setting everything down on the worktop. "It's a brand-new needle. I take the old ones down to the clinic, and they do me a trade."

"Wait a minute," Billy said, and even in his own ears it sounded like the beginnings of a whine. "I'm not so sure this is a good idea. I don't want to get hurt but I don't want to get hooked on anything, either."

"Nah," said the Junkie, undoing Billy's cuff button and starting to push back his sleeve. "That whole thing's just a myth."

"Really?"

"Really," said the Junkie. "I've been using this stuff every day for the past four and a half years. If there was anything to it believe me, I'd know."

"I'm just going to look over here," said Billy.

The Junkie seemed amused. "You really that scared of needles?" he said.

And Billy said, "I'm not scared of anything, I'm just going to look over here."

A couple of minutes later, he said, "Was that it?"

"That was it."

"You're pretty good at this."

"Thank you. Just relax and let it start to work on you. I've got to find a few things in the kitchen."

Billy lay back and closed his eyes. Maybe he could feel something already, he wasn't sure. He thought you were supposed to get a rush all at once like you were coming your brains out, but it wasn't happening that way. He wondered what would be next.

He knew even less about the art of tattoo removal than he did about the art of tattooing. Some people said it simply couldn't be done with any success, others that you had to go to a really expensive clinic and maybe even have skin grafts and everything. But then he'd heard that what they did was to use needles to hammer bleach down into the skin, deeper even than the inks that they were being used to eradicate, and he'd thought Well, it doesn't sound pleasant but it doesn't sound too complicated, either.

And then he thought, the kitchen?

And he thought Oh my God, he's going to use ordinary household bleach, and he started to sit up with the intention of getting out of the chair and heading for the door without a single look back; he could maybe just wear a bandage and tell people that he'd been burned and his hand was taking a long time to heal, and then he could settle in a new town and meet new people and he wouldn't have to go through anything like this at all…

And then a great sense of warmth and well-being hit him all at once, and it was better than coming his brains out because, to be honest, he'd always had this little problem of self-control that he never liked to talk about and always had to apologise for, and he sank back into the padded seat and, hey, wasn't it just the best and most comfortable chair in the history of mass-produced furniture?

"Getting any effect yet?" the Junkie said as he laid a few things out on the table alongside, and Billy said, "I dunno. Maybe."

He let his head fall back. It felt as if it was sinking into the padding about a foot deep or more. He smiled stupidly.

"Last chance to change your mind," the Junkie said.

And Billy said, "Do it."

The Junkie asked him to flex his fingers and he did, and then he had to ask the Junkie if anything was happening because he couldn't feel any feedback at all. The Junkie told him that was fine, and so Billy turned his face to the sweat-scented vinyl in the knowledge that when he sat up again, it would be over. He could move on, start again; and if anyone came looking, he could hold up his hands and say *Who, me?* with total confidence.

Move on. That was about what it entailed, because with or without the tattoo there was no going home. Thought about in the abstract, back when he hadn't actually been obliged to make the break, the notion had even held certain attractions; there was a lot of shit in his life that he'd always reckoned he could happily leave behind, a lot of arguments and all kinds of resentments, but somehow he couldn't see it that way any more. He kept thinking about his video collection. Every Saturday afternoon he liked to hang around street markets and car boot sales, looking for old stuff that the video libraries were selling off. He had all the *Halloweens* except for the first one, every one of the *Friday the 13th* movies, and almost a complete set of the *Police Academies* except for the one that was too new to have made it through the system yet. All lost. His mother would probably give them away or even just throw them out, the way she had with his comics all those years ago. Some of those comics would have been worth real money today. If he'd still had them, he'd never have needed to turn to crime at all.

Obviously, his troubles were all her fault.

He winced. Something hurt.

"Sorry," the Junkie said. "This isn't quite as sharp as I would have liked."

He'd been drifting. That wouldn't do. The last thing he needed would be to fall asleep and then wake up with the job half-done and the Junkie gone and his bagful of money gone with him. Even worse… what if the Junkie followed *Crimewatch*? Stranger things had happened. He'd know that the reward was more than the five hundred that Billy had offered, and Billy could wake up surrounded by police.

But if the Junkie had ever owned a TV, Billy reckoned that he'd probably sold or hocked it long ago. Not much danger there. But as far as the security of his kitbag was concerned, he'd already shown the Junkie what was inside.

Better to stay awake.

Concentrating his attention as best he could, Billy searched around for a conversational opener and then said, "How long have you been doing this?"

"About ten minutes now," the Junkie said. "It's not quite as easy as I thought. I'm trying to do it neat and there's all kinds of stuff in the way."

"I meant, how long have you been doing tattoos?"

"I don't do tattoos," the Junkie said.

This struck Billy as not a bad joke at all. He said, "So what's the big sign over the door and all the needles and stuff?"

"Oh, they're Steve's. He's the tattooist. But he doesn't open the shop on Wednesdays."

Billy frowned in his stupor. "So, who are you?"

"I'm Kevin. I just rent the upstairs from Steve. The roof leaks and it's a dump, but he lets me have it cheap as long as I pay him cash. I think it's a tax dodge. But I owe him more than a hundred in rent and he was going to throw me out; this means I can pay him off and have some left over."

Billy let his mind work on this one for a while, to no great effect.

And then he said, "But if you're not a tattooist, how come you know how to do a tattoo removal?"

There was a long silence.

And then the Junkie, his voice sounding as if it was coming from a long way away, said, "You wanted someone who could take off the *tattoo*?"

Billy sat up. He could only manage about halfway.

He looked.

The Junkie was sitting there on one of the hard chairs from by the wall, looking politely puzzled. He was spattered with red from the chin down, as if he'd been mixing up something nasty in a blender and had forgotten to put the lid on. In one hand there was a big, none-too-sharp looking kitchen knife; in the other, a towel that he'd been using to dab his working area clean. On the padded support before him, Billy's wrist had been tied down with a length of bandage that appeared also to be serving as a tourniquet.

But the most curious thing about the entire scene was the clear piece of daylight that was showing between Billy's hand and arm.

The Junkie said, "Don't judge it by what you see right now. It'll look much better when it's finished."

Billy gawped at the sight. Couldn't take it in. Still he felt no pain, no sensation at all from the shoulder down. The Junkie was watching his face, trying to guess his mood.

He was lost for words. Except, perhaps, for the phrase *Hanging by a thread*, which dropped into his mind unbidden and wouldn't go away.

He didn't dare move.

Not an inch.

He looked at the Junkie.

And the Junkie said hopefully, "Do I still get the five hundred?" ❧

# Restraint

§ "DID you get a look at the driver who forced you off the road?" The woman in uniform had pulled up a chair to put herself right alongside Holly's hospital trolley, so that she could speak close and keep her voice low.

Holly made the slightest movement of her head, not even a shake, and was instantly sorry.

The policewoman spoke again.

"Your son thinks it was your husband's car. Could that be right? We've called your house and there's nobody there."

Holly meant to speak, but it came out in an unrecognisable whisper.

"Where are the children?"

"Out in the waiting room. They've been checked over and neither of them's hurt. Your neighbours said you left after some kind of an argument."

"I'd like some water."

"I'll have to ask if that's all right."

Holly closed her eyes, and a moment later heard the sound of metal rings sliding as the policewoman stepped out of the cubicle. Only a curtain separated her from the Saturday night crowd out in Casualty, and a pretty lively crowd they sounded. She lay with a thin blanket covering her. They'd brought her back here after the X-rays. It was a relief to hear that the children were unhurt, even though it was what she'd half-expected. That short trip down the embankment would have shaken them up, but it was only their stupid mother who'd neglected to put on her own seat belt after making sure of theirs.

That car. It had come out of nowhere. But if there was one thing that Holly knew for certain, it was that Frank couldn't have been at the wheel.

Why? Because she and Lizzie had struggled to lift him into the boot of their own car, not forty-five minutes before. And assuming he hadn't leaked too much and no-one had lifted the lid for a look inside, he had to be lying there still.

He certainly wouldn't be going anywhere on his own.

The young policewoman was back.

"I'm sorry," she said. "I had to stop an argument. I forgot to ask about your water."

"Where's the car?" Holly croaked.

"Still in the ditch," the policewoman said. "The accident unit can get it towed away for you, but you'll have to sort out the rest with your insurers."

This was seductive. The linen smelled clean, and felt fresh. Holly was all but exhausted. She'd been lifted, laid down, tended to. It would be so easy to drift. The racket right outside was almost like a lullaby.

But her husband's dead body was in the boot of her car, and the police were all over it even as she lay there.

"Can I get that drink now?" she said.

As soon as the policewoman was gone, Holly tried to rise up on her elbows. The effort it called for surprised her at first, but she made it on the second attempt.

She was in her underwear, her outer clothing piled on a chair that stood against the wall. She started to climb off the trolley and it hurt, but it wasn't too bad; nothing grated and nothing refused to take her weight. Her head ached and she felt a great overall weariness, but there was no one part of her that screamed of special damage.

The floor was cold under her bare feet. She stood for a moment with her hand resting on the trolley, and then she straightened.

At least she could stand.

She tweaked open the side-curtain and put her face through the gap. In the next cubicle sat a young man on a chair, holding a spectacularly bloodstained dressing to the side of his head. He was in formal dress, with a carnation in his buttonhole and his tie all awry. He looked like the type who owned one suit and wore it for all his weddings, funerals, and court appearances.

"I wouldn't call you a shitsucker," Holly said.

He blinked at her, uncomprehending.

"The man you came in with just did," she said.

He was up on his feet in an instant, and as he flung back the outer curtain she got a glimpse of the scene beyond it. The rest of the wedding party was out there, arguing with the staff and with each other. The bride in her gown could be seen in their midst. They rose in a wave as the bloodied guest was spotted hurtling toward them, and then the curtain fell back as if on the world's most energetic Punch and Judy show.

That ought to keep her policewoman occupied for a while.

Holly could feel the adrenaline pumping now, flushing her of all weariness and pain, leaving her wired and edgy and ready to roll. She dressed as quickly as she could, and then instead of emerging into the open she started to make her way through one dividing curtain after another toward the end of the row. In the next occupied cubicle, an elderly West Indian man lay huddled under a red blanket. In the last sat a scared-looking woman with a small boy. They looked up apprehensively as she appeared out of nowhere.

"Sorry to disturb you," Holly said. "Where's the children's waiting room?"

It was around a corner and separated from the main area by a short passageway and a couple of vending machines. Under a mural of misshapen Disney characters stood a basket of wrecked toys, some coverless picture books, and some undersized chairs across which a sleeping form lay. She woke up Lizzie, and dragged Jack protesting out of the corner playhouse in which he'd made a den. He quietened suddenly when he looked at her face. She took them both by the hand and they followed a yellow line on the hospital floor toward the exit.

As they approached the automatic doors, Holly saw herself in the glass. But then the doors slid apart, and they sailed out into the night to look for a taxi.

In the presence of the driver they asked her no questions, and they gave her no trouble. Lizzie was twelve. She was dark, she was pretty, good at her lessons and no good at games. Jack was only six, a beefy little fair-haired Tonka truck of a boy.

The roads were quiet and the taxi got them to the place on the ring road in twenty minutes. It was a good half-mile on from where she'd expected it to be. The police were gone but the car was still there.

"Do you want me to wait?" the cab driver said, but Holly said no and paid him off.

She waited until the cab was out of sight before she descended to her vehicle.

The children hung back on the grass verge, by the deep earth-gouges that marked the spot where their car had left the carriageway. Spray-painted lines on the grass and on the tarmac showed where the accident unit had taken measurements. Down in the ditch, they'd left a big POLICE AWARE sticker on the back window of her Toyota.

The Toyota was old and it wasn't in the best of shape, but it was a runner. Usually. Right now it was stuck nose-first in the bushes along with all the windblown litter at the bottom of the embankment.

The keys had been taken, but Holly groped around in the wheel arch where she kept a secret spare. As she crouched there, she glanced up at the children. They were watching her, two shapes etched against the yellow sodium mist that hung over the road.

Her fingertips found the little magnetic box right up at the top of the arch, deep in the crusted road dirt.

"Got them," she said. "Come on."

Lizzie was nervously eyeing the Toyota as she and Jack came scrambling down.

"What are we going to do?" she said. "It's stuck here. We can't go anywhere."

"We don't know that for certain yet," Holly said, tearing off the police notice and then moving around to open the doors. She didn't know what the procedure was, but they couldn't have looked inside the boot. However quick the glance, Frank would have been hard to miss.

Jack climbed into the back, without an argument for once, and Lizzie got into the passenger seat.

Once she was behind the wheel, Holly checked herself in the rearview mirror. At least when she'd hit her head on the roof, her face had been spared. Her vision had been blurred in the ambulance, hence the need for an X-ray, but that had mostly cleared up now.

Still, she looked a sight. She ran her fingers through to straighten her hair and then she rubbed at her reddened eyes, but of course that only made them worse.

"Here goes," she said, and tried the engine.

It started on the second try. It was sluggish and it didn't sound at all right, but it caught just the same.

There was no point in trying to reverse up the banking, but she tried it anyway. The wheels spun and the car went nowhere. So instead she put it into first gear and tried going forward, squeezing on through the bushes.

For a moment it looked as if this wasn't going to work either, but with a jarring bump they lurched forward into the leaves. Switches bent and cracked as the Toyota forced its way through. She glanced in the mirror and saw Jack watching, fascinated, as foliage scraped and slid along the window only inches from his face. God alone knew what it was doing to her paintwork.

They came out onto what looked like a narrow limestone track, which was actually a soakaway at the bottom of the ditch. Staying in low gear, she began to follow its irregular line. After about a hundred yards she was able to transfer across to a dirt road, which led in turn to a lane. The lane took them under the ring road and then around and back onto it.

Once they were on hard tarmac again, Holly permitted herself to breathe. But not too much. There was the rest of the night still to be managed.

And then—perhaps even more of a challenge—the rest of their lives thereafter.

She hadn't seen it happen. She hadn't even been in the house. She'd come home to find Frank lying awkwardly at the bottom of the stairs and Lizzie sitting with her head in her hands at the top of them. It might have passed for an accident, but for the letter-opener stuck in Frank's neck.

He wasn't supposed to be in the house. The restraining order was meant to take care of that. He wasn't even supposed to come within a hundred yards of his daughter, regardless of where she might be.

So, technically speaking, by being in the boot of the car he was in breach of the order right now.

Holly's first thought had been to pick up the phone and call the police. Her second had been that perhaps she could first wipe off the handle and put her own prints onto it and take all the blame. Then a sudden rage had risen within her. She'd looked down on his twisted body and felt no horror, no awe. No anguish or dismay. Just cheated. Frank had contrived to poison their existence while he was around; was there to be no end to it even with him gone?

She'd made the decision right then. They would not enter that process. If they moved quickly enough, they could put him right out of their lives and make a clean beginning. It would be a credible move; Frank could make an enemy in the time it took him to buy a newspaper, and any suspicion would be dispersed among the many. She'd looked at Lizzie and told her exactly what she had in mind.

*We can't*, Lizzie had said.

So Holly had sat her down and for ten solid minutes had laid out the choices for her, making sure that she understood how much depended on the next few hours. What was done was done, she'd said to her, and there's no changing it now. Don't feel you're to blame. It isn't a matter of right or wrong. Your father made all the choices that caused this to happen.

It had worked. Kind of.

They couldn't use Frank's car. Being in the motor trade he'd use whatever vehicle was going spare on the lot, and of late he'd been favouring a red coupé that was hardly practical for the job in hand. So Holly had backed her Toyota into the garage on the side of the house, lined the boot with a plastic decorating sheet, and together they'd dragged Frank through the connecting door and manhandled his body into it. Handling him was less of a problem than Holly had expected. In the unpleasantness stakes, Frank dead was hard-pressed to match up to Frank in life.

Once he was safely stowed and covered in a couple of old towels, they'd driven out to collect Jack from school and then set off for the coast. Fish and chips on the pier, Jack. It's a surprise treat. We just have to make a call somewhere, first. Somewhere quiet. You'll stay in the car.

And then the accident, and the plan forced off-course.

But back on it, now.

✧

From the ring road, they got onto the motorway. The traffic was heavier here, and it slowed when the carriageway narrowed to a single lane. For a long time there was no visible reason for it, and then suddenly they came upon a surfacing crew laying down new tarmac under bright worklights; a colossal rolling tar factory that belched and stank like a dragon as it excreted a lane-wide ribbon of hot road, men with shovels and brushes working furiously in its wake, supervisors in hard hats chatting by their vehicles.

"Look, Jack," Lizzie said. "Big trucks."

"Big, big trucks!" Jack said with awe, and turned in his seat to watch through the back window as they left the staged drama behind.

"You like the big trucks, don't you, Jack?" Holly said as the lanes cleared and the Toyota picked up speed again, but Jack didn't answer.

Holly couldn't put a finger on it, but the Toyota didn't feel quite right after the accident. She could only hope that it wouldn't let them down, and that the outside of the car wasn't messed up too much. A police stop was something that she didn't dare risk.

The next time she checked on Jack, he was asleep. His mouth was open and his head was rocking with the rhythm of the car. He slept the way he did everything else... wholeheartedly, and with a hundred per cent commitment.

For a moment, Holly experienced a sensation in her heart that was like a power surge. This was her family. Everything that mattered to her was here, in this car.

And then she remembered that Frank was in the car with them, too. Good old Frank. Consistent as ever. Bringing a little touch of dread into every family outing.

They left the motorway, took a back road, and drove through a couple of darkened villages. There was a place that she had in mind. Out to the north and west was a great bay whose inland fields and marshes were almost unknown beyond the region. At low tide, saltings and sand-flats extended the land almost to the horizon. Much of what was now solid ground had once been part of the sea. In places the sea was claiming it back, pushing the coastline inland so that fields and even some roads were being lost forever. Hide something well enough in the part that was disappearing, and...

Well, she'd have to hope. It was the best she could come up with.

Somewhere along here there was a causeway road that had once led to a farm, long-abandoned. People had trekked out to it for a picnic spot when there was something to see, but then the shell had become unsafe and it had all been pulled down. Now there was just rubble and the lines of a couple of walls, and that only visible at a low spring tide.

They crawled along, following the causeway with the Toyota's dipped beams. It didn't so much end as deteriorate steadily for the last couple of hundred yards. The concrete sections of the road had become tilted and skewed as the ground beneath them had given up any pretence of permanence. The sections had drifted, and in places they'd separated completely.

She had to stop the car and get out to locate the cesspit. When she turned back, Lizzie was out of the car and standing beside it.

She was looking around and she said, "Have I been here before?"

"Once," Holly said. "Before Jack was born. I brought you out here to show it to you, because it was a place my mother and father used to bring me. But it had all changed."

Lizzie tried to speak, but then she just nodded. And then her control went altogether, and her body was suddenly convulsed with an air-sucking sob that was shocking both in its violence, and in its unexpectedness.

Holly moved to her quickly and put her arms around her, holding her tightly until the worst of it passed. There in the darkness, out on the causeway, with the moon rising and this thing of such enormity to be dealt with. It would be no easy night, and no easy ride from here. Holly was only just beginning to appreciate how hard her daughter's journey would be.

"I can't do this," Lizzie whispered.

"Yes we can," Holly told her.

They got him out of the car into the pool and he floated, just under the surface, a hand drifting up into the pale shaft of dirtwater light from the Toyota's beams. The first stone sank him and then they added others, as many as they could lift. A sudden gout of bubbles gave them a fright. Holly was convinced that it caused her heart to stop beating for a moment.

They stood watching for a while to be sure of their work, and Holly sneaked a glance at Lizzie. Her face was in shadow and impossible to read.

"We should say a prayer," Lizzie said.

"Say one in the car," Holly said. "We need to get back and clean up the stairs."

Back on the motorway she watched for police cars, but she saw none. She *did* become aware of some lights that seemed to pace her for a while, but when she slowed a little the vehicle drew closer, and she was able to see that it lacked the telltale profile of roof bar and blue lights.

They had unmarked ones, of course. There was always that risk.

After a while, the headlamps in her mirror began to irritate her. She slowed even more to let the car pass, but it didn't. So then she picked up speed and tried to leave it behind; two minutes later and as many miles on, it was still there.

It surely meant nothing, but now it was making her nervous. Lizzie seemed to pick up on this. She saw Holly's frequent glances in the mirror and turned herself around in her seat, straining at her belt to look out of the back window.

"It's the same car," she said.

"What do you mean?"

"The one that pushed us off the road."

"It can't be," Holly said.

Lizzie clearly wasn't certain enough to argue the point.

"Well, it's similar," she said.

Holly increased her speed even further, up and over the limit, and the wheel began to vibrate in her hands as if the Toyota was beginning to shake itself apart. It couldn't be the same car. She couldn't imagine who'd want to follow her, or why.

It seemed to be working. They were leaving the other car behind, but then she saw something out of the corner of her eye. She looked down. The oil light was on, the brightest thing on the dash, and the one thing she knew about a car's oil light was that on a screaming engine it signalled imminent disaster.

She slowed, but it didn't go out. Other warning lights started to flicker on around it. So Holly quickly put the car out of gear and indicated to move off the motorway and onto the hard shoulder.

They coasted to a halt. The engine was already silent by the time they reached a stop. It had died somewhere during the deceleration, she couldn't be sure when. As they sat there, the cooling engine block ticked and clanked like coins dropping into a bucket.

In the back, Jack was stirring.

"Fish and chips on the pier," he said suddenly.

"I'm sorry, Jack," Holly said. "It's got too late. Another time."

The other car was pulling in behind them, hazard lights flashing. Right then a big bus passed them at speed in the inside lane, and its slip-stream rocked the Toyota on its wheels.

"Who is it, then?" Lizzie said, peering back as the other car came to a halt about fifty or sixty yards back.

"I don't know," Holly said. "Nobody."

Jack said, "Is it daddy?"

Holly looked at Lizzie, and Lizzie looked at her. There was a risk that Jack might have picked up on something then, but all his attention was on the road behind them. The following driver was getting out. Just as the car was an anonymous shape behind the glare of its own headlights, the driver's figure was a slip of shadow against the liquid stream of passing traffic.

"No, Jack," Holly said, an inexplicable anxiety rising up within her. "It can't be your daddy." She glanced down at the dash. All of the warning lights were on now, but that meant nothing. Everything always came on when the engine stalled.

"It *is*," Jack said.

Holly could tell him it wasn't. But she couldn't tell him why.

She heard Lizzie draw in a deep and shuddering breath, and let it out again. She found her daughter's hand in the dark and squeezed it once.

Traffic flew by, and the driver kept on coming. He was silhouetted against the flashing hazard lights of his own vehicle, pulsing like an amber heart.

Maybe he was your regular Good Samaritan, coming to offer them a hand.

Or maybe he was one of any number of things, as yet unrecognised and uncatalogued.

"He's been in the rain," said Jack.

Forget the oil pressure. Forget the ruinous cost of a thrown piston or a seized-up engine. Suddenly it was far more important to get herself and the children away from this spot.

But all the Toyota's power seemed to have gone. The engine turned over like an exhausted fighter trying to rise after a long count. She tried turning off the lights, and as their beams died the sound of the starter immediately improved.

It barked, it caught. All the warning lights on the dash went out, including the oil. She crashed the gears, checked her mirror once, and pulled out. Right now her only concern was to get moving again.

Jack was turned around in his seat, straining to see.

"Who is it, if it isn't daddy?" he said.

"It's nobody," Holly said. "Face forward."

"He's running after us."

"Jack," she said sharply, "how many times have I got to tell you?"

She was expecting him to give her an argument. But something in her tone seemed to make him decide, and he complied without another word.

Nothing that she was supposed to hear, anyway.

"It *was* daddy," she heard him mutter.

She knew it wasn't, but the thought was planted now and it spooked her. The sooner this was over with, the better. She wondered how they'd recall this night. Would it be etched in their minds so they'd relive it, moment by moment, or would it move to the distance of a remembered nightmare?

Jack must never know the truth. For him, the story would have to be that his daddy had gone away. He'd keep on looking forward to his father's return, but in time he'd grow and the hope would fade and become part of the background noise of his life.

For Lizzie it was going to be a lot trickier. But at least she was safe from her father now. Whatever problems she might have in dealing with the deed and its memory, that was the thing to keep in mind.

Over a wooded hill, down into a valley, heading for home. Out there in the darkness were the lights of all those small towns that didn't rate exits of their own, but were linked by the road that the motorway had replaced.

That following car was back in her mirror. Or perhaps it was some different car, it was impossible to say. All she could see was those anonymous lights. This time they were staying well back.

Here came the roadworks again. Same stretch, opposite direction. Again, one lane was coned off and the carriageway lights were out. A few moments after they'd crossed into this darker territory, the driver behind her switched on his beams. They were the pop-up kind. She saw them swivel into view like laser eyes.

Just like on Frank's coupé.

Jack said, "Can we have the radio?"

"Not right now," Holly said.

"It was working before."

"I'm trying to concentrate."

He was closing the distance between them. Holly knew she couldn't go any faster.

She looked down and saw that her ignition lights were flickering and that, once again, her oil warning light was full on.

They passed what remained of a demolished bridge, with new concrete piers ready to take its wider replacement. Beyond the bridge site, just off the road, stood a mass of caravans and portable buildings. It was a construction village, a shantytown of churned up mud and giant machines. A temporary sliproad had been bulldozed into the embankment to give access to works traffic.

Holly waited until it was almost too late. Then she swerved across the lanes and into the sliproad.

Something thumped against the car, and in the mirror she saw one of the cones go tumbling in her wake. The car behind her was swerving to avoid it. It made him overshoot the turnoff, so he couldn't follow her. Now he'd be stuck. The traffic wouldn't allow him to stop and back up again. He'd be heading in the same direction for miles and miles.

Good Samaritan? Good riddance.

All the lights in this temporary settlement were on, yet nothing moved. Jack was craning, eagerly looking around the various site office buildings as they entered the main area. But Holly got in first.

"Yes, Jack," she said. "They have big trucks here."

It was almost as bright as day, and completely deserted. The yard was floodlit and every portakabin office had its lights on. Holly could see through all the uncurtained windows that every one of the offices was empty.

She slowed, and stopped, and looked around.

A few vans, a couple of big diggers. Some concrete bridge sections waiting to be trucked out and assembled elsewhere. The site had the look of a frontier fort, obviously not intended to be here for ever; but it was hard to believe that the scars it would leave on the land could ever easily heal.

They would, of course. The big machines would simply put it all back when they'd finished. It wouldn't quite be nature, but everybody would be going by too fast to notice.

She got out. There was the sound of a generator, banging away somewhere in the background.

"Hello?" she called out, and then glanced back at the car.

Jack and Lizzie were watching her through the side-windows. Pale children, out on the road past their bedtimes. They looked hollow-eyed and tired. Jack with his little round face, Lizzie like a stick-version of the teenager she'd soon be.

Holly gave them a brief smile, and then moved out to look for someone. She didn't want to get too far from the car. She didn't want to let them out of her sight.

She called again, and this time someone came out from behind one of the buildings.

He stood there, and she had to walk over to him. He looked like a toothless old shepherd in a flat cloth cap, knuckly hands hanging down by his sides. He could have been any age, from a well-preserved seventy down to a badly done-by fifty. Too old to be one of the road gang, he looked as if he'd been on road gangs all his life.

She said, "Is anyone in charge around here?"

"Never, love," the man said. "They all do what they sodding well like."

"Well... what do *you* do?"

"I'm just the brewman."

Holly looked around her at some of the heavy plant that stood under the lights, looking as if it had all been airdropped in to remodel the face of Mars.

She said, "I've been having trouble with my car. Is there anyone who could have a look at it for me? I've got some money."

"Andy's the mechanic," he said.

"Is he here?"

"He's never here."

"Is it worth me waiting for him? Can I do that?"

"You can do whatever you want," and then added, as if it was his all-purpose charm to ward off evil, "I'm just the brewman." And then he trudged off.

She went back to the car.

"I'm fed up of this," Jack said.

"I can't help it, Jack," Holly said. "Try to understand."

"No," he said, barking it out like a little dog with all the passion and venom he could manage.

Rather than argue or get angry, Holly got out of the car again to watch for Andy the Mechanic.

The site wasn't quite as deserted as it looked, but it took a while to become attuned to it and to pick up the signals; the sound of a door opening and closing somewhere, a glimpse of a figure passing from one building to another.

She paced a little. She looked toward the motorway. For something to do, she raised the Toyota's bonnet and took a look at the engine in the vague hope that her car problems might have some blindingly obvious solution. But it looked like engines always did to her, grimy and complex and meaningless. There was a smell as if something had been burning, and when she held her hand out over the block she could feel the heat rising from it. She poked at a couple of the leads, to no effect other than to get her hands dirtier than they already were.

A voice called out, "Are you looking for someone?"

A man was walking across the open ground toward her. He was short, dark, powerfully built. He had at least six upper teeth missing on one side, but from the way that he grinned the loss didn't seem to trouble him.

"Would you be Andy?" she said.

"I might."

"Then I'm looking for you."

She quickly explained her problem in case he started to get the wrong idea, and he moved her out of the way so that he could take a look. It didn't take him long.

"Look at your fanbelt," he said. "If your drawers were that slack, they'd be down around your ankles. When that starts to slip, your battery runs down and you run out of power."

"Is it hard to fix?"

"If I said yes, you'd be more impressed," he said, and it was then that he noticed the two children inside the car. They were staring out at him.

"Yours?" he said.

"Yes," Holly said. "We've been to the seaside."

He looked at her, and then he looked at the car.

And then he said, "You take the kids and wait in the brew hut while I have a go at this. Tell Diesel to make you a cup of tea."

"Is Diesel the brewman's name?"

"It's what his tea tastes like, as well."

The brew hut was the oldest-looking and most battered of the site buildings. It was up on blocks, and reached by three stairs. The floor sagged as they stepped inside. There were about a dozen folding card tables with chairs around them, and a sense of permanent grime every-where; it was as if engine oil had been ground into the floor, rubbed into the walls, coated onto the windows.

The brewman was sitting by a plug-in radiator, reading a copy of *The Sun*. It wasn't a cold night, but the radiator was turned up high and the air inside the hut was stifling. He looked up as they entered.

Holly said, "Andy told us to wait in here. Is that all right with you?"

"Whatever you like," the brewman said. "I'm Matty."

"He said you were called Diesel."

Matty's face fell, and he looked out of the window.

"The bastard," he said, and he got up and stamped off.

Given his mood and the likely state of his crockery, Holly decided not to press him about the tea. She ushered the children onto grimy plastic seats that stood against the wall. On the wall itself was tacked a selec-tion of yellowing newspaper cuttings, all of them showing the debris of spectacular motorway crashes.

Jack said, "It stinks in here."

"Shh," Holly said.

"It *does*."

She couldn't tell him it didn't, because it did. And she couldn't agree that it did in case Matty was listening. So she only said, "It won't be for long."

They waited. There was a clock on the wall, but it was wrong. Jack swung his feet, Lizzie stared at the floor. Outside, a massive engine began to rev up somewhere close behind the building, making their chairs vibrate.

Jack said, "I'm bored."

"Play I-spy," Holly suggested.

"I'm not playing with him," Lizzie said. "He can't spell."

Holly said, with an unexpected tightness in her tone, "Then why don't we all just sit here quietly?"

There was silence for a while and then Lizzie muttered, rebelliously, "It's true. He can't."

And Jack agreed with her. "I've got a giant brain," he said, "but I can't spell."

Holly covered her eyes. She wasn't sure whether she was laughing or crying and the two children, equally uncertain, were watching her closely for clues.

This night would pass. It would somehow all be fine.

Keep thinking that, she told herself, and it might even come true.

"Mum… " Lizzie said.

Holly looked at her and saw the unease and the apprehension in her eyes. She might be sharp, but she was still only twelve years old.

"When this part's over," she said, "What then?"

She was choosing her words carefully because of Jack, but Holly knew what Lizzie was trying to say.

"We'll carry on as normal," she said.

"Can we do that?"

"We'll have to," Holly said.

There was a tap on the window. Andy was standing there outside, raising himself up on tiptoe so that he could look in, and he beckoned to her.

She went out, and they walked over to the car together. He told her he'd left the keys inside it.

"Best I can do," he said. "I've tightened your fanbelt and cleaned off your plugs. They were blacker than Matty's fingernails."

"Thanks, Andy."

"You've got a lot of oil down there. I don't know where it's coming from. You might need a new gasket."

He showed her what he'd done and got her to feel the difference in the fanbelt, which she pretended to appreciate. She offered him twenty quid and he took it with no embarrassment. Then she went back for the children.

The brew hut door was open. Lizzie was alone inside.

Holly said, "Where's Jack?"

Lizzie had slumped down into her coat as if it was a nest, hands in her pockets and legs outstretched, looking at the toes of her shoes as she clacked them together. She said, "He followed you outside."

"I didn't see him."

"He wanted to look at the big trucks."

Holly went out. Jack hadn't gone over toward the car, or she'd have seen him. She stood in front of the brew hut and called out his name.

Nothing.

Lizzie was in the doorway behind her now.

"It's not my fault," she said defensively.

Holly went around by the side of the brew hut and found herself in an area lit by the most powerful of the overhead floodlights. Under the lights stood a few parked cars and a variety of dormant machines. She could hear the massive engine whose note had been shaking the brew hut's foundations, and could tell that it was somewhere close.

She looked back and saw that Lizzie had followed her some of the way.

"You look around the buildings," Holly said. "I'll look here."

She didn't wait to see how Lizzie responded, but started to make her way through the machine yard. It was like a giant's bazaar of heavy engineering, the night sun casting deep, dark shadows under the gear. These were machines for ripping up the land, and they had spikes and claws and teeth on a saurian scale. Encrusted with clay and battered by hard use, they stood like bombed-out tanks.

She hauled herself up and looked in the cab of a well-rusted bulldozer on tracks. Jack wasn't in it, but by hanging on she could look out over the yard. Down the next row, a wagon was being inched up onto a flatbed trailer by some driver she couldn't see. The tyres on the wagon were enormous, and the ramps were bending under its weight.

She looked all around and called Jack's name, but she had little chance of being heard. The big engine roared and the great tonnage slowly rolled. In her mind's eye she saw Jack crushed or falling or struggling to get free of some unexpected snare. She saw gears turning, teeth meshing, pulling him in.

She called his name again, louder, and then hopped down to continue the search. She stumbled a little when she landed. The ground here was nothing more than churned-up dirt into which stones had been dumped to give it some firmness. It was no playground.

"Jack!" she called, moving forward.

As she came around by the bulldozer onto a firmer stretch of concrete road, she saw him. She could see all the way to the perimeter fence, where he was climbing.

Climbing? What was he *doing*?

And then she understood, and started to run.

It was a storm fence, about eight feet high. Jack was already over the top of it, and climbing down the other side. The fence rocked back and forth under his weight as the concrete posts shifted in their holes, but he clung to it like a bug; its close weave offered ideal purchase for his small feet and fingers.

Holly stumbled on the rough ground, but caught herself and went on. On the other side of the perimeter fence was an unlit country lane.

Out on the country lane stood the red coupé with the pop-up headlights.

"Hey," she shouted. "Hey, Jack, no!"

He was descending with his face set in a look of utter concentration. Behind him, the car was making a low purring sound with its engine off but its electric fan sucking in the cool night air. The driver hadn't stepped out, and she could barely see anything of him. She could only guess that he was watching her.

Holly reached the fence, looking through it and up at him. "Jack," she said. "Come down, Jack, please. You can't go over there. That's not your daddy. Believe me. There's no way it could be."

But Jack didn't look at her, and didn't even show any sign of having heard. He was moving like a monkey. He reached down with his foot, found another space in the diamond pattern, and hooked his scuffed trainer into it before lowering the rest of his weight.

She could touch his fingers as they hooked through, right in front of her eyes; her breath through the wire could fall onto his face. "Jack," she said, "no!"

But he wouldn't look at her, and although he was only inches away she couldn't reach him. She was powerless.

"Jack," she said, "Look at me, please. Don't do this. Don't go to him."

She made a move as if to try and catch his hands through the wire, but it was pointless. She couldn't hold him if she caught him. All she could do was risk hurting him.

"Lizzie's looking for you as well," she pleaded. "Oh, *Jack...* "

He jumped, and hit the dirt on the far side with a thump. Holly made a leap at the wire and felt the entire fence lean before her, but she didn't have his agility and couldn't begin to climb the way that he had.

He was running for the car, now, and the car's passenger door was opening to receive him.

Holly was screaming, although she didn't immediately realise it. The car door slammed and its laser eyes opened. The engine started, and its nose swung around as it began to turn in the narrow lane.

Her hands were up at the sides of her head. She'd heard of people tearing at their hair, but she'd always thought it was just an expression. She looked around wildly.

Then she started to run along the inside of the fence, ahead of the turning car.

The country lane ran close on the other side. If there was a gap anywhere, she'd get through it. The car wouldn't pass her. No way was she going to let that happen.

Here was a gate. It was a back way into the site, little-used. A big double gate, wide enough for a lorry but chained and padlocked in the middle. There was enough play in the chain to make a gap of a foot or so.

It was a squeeze, but not an impossible one. She came out on the other side and all that she could see were the twin lights, the laser eyes of the beast that she had to impede.

She put on a burst and dived into its way, sliding to a halt in the middle of the lane and raising both of her hands. When it hit her, she felt nothing other than her own sudden acceleration; no impact, no pain, just the instantaneous switch from rest into motion as her legs were knocked from under her and she was spun down the side of the car.

Afterwards she'd never know whether she really saw it or only imagined the memory, but Holly went down hard in the wake of the moving car with a mental picture of her son's blank face only inches away on the other side of the glass.

She lay there.

She couldn't move. She could hear that the car had stopped and she wanted to lift her head to look, but nothing happened. Oh God, she was thinking, I'm paralysed. But then when she made an enormous effort, her hand came up and braced itself against the ground. As she was doing it, she heard a car door opening.

She wasn't paralysed, but she'd no strength. When she tried to push down with her hand to raise herself, her arm trembled and nothing happened.

Someone was walking up behind her.

Before she could muster the energy to turn and look, strong fingers gripped the back of her head and thrust her face down into the mud. In an instant, she was blinded and choking.

She found her strength now, all right, but it did her no good as a sudden knee in her back pinned her further to the ground. She struggled and flapped like a fish, but her face stayed under. The blood roared in her ears and lights exploded before her eyes.

Then in an instant, the pressure was off.

That first deep breath nearly drowned her on the spot, as she sucked in all the mud that had filled up her mouth. She retched and coughed, blowing it out of her nostrils and heaving up what she'd both swallowed and inhaled.

She felt a lighter touch on her shoulder and lashed out, only to hear a cry from Lizzie. She was there when Holly's vision cleared, keeping back and holding her arm where she'd been struck.

"I'm sorry, mum," she said.

Holly stared dumbly for a moment before an understanding started to form. Lizzie was backing toward the waiting car.

"No, Lizzie!" she said. She tried to rise, but one of her legs wouldn't support her.

"I know how you want me to feel about it, but I can't. I wish I could. I'm sorry. It's never going to be right after tonight, whatever we do. Ever."

Holly made another massive effort and this time made it up and onto her feet, putting all of her weight onto the uninjured leg.

"Wait," she managed.

Lizzie had reached the car.

"I'm the one that he wants," she said. "But he'll take Jack if I don't go with him."

The passenger door popped open about an inch.

"I'm sorry," she said again, and she reached out and opened it all the way.

Holly wasn't close enough to see how it worked, but Jack popped out of the vehicle as if propelled on a spring. He landed on both feet, and Lizzie quickly slipped around behind him and into the car.

The door closed like the door on a well-fitting safe, and the car's engine started to rev. It was all as swift and as decisive as that.

Holly started toward them, half-hopping, half-limping, but the car was already moving off and starting to pick up speed.

"Frank!" she shouted. "You bastard! Give her back!" and at the sound of her voice, Jack seemed to wake as if from a daze.

He looked about, as if suddenly remembering something, and spotted those red tail lights receding off into the darkness.

He gave a strangled cry.

"Dad!" he called out, and started to run down the lane after the car, slapping down his feet so hard that the ground almost shook.

Holly hadn't yet reached him, and her cries couldn't stop him. Neither of them had any chance of catching the car. But both of them tried.

She caught up with him a full ten minutes later, still standing on the dark spot where his breath and his hopes had finally given out.

"He forgot me!" he wailed. Holly dropped to her knees and pulled him to her.

For once, he let her hold him. ❦

# The Plot

§ IT WAS a grey February morning in the Northern hills and Matthew Price, vicar of a rural parish, was crossing the graveyard that stood between his parsonage and the church. The church stood above the town, and the churchyard was exposed. The wind had driven a rim of last night's hail around the headstones, piling it up against them in a shallow tide of gruel.

There was only a short dash to make, but the wind was bitter. Matthew kept his face turned from it, and failed to see the young woman until she stepped out into his path.

She was red-haired and pale. Her thin shawl plastered to her and her dress whipped around her legs. She was nineteen.

"Mary," said Matthew, taking a moment to overcome his surprise. "You should not be out."

"I am well enough," the young woman said. "And someone sits with my daughter."

"Your daughter? Where is she now?"

"In the cot the parish gave me."

He was shocked at this news.

"Still?" he said. "A week has passed."

"She keeps well enough in this cold."

"Mary," Matthew said. "You must bury her."

She looked away. A tendril of hair fell across her face, and she pushed it aside.

"Not in your unhallowed ground, Reverend. Will you not relent and baptise her?"

"Baptism is for the living."

"She looks just as she did in life," Mary offered.

Matthew felt something close to despair as he looked upon her. She meant her words to be taken seriously. It was as if she hoped that, with a little haste and a show of conviction, even God himself might be misled.

The young girl was returning his gaze with a mixture of wariness and defiance. She had a face that was doll-like and pure when she washed it, save for a faint childhood scar that divided her right eyebrow. She was without family and without much education; and now she was without her child.

"Walk with me to the church," he said.

The path took a haphazard course through the yard, cutting this way and that; here around an iron-railed sepulchre, there to avoid an angel. These were the tombs of country families who built their graves like they built their houses; solid, massive, ugly, and for all time.

Matthew said, "I don't say no to punish you, Mary. God makes provision for the unbaptised."

"Amongst the suicides and heathens."

"In limbo."

"A place of nothing."

"Limbo is not a place of nothing, Mary. It is a state in which the innocent can look forward to the day when they receive God's grace."

"And be denied it until then."

There was no persuading her. What she lacked in sophistication, she more than made up for with directness and tenacity. As they reached the church's oak door he said, "Why did you not bring the child to me before she died?"

"The midwife said she was too poorly to be moved."

"Then you had only to send word of your need," he said as he unlatched the door and pushed it inward, "and I would have come to you."

"I came to ask," she said. "But I was turned away."

He turned back and looked at her in dismay.

"When?" he said.

But she had stopped at the threshold. She looked in and all around, like a person whose way had been barred by an invisible hand. She took in every corner of the cold church, as if to remember it.

"I will not enter this house," she said.

"Mary!" he said, but she had nothing more for him. She turned and walked away.

He tried to follow, but he could not catch up with her. He stopped at the church gates and watched her departing figure as she descended the hill. It was a cobbled street that ran down through the middle of town to the river and the mill. It did not run straight, and in less than a minute she was lost to his view.

Matthew went back inside, and closed the door. The chill of the wind gave way to the bone-cold stillness of stone. There was an iron stove against the church's third pillar. Jacob had cleaned out the ashes and laid a new fire the night before, and it waited now to be lit. Jacob had begun his working life as the gravedigger's boy. Now in his sixty-eighth year, he served the parish as verger, sexton and churchwarden.

By the time of the morning service the stove was glowing, the pipes were clanking, and the difference they made was imperceptible. It was a midweek matins, and poorly attended; the usual roster of widows and cripples and indigents. They hurried for the best pews near the stove, and gave up their places to no-one.

The coughing was louder than the singing, and a mite more musical. Not for the first time, Matthew looked over his midweek flock and reflected that the people who clung most fiercely to their God always seemed to be the ones who'd received the worst of his favour.

But perhaps even a God could go too far. Matthew spoke the words and led the hymns, but his thoughts were elsewhere. They were of Mary Tolliver and in particular of her child—one scant week of life, and an eternity dead.

Back at the parsonage, the service over and his body chilled to the core, Matthew did his best to warm himself at the big fire in the kitchen. He could hear Mrs Temple moving around upstairs. He waited for her to appear and then, when she did not, moved to the stairway and called to her.

Like Jacob, Constance Temple had been a fixture when he'd come to the parish. And like Jacob, she'd embraced Matthew's new ideas for managing the household while somehow managing never to act on any of them. He felt guilt as he listened to her descending. Her back was as straight as an artilleryman's, but she moved with the slow dignity of joint pain.

When she was with him, Matthew said, "Mary Tolliver was waiting for me in the churchyard this morning."

"Was she," Mrs Temple said, in a tone that somehow took the query out of the words and gave them a critical edge.

"Did you ever turn her away from the door?"

"I turn away anyone who will not disclose their business."

"You must have known her business. Everyone in the village is aware of her state."

"And a fine state it is. There's a word for her and there's another for her child."

"Please don't speak it."

"I would not soil the air."

So that was it. Matthew knew that if he argued further, Mrs Temple would remain calm and he would grow more agitated and in the end, she would acknowledge no fault and nothing would change. Her opinions had stood for a long time, and their foundations went deep. For two years he'd been trying to persuade her to bring in a housemaid to help with the more onerous tasks. She would listen and promise to consider, but nothing would be done. He might as well argue with the land itself.

He said, "She lodges in Mill Row, does she not?"

"Along with the rest of them."

The rest of them being unmarried mill girls and servants who lived out. Some had privacy in rented rooms, most had to share. The Row had a certain reputation.

"Thank you," Matthew said.

He had a funeral to conduct that afternoon, and an important letter to write in the evening. Perhaps a few hours would give Mary time to regret her words and reconsider. First thing tomorrow, he would seek her out and see to what extent the church's forgiveness might move her.

But it was not to be. At four in the morning, he was awakened by the barking of Jacob's dog. The dog was as touchy as its owner and often barked at any sound in the night, but would normally fall silent after a while. This time it did not. Matthew climbed out of bed and moved to the window, where he looked down and saw the light of a lantern moving in the churchyard. He dressed over his nightshirt and went out.

He found Jacob standing over the grave that he had filled in only a few hours before. The wreaths and flowers had been scattered from the freshly-turned earth, and some of the exposed mound had been excavated.

"Grave robbers, Reverend," Jacob said. "In this day and age."

Matthew had him raise the lantern higher, and studied the work. A piece of broken fencepost lay close by. Someone had been scraping into the dirt with it, to little effect.

"They don't seem to have achieved much with their efforts."

"And the hard work already done for them, as well," Jacob said contemptuously. "That ground was like iron when I broke it."

But Matthew's gaze had been led to the dog, quiet now and sniffing around at some short distance.

"I think our dead are safe from an earthly resurrection," he said. "I suspect a different motive."

They moved over to where the dog had stopped, and Jacob shooed it away. It hovered at the furthest reach of the lantern's throw as Matthew bent to inspect the bundle it had found.

"Not here to raise a body," Matthew said quietly, "but to leave one."

It was the body of a week-old child, pale as the marble angels and wrapped in stiff linen.

"In another's grave?" said Jacob.

"Where better to lie undiscovered?" said Matthew. "Please. Steady me."

Rising with the child, he felt the usual rush of blood from his head and waited, the sexton's hand supporting his arm, until the dizziness abated.

Once he was confident of his balance again, he had Jacob light the way to the church. The dog followed behind.

"I should fetch the constable," Jacob said.

"Wait until the morning," Matthew said. "If call him we must."

He laid the dead child before the altar in the side-chapel, and took a seat in the front pew. He said a prayer, but once again found his thoughts taking him to a place where he felt less than comforted. He wished that Mary had not fled before he had arrived. He wished that he could have sat here with her in the presence of her daughter, and persuaded her back to God. She was distraught, and it was natural. She retained her sense of what was right, or she would not have attempted to place the child in consecrated ground. Were she truly lost, consecrated ground would mean nothing to her.

If only he could make her see that even to deny God was to acknowledge his presence. Matthew's fear now was that this failure to secure a burial in the churchyard might drive her farther from the light. Wasn't that it? Wasn't that the source of his discomfort?

But faced with the dead child, its eyes closed, its mouth open, its cold fingers crooked, an ivory doll from a nativity scene, Matthew was not so sure. He could feel no sense of justice at the exclusion of its soul from heaven. Not for a promise of eventual bliss, not for even for the briefest moment.

He'd baptised many children. He'd performed the service so many times that sometimes his mind wandered as he said the words. The water came from a tap in the churchyard. Godparents stumbled through vows they could neither repeat nor remember. The child knew nothing of its state before, nor of any difference after.

He put his head in his hands. He wore the robes and stood for the Church's authority in all things spiritual. But could it be that, if there was a conflict here, his sympathies were not entirely where they ought to reside?

After a few moments, he had regained himself. Mary Tolliver's bitterness might be justified, but it was not right. If he allowed his sympathy to undo him, he could be of no help to her. Ministers must not question their duties.

Allow them that option, and even the Kingdom of Heaven might fall.

There were stars still visible in the morning sky as Matthew and the Constable made their way to Mill Row. Matthew had not slept. The Constable had been roused early, and had little to say. Matthew was directed to a communal loft that ran the length of four stone cottages in the roof space, where more than thirty young women and girls made a home. Some slept on mattresses on the floor, others had strung up blankets for privacy. The girls were awake and dressed but many had yet to leave for the mill.

Matthew recognised some of them. There were other churches and chapels in town, but Mill Row fell within his parish. The girls were reluctant to speak, until Matthew caught the Constable yawning and sent him to find a chair.

He learned that Mary Tolliver had made a brief return to collect some possessions but had fled before first light, telling a few close friends that it was her intention to make her way to the city. The nearest city was at least two days' walk away for a person in the best of health, and Mary was still weak from childbirth.

"Has she lost her wits?" Matthew said. "She could die on the road."

"She spoke of a married sister," one of the girls said.

"In town?"

"In her old life."

As Matthew was leaving, he noted that the cot from the parish stood out on the landing. Mary's space had already been claimed by another.

A plan of sorts had begun to form in Matthew's mind. There seemed little that he could do for Mary now, and the course that had suggested itself to him was hardly a correct one. But it had a sense of necessary decency about it.

As they walked from the Row and over the river he conversed with the Constable, and easily persuaded him to take no further interest in the matter. He argued that any offence here was spiritual, and need not trouble the law. The Constable offered no argument in return.

Then Matthew made an early call at the offices of Henry Munby, the solicitor who handled all of the parish's legal affairs. An hour with Munby got his designs off to a start, and he climbed the hill back to the parsonage with renewed purpose.

He found Jacob, and walked with him to the place where the churchyard ended and the moor began. The division was marked by a stone wall with a gate in it. Beyond the gate was an unmade path that led off into rolling hill country and a sea of ferns. It was lush in summer, blighted now. By the gate stood a massive elm.

Matthew said, "I want a child's grave dug under that tree."

Jacob gave him a suspicious look. "I can't dig if it's not church land."

"It will be. I've taken steps to acquire the plot outside the gate. It won't be consecrated, but I can bless the ground and the child that lies in it. And Jacob... please. Tell no-one for now."

He did not mean to, but he glanced toward the parsonage as he said this. And Jacob brightened; any scheme that merited Mrs Temple's disapproval was guaranteed to secure his.

The job would take Jacob the rest of the day. He went off for his barrow and tools, and Matthew went to the church. He'd closed it up with the dead child inside, locking the doors and keeping the keys on him. His intention had been to send a local undertaker with them to collect the body, but that intention had now changed.

If the church had made no provision for the unbaptised, he would make his own. It was not unknown for a churchyard to have sections both consecrated and unconsecrated. As communities grew, people took less of an interest in the fates of the strangers around them. An unknown suicide might rest in an anonymous corner nowadays, where once they would have been banished to a crossroads burial. There was even a time set aside for such interments, the grim hours between nine and midnight.

So might it be here. This bastard child could be denied the full service of burial, but need not be denied Matthew's prayers or his compassion. And if no-one else knew of it, then none need debate it.

They laid the child to rest that evening, wrapped in the simple linen in which they'd discovered her. Jacob and his dog were the only witnesses. There was no marker but Matthew made a careful drawing of the spot, measuring and noting the distances from gateway and tree. It was important to have a record, in case the plot should ever be needed again. Mary Tolliver was not the first of her kind, nor did he expect her to be the last.

It was more than a week later when Matthew read of a theft at a coaching inn that stood out on the city road some fifteen miles from town. Baggage had been left unattended for a few minutes when a horse had thrown a fit, and a young woman had seized this opportunity to rifle the passengers' goods. She'd left valuables and fled with only money, but a substantial sum of it. A reward was being offered by the carriers. She was described as pale and red-haired, and bedraggled from the road. Those who'd seen her before the theft described her as 'glocky', or half-witted, talking to herself and shunning company. She'd been begging money for herself and her child, although no child was seen with her.

It was little enough to go on, but Matthew was convinced. Red-haired, bedraggled, an imagined child—it seemed likely to him that Mary Tolliver was the thief. If so, she was pursuing a downward course. And pursuing it in a way that he had done nothing to prevent.

But perhaps he might act to halt or even reverse it. More than anything, he wanted to show her the plot under the elm and to tell her of the blessing. Her child might not lie in the Bishop's ground as she'd wished, but she surely lay in God's own earth.

Letters were sent that same day, and replies received the next. A curate from the adjacent parish would take over his duties during a few days' absence. A carriage and driver were borrowed from the Wetherbys, a local family who were rich and had several and could be persuaded that the loan of a spare would gain them some extra credit with the Almighty. Matthew weathered Mrs Temple's disapproval as she packed for him.

"Be sure you let Jacob carry your bag," she said.

"That hardly seems right," said Matthew. "He's close to seventy years old."

"And he spends all his days in a hole with a shovel," Mrs Temple said bluntly. "He's used to the strain. You've had your doctor's warning."

He reached the coaching inn at around three in the afternoon. He gave the driver a shilling, and half an hour to spend it in. Matthew himself had no appetite, and was relieved to stand on firm ground for a while and not be shaken. He took a walk around the yard. He watched the horses being watered, and spied a white-bearded, bald-headed man in a tattered army coat, striding about with a hefty staff and slamming the end of it down on the cobbles whenever he stopped. His frame was aged, but his gaze was fierce.

Matthew caught his eye. Aware of his attention, the old man drew himself up a little taller.

"A formidable weapon," Matthew observed.

"And I'll use it," the old man said, "before I see property interfered with again."

"I take it you speak of the woman who rifled the luggage."

"She took advantage of her sex and struck at me like the harpy she was." He tapped his waistcoat with his finger, just below the breastbone. "Struck me right here and drove the breath from this old body. A pitiable object she made of me."

"Would you know her again?" said Matthew.

"In an instant," said the old man. "And so might you, by the mark on her brow."

And he touched a finger to his own white eyebrow, in exactly the place where Mary Tolliver's had been divided by some long-forgotten hurt.

Once in the city, Matthew took a room in a small commercial hotel and sent the carriage driver home. He ate little and retired early. His stomach was unsettled and his head ached. Matthew did not travel often, and when he did he rarely travelled well. The ache was still there when he woke, dull and specific like a blunt nail in the brain. But he ignored it, and with breakfast it faded.

After the small mill town that he was accustomed to, stepping out into the streets of the city both excited and threaten to overwhelm this country parson. So many people. So many streets. The noise, and all the smells. But it was only novelty, and it soon began to pass.

He began his search with the aid of a sixpenny gazetteer and a street map. His plan was to visit every hostel and charitable institution, but after three or four of these he began to realise that he was wasting his time. All had some form of religious patronage or other association, the very thing that Mary had set herself against. Even the hospitals bore the names of saints.

But a sister had been mentioned. A married sister, so she would not be a Tolliver. But she had been a Tolliver once. Matthew abandoned his tour of charity houses and set himself instead to visit the various parishes of the city, asking to see their marriage registers. He was dismayed by the scale of everything—the distance between parishes, the sheer number of them, the size of the record books in each. His own modest register recorded perhaps a dozen weddings in a year. These churches were putting them through like factories.

On the second day of his search he found a likely candidate, married seven years past. The wedding of one Albert Wardle to one Dorothy Tolliver, spinster of this parish. He took a note of the husband's address, and found the house in a dark terrace by a canal. Here lived Albert's mother, widow of the one-time lock-keeper. From there he was sent to the tenement where Albert now lived with his fast-growing family.

Dorothy Wardle received him with eagerness and some embarrassment at the state in which he found her. Her husband was at his job in the docks, and her children were everywhere around them. Matthew counted six, or it might have been eight. They moved about too much, and too quickly. Not all were her own; she minded the children of neighbours for payment.

Mary had been to visit her, but she had not stayed. She'd looked weary, but she had new boots and nearly-new clothes. Dorothy was shocked when Matthew told her of the theft that had paid for them.

"She said it was money she'd saved," Dorothy said. "She told me that her mind was set on something to buy with it. That was her reason for coming to town."

"Did she say what she intended to buy?"

"No."

"It is important that I find her," Matthew said. "I believe that I bear some responsibility for the course that she follows."

"Surely not, Reverend."

"Although I did not judge her, I fear I left her feeling judged. Might she return here, do you think?"

"I could not swear to it. But her parting words had the sound of a goodbye."

She had to break off their conversation for a moment, to scold one of the smaller children who was picking mouldy wallpaper from the wall and eating it.

Matthew said, choosing his words with delicacy, "Did she seem… entirely herself to you?"

He could see that Dorothy understood his meaning well enough. But she shied from it. "How else would she seem?" she said, uneasily, and her very unease was the answer he sought.

He said, "Do you know where she went to from here?"

"She'd a list of some addresses that she wanted to visit. I gave her Albert to lead her. Albert!"

A boy of six or seven came forward. His head was the shape of a battered turnip, his eyes the eyes of a frightened doe.

Dorothy said, "Show the Reverend the penny that Aunt Mary gave you."

Albert produced a grubby handkerchief and carefully unfolded it. From its heart, he took out one new penny.

"Very shiny," said Matthew. "If I can match it with another, can you tell me where your Aunt Mary went?"

"Albert does not speak," Dorothy said. "Will you not sit for a while, Reverend? You seem drained by your journey."

"I shall rest once she is found," Matthew said.

Albert might not speak, but Albert could lead, and so Matthew followed him through streets and down alleys and into a district of warehouses and sweatshops. Albert hopped and ran, dodging through handcarts and porters laden with bales and bolts of cloth, and every now and again would stop and look back to see that Matthew was still with him. More than once, Matthew feared that he'd lost sight of the boy. At the next glimpse, off he went again.

Beyond the warehouses was a broad street, and beyond the street was a sooty park with factory chimneys in the distance. The houses around the park were tall and fine and many had porches and railings. The pavements here were broad, and flagged with stone. At the end of the avenue leading up to the park gates stood a white tower. Here, Albert stopped.

An engraved brass plate was fixed below the bell-pull.

"She had you bring her *here*?" Matthew said. "Are you sure it's the right house?"

Albert stared up at him and waited for his penny.

By the time Matthew had done ringing the bell, the boy had disappeared. Looking around for him, he missed seeing the door open and turned quickly at the sound of it.

He was surprised to find himself faced by a man whom he guessed to be the householder or tenant. He'd expected a servant. But no servant would appear at his master's door in a faded Turkish robe and carpet slippers. The man before him was pale and fair, his face strangely undefined and smooth. He had a fringe of beard around his chin.

He took in Matthew's clerical garb and said, "Arthur Halifax, sir. How may I help you?"

"I seek a young woman with a scar on her brow," Matthew said. "She was led here."

"Won't you come in?"

On entering, Matthew perceived the white tower to be a house of books and cats. He saw the books everywhere—on shelves down the hall, on shelves in those rooms that he could see into, stacked in deep piles on the treads of the stairs leaving barely enough room for a person to ascend. The cats he didn't need to see at all.

There was nowhere to settle, but Arthur Halifax led the way down the hall and into a kitchen and scullery at the back of the house. It had a view over a yard filled with broken furniture and rolled linoleum.

After Matthew had explained himself further, Arthur Halifax said, "She was here. She was lucid. She was bright and composed. But she had a strange idea of the kind of service that I might do for her."

"Your plate declares you a bookseller, yet I see no shop."

"I have no use for a shop. I seek out rare volumes for particular clients. I suppose some might imagine that because I handle knowledge, I must therefore be in possession of it."

"What service did she ask for?"

"Help in obtaining the unobtainable. She had made a list of many items—I cannot remember them all. But they were odd. The life of a dying child, a face of innocence, the power of a serpent's poison. As if these were things that one might touch and trade. And yet she asked with such sweet earnestness that at first I thought the flaw was in my understanding, and that her requests were no less than reasonable."

By now Matthew had noted that Arthur Halifax had eyes that did not entirely fix upon the person that he was addressing, but rather on some point in space to one side or the other. Yet he seemed sufficiently aware of who or what he was looking at.

Matthew said, "She has suffered much, of late. Her grasp may not be complete."

"Is she kin to you? My sympathies if she is."

"A parishioner. I have made it my task to bring her home."

Halifax nodded, slowly, and then picked off some cat hairs from the front of his robe.

He said, "However strange her purpose, it seemed to be sustaining her. But a fire that burns so brightly can never burn for long. Search where you will. But may I suggest that you also call on the madhouses."

Leaving his company, Matthew found himself wondering whether the volumes that left the house bore the same feline history that his clothes now seemed to carry. He took a brisk walk around the park, flapping his coat to dispel the odour, while he considered what his next step ought to be.

It was surely as he'd begun to fear. Grief and frustration had unbalanced her mind. It was mainly on the public stage that mad people gibbered and rent their clothes; in life they often presented themselves with no perceptible change, save that their aims and reasons followed a logic entirely of their own, until self-neglect or some worrying encounter drew attention to their state.

He could return to the sister's house and see if Albert would be good for a second address. Or he might try to determine from which directory or magazine's advertisement columns she had compiled her list. But his time was limited. As was his money, and as were his energies. There seemed little point in continuing his pursuit at a distance that he could never diminish.

He sat on a bench by a stone urn that had been blackened by factory air, and took out his sixpenny gazetteer. No asylums were listed; but he did find an entry for the city's Lunacy Commission, at an address close to the courthouses. If her state grew worse, eventually the Commissioner would come to know of it.

And so, early that evening, the Reverend Matthew Price found himself before the gates of a public asylum on the outskirts of town, its high brick walls surrounded by open fields and its barred upper windows opened to the clean country air. In his hand was a letter from the

Lunacy Commissioner. In his heart, sadness and dread. The gate-keeper let him in and led him up the driveway toward the home of the Superintendent.

The asylum was not one building but many, occupying an estate of its own. Were it not for the workhouse-style construction of its wards it might have been taken for a veritable village of the unfortunate, with a duck pond and a chapel and a farm manned by inmates to supply its needs. It had a one-platform railway station with a line that ran out from the city, with special trains for visitors at weekends.

There had been twelve new admissions in the month. Three of these had taken place in the past week and one of them had been of a young woman of roughly Mary Tolliver's age and description. This woman had been found screaming and breaking mirrors in a public house, and had to be prevented from tearing at herself with the shards. When they took the broken glass from her, she attempted further damage to herself using her nails. Her clothes had been good but were ruined, and when committed she was penniless.

There was a trade in pauper lunacy, Matthew knew. With a grant of seven shillings a week for their keep, they could find themselves sped from the streets and into a system from which they might find it hard to escape. If she was here, the fault was his. And if she truly was mad, then here she would probably remain. Here or somewhere else like it, perhaps for the rest of her days.

His letter was read, and an attendant summoned to take him to view the patient. As he followed the attendant down the corridor, he felt his pulse racing and his heart pounding. A part of him hoped that he would find himself facing some stranger. But to have such a hope was to wish a misfortune onto someone that he did not even know. All the same, if the misfortune was a given, would it be wrong to feel relief?

They passed day rooms where inmates warmed themselves, and then left one building and passed through yards and airing courts into another. Matthew felt as if he were moving deeper and deeper into a place from which all sense of the world outside was being lost. They came to a locked cell; he waited alone as the attendant went for a key.

She lay on a cot with a single blanket. There was little chance of her clawing herself now. Her arms had been bound from her fingers to her elbows, and some blood had seeped through the bandages.

His heart sank as he crouched beside her and, sensing his presence, she turned her face toward his.

"Do you know me?" he said.

Her eyes showed no recognition.

"Can you remember your name?"

Her bandaged hand went to her face, but stopped short of touching it.

From behind him, the attendant said, "Tell the reverend your name."

Matthew winced at the sharpness of his tone and would have remonstrated with him, but the young woman said, "My name is Bridget Fagan."

"No," Matthew said.

"My father was a bricklayer."

"Your name is Mary Tolliver. You had a child that died. Do you understand me? Think on it, Mary. Grief has driven you from your senses."

Her gaze wandered from him, past him, taking in the room as if she'd never seen it before and could not comprehend its planes and angles now.

"I broke a mirror in Molly's shop," she said.

"Do you understand me, Mary?"

"My name is Bridget Fagan."

Matthew was growing dizzy. He knew that he ought to stand.

"May God forgive me," he said. "Have I found you too late?"

And in that moment it was as if a veil had dropped, and her eyes fixed on his and grew fiery, as she said in a low whisper that the attendant could not hear, "Too late for you, Matthew."

Startled, Matthew drew back. He tried to rise, but halfway up his balance failed and he stumbled and had to grab for the rail at the end of the cot. He missed it, and would have fallen had the attendant not reached him in time.

Normally these episodes would pass in a moment. This one did not.

There was no chair in the room. The attendant lowered him to sit with his back against one of the walls, and then ran for a doctor. Matthew felt as if he was in a sea, a blood-warm sea, and he was rising and falling with its motion. Each rise and fall, he knew, was a beat of his heart. Each surge of the tide was a flush of his life's-blood through his head, the barriers broken, its flooding unchecked.

He saw the young woman sit up, and swing her legs off the cot. Her bandaged arms were like paws, blunt and bloodied. She sat there, staring at him. Her face was slack. Where for a moment there had been fire, now there was an absence behind it. He could see that there were red marks on her cheeks where scratches had been made and had begun to heal.

She rose to her feet, and began to move across the room toward him. Crouching down, she stared blankly into his face. He tried to speak, but it was as if a great weight had been hooked into the corner of his mouth.

Her gaze roved over his features. Something flickered there.

Then she rose and returned to her cot.

The attendant arrived with the doctor no more than a minute or two later. The doctor spoke to Matthew in scrambled words that he could not understand. Beaten and drained, he did not even try to listen. He knew only one thing.

The young woman on the cot had the face of Mary Tolliver.

But the face bore no scar.

Matthew's greatest fear, as the days passed, was that they would keep him here and he would eventually be forgotten. How easily that could happen. He was unable to speak, or even move. He lay in a whitewashed room with a wooden cross upon the wall. Weeks seemed to pass without news, and no-one ever thought to tell him anything. Or did they tell him, and he failed to remember?

Some days a female inmate was sent to sit with him and read aloud from the bible. She read random pages, without order. But even then the scriptures retained their power; he began to feel a limited strength returning to his left arm. After a while he could lift it a few inches from the bed and push against the mattress with his knuckles. With persistence, he might soon be able to grip.

Then, one day, instead of a lunatic with a bible at the end of his bed, there was Jacob. Nervous and uncertain, with the brim of his old hat clenched in his hands and a suggestion of tears in his eyes. Jacob had come to take him home. He'd brought a wagon borrowed from the next parish and a fourteen-year-old girl to nurse him on the journey.

His doctor gave him a final examination, and a few parting words.

"I am encouraged by your recovery," he said, "As you should be." And he held Matthew's face in his hands and turned it, first this way and then that. "I am optimistic that the power of speech may return, and I see no reason why your power of movement should not continue to increase. I have known patients with your condition make a full and complete recovery. But their attacks were less severe. And they were younger and stronger than you. I think you should continue in hope. And be grateful for whatever you receive."

Two of the asylum's attendants dressed him for the journey in the clothes in which he'd arrived. They bundled him in blankets, sat him in a chair, and then carried man and chair down to the yard where the wagon waited. They sat him in a corner of it, and wedged him there with pillows and cushions.

Jacob drove the horses. The child sat with Matthew and watched. Where the road was rough and he started to slide, she moved over and righted him. She was small, but surprisingly strong. When they stopped at the coaching inn where he'd talked to the old soldier, she fetched water and held the cup to his lips. As Matthew drank, he raised his eyes to her face. It was unfamiliar to him, but he saw the scar that divided her brow. Their eyes met, and he knew.

She settled opposite and watched him for the rest of the journey.

He ached to tell her of the plans he'd had to make amends. Of the plot of ground and the quiet grave under the elm, of the prayers he'd said, of the prayers he'd hoped they might say together. But it was all hollow. It had been for his comfort, not for hers. Salve for his conscience, where there could be no balm for her pain.

The child disappeared after they'd reached the parsonage. Jacob was joined by the blacksmith from the Wetherby estate. They didn't use a chair but faced each other and gripped each other's elbows to make a seat on which they carried Matthew to the house, one to either side. The toes of his dangling shoes skimmed the longer grasses, as if he hovered above the ground without touching it.

"See, Reverend?" gasped Jacob as they shuffled him up the path. "See what it is to fly with the angels."

Mrs Temple was waiting to see them in, and directed them toward the sitting room. Matthew saw that his bed had been brought downstairs. He had not been forgotten, as he'd feared. He had never been forgotten.

Mrs Temple took off his shoes, and they laid him on the bed in his clothes. She sent the men away and then stood before him. He tried to smile. He knew that his effort would probably look bizarre.

"Oh, Reverend," she said. "Matthew. Promise me you will not give in to despair, and I shall do the same. We may question God's will but we cannot hope to know his mind."

Her use of his name did not escape him. He had never heard her be so familiar before.

She went on, "This is Bridget."

Matthew was able to turn his head sufficiently to see that the young girl had entered the room, and was standing behind Mrs Temple. "She'll be helping me to care for you," Mrs Temple said. "She came to us with a reference from your asylum doctor. You see how God provides?"

But Matthew could remember that when she'd arrived with Jacob to collect him, the asylum doctor had shown no sign of knowing her.

That night, Mrs Temple fed and bathed him, and then she retired and the girl named Bridget came in to sit with him.

The hour grew late, and the house grew quiet. Jacob's dog barked once, and far away. Bridget sat with the oil lamp dimmed, and an open book unread on her knees. Her eyes were on him, and she never seemed to blink. Matthew thought back over that mysterious list... the life of a child, a face of innocence, the power of a serpent's poison. What did it mean? And what else might it have contained?

He saw her lay aside the book. He watched as she drew a plain silk handkerchief from her sleeve. She reached for his water glass on the bedside table and spread the handkerchief over it, pulling the silk tight so that it stretched across the opening like the skin of a drum.

Then she raised it to her lips and tilted back her head, unnaturally far. He saw teeth that were hooked like cats' claws, but only for an instant; they burst through the tight silk with an audible pop, and then he saw a milky fluid dribbling down the inside of the glass as she chewed at the fabric.

When she was done, she unhooked herself from the silk and used it to wipe her lips before returning it to her sleeve. There was now about an inch of cloudy water in the glass.

Moving with a rustle as her dress brushed along the length of the sheets, she brought the glass to him. She reached across the bed, and he felt her breath against the exposed base of his throat where the collar of his nightshirt began.

She picked up his left hand and, bringing it across his chest, wrapped the fingers of it around the glass. He hadn't the strength to resist her. With her hand over his own, she raised the glass to his lips.

As he felt its touch, he heard her whisper close to his ear.

"By your own hand," she said. The first and the last words he would hear from that mouth.

And then she tipped the poison into his.

Constance Temple, a light sleeper who refused any opiate to ease her pain, was alerted by a scream from the girl followed by the sound of a glass breaking. By the time she reached the sitting room, it was too late. Matthew had half-slid out of his bed and onto the floor, and was stone dead.

The girl named Bridget had backed off as far from him as it was possible to get, and was distraught.

"I saw him with the glass and dashed it from his lips," she said, "but it was too late."

Mrs Temple carefully picked up the intact base of the glass. There was a drop of white fluid in the angle. She sniffed it briefly, and recoiled.

"But I thought he could do nothing for himself," Bridget said.

"Perhaps he exaggerated his infirmity," Mrs Temple said, carefully setting the broken glass down, "so no one would interfere." Then she looked at Bridget.

"Hush, child," she said. "Do not be afraid. Nobody will blame you."

And no one ever did, although no one could account for the poison. Bridget vanished soon after, and the one person who might have explained it was no longer of this world.

There was hope of some leeway, but the Archbishop was adamant. The child's account of the parson's last moments left no room for doubt. The Word of the Lord was clear: *Know ye not that ye are the temple of God, and that the Spirit of God dwelleth in you? If any man defile the temple of God, him shall God destroy; for the temple of God is holy, which temple ye are.*

So Matthew Price, servant of God and defiler of his temple, was buried outside the churchyard in the very plot of land that he'd been securing for others' use. He was laid to rest one week after his suicide, sometime between the hours of nine and midnight. Only Jacob knew the hour for sure, and Jacob made no note.

It may be assumed that he'd have needed help with the body. It's possible that Constance Temple may have been at the graveside. A woman was seen there, it was said.

But all that can be said with certainty is that Matthew ended his earthly existence with no prayers, no marker, and no eternal company in the ground save that of one unshriven babe. ❧

# Doctor Hood

*9* AT THE top of the narrow garden, Miranda climbed the steps to the front door of her childhood home and rang the bell. Then she waited.

No lights were showing in any of the windows. The lane on which the big house stood was a pocket of old-fashioned stillness in the city, tucked-away behind the Cathedral and especially quiet at this hour of the night. You turned in through a gated opening half-hidden from the main road and seemed to enter an older, gentler, and more tranquil world. The lane was narrow and tree-lined. It wasn't maintained by the city but by the residents, who mostly left it alone.

She gave it a minute before producing her key and letting herself in.

"Dad?"

Now she stood in the hallway, and waited for an answer that didn't come. She set her overnight bag down on the floor. There was light somewhere upstairs but none down here at all, apart from the watery street lighting that shone in through the windows.

Miranda started to ascend, calling to her father as she went.

There was apprehension in her, but she wouldn't acknowledge it. She'd come here to establish that nothing was wrong. Not to flirt with dread. Dread's day would come regardless, she'd learned. Why spoil other days by anticipating it?

The next floor was also dark. The light came from the one above, where her old room had been. She stood on the landing and looked up the stairs.

"Dad?"

Something moved in the darkness behind her.

She spun around. In the space of an instant she felt her heart rate spike and a cold shockwave pass through her. It seemed to take the breath from her body while lifting every fine hair on her skin.

"God Almighty," Alan Hood said, no less taken aback.

He was a pale and insubstantial shape in the darkness, but as he moved forward into the light she could see him better. He had some sort of technical device in his hand that he glanced at and then shoved into his pocket.

"Where did *you* appear from?" he said. "You frightened the life out of me."

"I let myself in," Miranda said. "What was I supposed to do? You didn't answer when I rang the bell, and that was after I'd been trying all night to phone."

"Well, why not just call me tomorrow?"

"Well, why do you *think*?"

It came out a little more stridently than she'd intended, but it gave him an accurate snapshot of her mood. What could he expect? That she shouldn't worry? Her father lived alone in this enormous empty house, and she lived a hundred miles away.

He ran a hand through his uncombed hair and glanced all around him, in an attitude that was somewhere between distraction and embarrassment.

"I suppose I can see what you mean," he said, and then, "Why don't we go downstairs?"

She couldn't help looking at him critically as he moved past her. His clothes were clean, but didn't match and looked as if they'd been slept in. He was turned out the way a man might dress for gardening.

As she followed him down, the thought in her head was both an uninvited and an unwelcome one; *He's doing his best, but he's looking old.*

He apologised for the state of the kitchen, as well he might.

"I'm due a tidy up," he explained.

Miranda looked through towers of pans and dishes at the phone extension on the wall. This was the message phone. No wonder there'd been no answer when she'd called.

"Why's it unplugged?" she said.

Her father had to move some of the dirty stuff in the sink just to get the kettle underneath the tap.

"I was working on something," he told her as it filled. "I needed to concentrate."

If he'd disconnected the bedroom phones as well, her attempts to raise him must have rung out unheard in the basement.

There were no clean mugs, but he rinsed a couple and set them on the kitchen table. As he was pulling out a chair, she said to him, "Your head of department called me. He got my number from your doctor. He wanted to talk about something."

He looked at her in puzzlement as he sat. "What, exactly?"

"He didn't say. Just left me a message."

"And you couldn't leave it until the morning?"

"No."

"You didn't have to race over. Everything's fine."

"It doesn't look it," she said, and waited.

He looked around and past her, anywhere but at her. He clearly didn't have a ready or an easy answer to her concern.

"I don't know how to say this," he said. "Which is why I haven't tried. But since you've come all this way and you're obviously worried, I'd better tell you. I've been aware of your mother."

"That's no surprise," she said. "There can't be a thing in this house that doesn't remind you of her."

"More than that."

His gaze was on her and steady now, and she didn't like the way it was making her feel.

"What are you saying?"

"It's a perception thing," he said. "You want the science of it? There's no obvious cause but there can be a definite physical effect. The temperature falls. The electromagnetic potential at a given point changes. I can measure it. I'm not about to start believing in ghosts," he added quickly. "But maybe this is what makes people fall for the idea."

"Ghosts? Jesus, dad… "

"That's exactly my point."

"So being you, of course you've got to study it."

"I can't dismiss any of it, can I?" he said. "It's first-hand experience. The alternative is to pretend it didn't happen. How professional would *that* be?"

What she really wanted was for him to stop right there, to change the subject, or even better to tell her that he wasn't really being serious.

Anything that meant she wouldn't have to deal with this.

She said, "What form does the awareness take?"

"Mental certainty," he said. "For no apparent reason. Nothing seen, nothing heard, I just know she's there. While I fully accept that she isn't."

"All the time?"

"No."

"Okay. Right."

There was an awkward silence.

"So how's everything at your end?" he said.

Pausing on the way to collect some bedding from the half-landing cupboard, Miranda trudged up the stairs that had once been so familiar to her. Most of her childhood and all of her teenaged years had been spent in this house. She'd never imagined there could be a day when it wouldn't feel like home. But the day had come, nonetheless.

The suite of attic rooms had been her exclusive territory. The Independent Republic of Miranda. They'd redecorated the one room she'd painted black, but otherwise they'd left everything pretty much as it was. Now she saw cables on the upper landing and boxes in some of the rooms. They were the like the boxes that computers came in.

So what was the purpose of all this? When she elbowed open the door to her old bedroom, a sudden flash half-blinded her and she almost dropped the linen right there.

On a tripod in the middle of the room, a Polaroid camera spat out a print.

"Oh, for fuck's *sake!*" she said, and when she'd tossed the linen onto the bed she lifted the entire apparatus, tripod and all, and shoved it out onto the landing. There were microphones in the corners of the room, and they followed the camera along with their cables.

Lying in her old bed, in her underpants because she'd forgotten to bring nightwear, too exhausted to stay awake, too upset to go to sleep, her mind wandered a little and then settled into its well-worn small-hours track. The one she never chose, but couldn't avoid.

Just like tonight, for her it had started with a phone call. She'd made the same long drive, although she remembered nothing of it. At the hospital she'd found her father waiting, rudderless and dazed; Miranda had more or less had to take over, talking to the medical staff and then repeating their words for her father, who wasn't listening. She was, she realised, playing a part in a sad and sorry spectacle. The great Doctor Hood, major figure of international science, one-time Nobel co-nominee, the Northern Hemisphere's leading authority on Dark Matter, rendered almost childlike by personal disaster.

He'd discovered his wife at the bottom of the stairs, where she'd been lying for some time. But it wasn't a simple matter of a fall. For a week or more she'd been suffering from persistent headaches and had been sleeping for as many as twenty hours out of the twenty-four. The best guess was that she'd woken alone in the house and been unsteady or disoriented. Further investigation showed an unsuspected brain tumour that had already grown to inoperable size.

Over the next few weeks, they moved her from ward to ward and tried different combinations of drugs to reduce the cerebral swelling and raise her from the coma she'd fallen into. It had worked for a few days and for a while they'd had her back, lucid and aware even though her thinking had been a little strange. But then she'd relapsed and died. It had been a rapid decline, but at the time it had seemed to take forever.

w this. With her mother gone, her father was falling apart. It didn't seem fair. So much that she'd always taken for granted was no longer there. Much of the pain she felt was that of a lifetime's support system being kicked away. When she tried to explain it to Dan, his idea of sympathy was to match her troubles with competing ones of his own.

She'd been pressed into membership of a melancholy club where the options were limited. One either died young, or eventually one joined it.

Like it or not, she was the grownup now.

She was first downstairs the next morning. The day was a bright one. After loading the dishwasher and setting it going, she went into the basement and did the same with the laundry.

He hadn't quite been letting himself go. Most of his clothes were clean, and had been hung to dry on fold-out racks. Miranda suspected that they'd probably stay there until he came to wear them, skipping the need for an iron to press them with or a closet to put them in.

The mail arrived, and she went back up to get it. Her father appeared then, bleary and tousled, in a paisley bathrobe knotted over mismatched pyjamas. He followed her into the kitchen.

"This place is a tip," she told him.

"I know."

"Then why don't you do something about it? Where's Mrs Llewellyn?"

He settled back into the place where he'd been sitting the night before.

"I let her go," he said.

"Why?" Miranda said. "You've had her for years."

"She kept offering to stay late and cook me a meal. And I don't think that feeding was all she had in mind. You know what I mean? I'm not up for that."

"If I mark up the Yellow Pages for you, will you promise to sort out a replacement?"

"Yes, miss."

"I'm serious, dad. It's such a big place. You don't want it turning into a sty. Once it gets past a certain point you'll be like one of these old guys the council sends a hit squad to fumigate."

"Thanks very much."

"You know what I mean."

"When I'm done with the observations I'm making, then I'll get a housekeeper in. I don't want someone fussing around and messing up the data."

Miranda set coffee in front of him while he looked through the day's letters. He glanced at each and then laid them aside without opening any.

She waited until he'd gone for a shower before letting herself out of the house and heading over to the University.

∞✕∞

The physics block was way out at the back end of the campus, the last major building before the playing fields and the sports centre. It had won architectural prizes in the 'seventies and was hideous beyond belief.

Duncan Dalby was neither as senior nor as well-qualified as Miranda's father, but even Doctor Hood would have to agree that Dalby was a better choice for department head. He might have been a mediocre scientist, but he was a born administrator.

Informed of her presence, Dalby came out of a budget meeting to see her.

"Do you have any influence with your father?" he said.

"Why?" she said.

"Because, to be frank with you, he's giving me problems I can't handle."

"So you're asking me, can I tell him what to do? You're talking about the infamous Doctor Hood."

"Thanks to whom we've got a physics department that's on a par with the best in Europe. But for how long? Someone needs to make him aware of what will happen if his behaviour doesn't change. I can't get through to him. I was hoping that you might. The only times he ever makes an appearance, it's to help himself to equipment which he doesn't account for. He's done no teaching. He's got five postgraduate students who've been getting no supervision. Our participation in the dark matter project's fallen through and I can't pin him down to discuss it."

The Dark Matter Project was an EU-funded venture to build a specialised particle detector at the Bern underground laboratory in Switzerland. Alan Hood had been one of its most active lobbyists, and had been an obvious choice to chair the project's governing committee.

"Look," Dalby said, "I know he's had a tough time. But it's been nearly a year."

"He isn't losing his mind," Miranda said. "He's coping."

"Not professionally, he isn't."

"I'll talk to him," she said. "I'll see what I can do."

Five people were waiting for her in the building's smart but draughty foyer. Three young men, two young women. They were all older than the average undergraduate, but not by much. Their spokesman looked as if he was at least part-Chinese.

"Are you Miranda Hood?" he said.

She was wary. "Yes?"

"Can we speak to you?" he said. "We're your father's research students."

They all went over to the Union bar. The lunchtime rush hadn't started yet and they had their pick of the circular tables. One of the researchers brought teas and coffees from a machine on the counter where you fed it a plastic sachet and it peed you a drink.

The part-Chinese boy's name was Peter Lee. He told her, "We're all just marking time with our own research. Duncan Dalby wants us to inventory everything in the labs for a full picture of what's gone missing."

"We daren't tell him exactly what's involved," added a young woman named Kelly. "There's a thermal imager alone gone missing that's worth fifty thousand. Have you any idea what he's doing with it all?"

"If I were a scientist," Miranda said, "I might be able to tell you. As it is… "

She was still hesitating because her natural instinct was to defend her father, but she couldn't come up with any account of his activities that didn't put him into a bad light. Poor old Doctor Hood. Poor old man. Those whom the gods would destroy, they first soften up with a whiff of the occult.

She still hesitating when the time alarm on her phone went off.

"Oh, shit," she said as something dawned on her.

Peter Lee made a polite face. "Something wrong?"

"Can you excuse me for a second?"

She left them talking amongst themselves and moved to an empty table, where she took out her organiser and ran through her schedule for the rest of that day. Miranda made her living as a private singing teacher, mostly coaching teenaged sopranos through the ABRSM grades. She wasn't going to make it back in time to take any of her lessons, it was as simple as that. She'd have to be on the road within the hour, and that clearly wasn't going to happen.

By the time she'd finished making calls and leaving messages, the bar was filling up. Of the physics department party on the next table, only Peter Lee was left waiting.

"Sorry," Miranda said as she rejoined him, and he shrugged and smiled as if to say, not that it didn't matter, more that it did and he'd be lying if he pretended otherwise.

Miranda said, "What's the chance of getting a list of the missing gear?"

"Tricky," he said. "Nobody knows exactly what's gone. We've spent many an hour trying to work out what he might be using it for. Why?"

She was thinking of the cardboard cartons up in the attic. She'd peeked into some of them, and they hadn't even been unpacked. "Maybe we can get some of it back to where it came from."

"The gear's not really the main issue for us. It's more about the academic ground we're losing."

"But it's a place to start."

She walked in the open for a while, wondering what best to do. She was hardly up to this. She felt like a person charged with stopping a rock slide, armed only with a couple of sticks and a handkerchief.

When she finally got back to the house, the day was all but over and there was a note waiting for her on the door.

*Experiment in progress*, it read. *Enter via back door.*

In no mood to be messed around, she used her key and walked straight in.

The first thing that she noticed was a deep bass *wub-wub-wub* sound permeating the entire building and pitched so deep that she mainly felt it through the soles of her feet and in the pit of her stomach. The neighbours were probably watching their furniture walking around on its own and asking themselves what the hell was happening. As Miranda moved toward the foot of the stairs there was another flash, just like the one she'd experienced the night before but this time from a different camera. This one had a motor drive. It was aimed at the spot where her mother had fallen.

The throbbing noise stopped abruptly. She could hear him heading down. She didn't wait, but went up the stairs to meet him.

"Didn't you see the note?" he called out.

"Yes," she shot back, "I saw the note. You want to carry on like Professor Branestawm, fine. Just don't expect me to pretend this is normal and play along with you."

They met up on the middle landing, where there now stood a loud-speaker that wouldn't have been out of place at a Grateful Dead concert.

"What do you mean?" he said.

She looked at the speaker, and wondered how he'd managed to get it up the stairs without help. Her mental picture of his struggle didn't help his case.

"I'm not going to humour you in this," she said. "You are seriously making an idiot of yourself while your students' careers are going down the toilet."

"What have *they* got to do with anything?"

"Given the consideration you've shown them, nothing! That's my point!"

"Who've you been talking to?"

She took a deep breath and steadied herself and then she said, "I can imagine what it's like for you. It almost made sense when you explained it to me last night. But to everyone else you're coming over as a... a... "

"A nutcase?" he suggested.

It was as good a word as any, and more polite than most of the ones she'd been thinking of.

"They're making plans, dad," she said. "Everything you spent your life putting together, you're losing it all."

To her irritation, right at that moment her phone timer went off again. Or did it? As she pulled her phone out, her father searched around and produced an identical one of his own.

"It's mine," he said, killing the beeper. "I have to be somewhere." He slid past her without touching her and started to make his way down the stairs.

"That's right," she called after him in exasperation. "Walk away."

From down at the rack in the hallway, shrugging into his big overcoat, he looked back up at her and said, "Walk with me, then."

What had once been a densely settled part of town was now a wasteland. Some of the old pubs had been left standing, only to turn rough and then die in their isolation. Now they stood amidst blown litter and weeds, bereft, boarded and vandalised.

Hood said, "Your grandfather used to look at the houses and say he could remember when all this was fields. I wonder what he'd say now."

Miranda walked on with her head down, and didn't respond.

Without changing his tone, her father said, "I do know what you're thinking. The simple fact of it is that I can't deal with anything if I don't deal with this."

"Can't you deal with it outside office hours?"

"If it's any consolation, I find it all as ridiculous as you do. I'd love just to nail it and get back to normal."

Not quite everything had been razed. A pillarbox here, an old church up ahead. Miranda was taking her father's words on board when she realised that not only was the old church not deserted, but it was their destination.

Some cars stood on the street. Bodies were getting out of them and one or two elderly-looking people were already going into the building. One of them waved, briefly.

Her father raised a hand in acknowledgement.

Miranda's heart sank.

On the pavement outside the door, as her father was making his way in, she stood and looked up at the hand-lettered board above the entranceway.

It had been nailed over the original church sign. It was in Gothic script, painted by a non-professional with only an approximate idea of what Gothic script ought to look like.

It read *LANE ENDS SPRITULIST CHURCH* and underneath, in smaller letters, *Healing, Open Evenings and Sunday Services.*

Someone behind her said, "Don't be shy!" and a batty-looking woman just inside the doorway called out, "You must be Miranda! Come in! Come in!"

And before she knew it, she'd been swept inside.

The building was in bad shape but it was still recognisably a church, albeit a peeling and crumbling one. The congregation numbered about thirty, and Miranda was the youngest amongst them. Everyone was in a group at the end of the nave, chatting enthusiastically. The woman who'd greeted her by name made something of a fuss of her and offered to take her coat, urging her to have a seat by one of the pillars with a radiator.

"They're the most popular spots," she explained. "They always go first." The woman was wearing a blue cardigan and had a lazy eye. Miranda had to make an effort not to glance back over her shoulder to see who she was talking to.

Her father was a few yards away, in the middle of the group. It was obvious that he was some kind of a regular here. As soon as she could, Miranda disengaged herself and moved to his side.

"I'm not staying," she said in a low voice when she had his attention. "I'll see you back at the house."

"Don't leave now," he said. "You might learn something."

"*Dad…* " she said, but was unable to continue as an excited murmur rose up at the appearance of a late arrival. He was standing in the doorway, and a couple of senior members of the congregation broke away to greet him. He was one of the worst-dressed men that Miranda had ever seen.

"That'll be Doctor Arthur Anderson," her father murmured to her. "He's come over from Leeds."

Anderson was a shrunken-looking homunculus in a brown checked suit that looked as if it had once been put through the wash with him inside it. The points of his waistcoat were curling up even more than the tips of his shirt collar. With this costume and his wispy moustache and a chin that almost vanished into his neck, he'd have passed for Ratty in a low-rent theatrical production of *The Wind in the Willows*. He was declining a cup of tea, rubbing his hands together, expressing a wish to be getting on with it.

"Doctor of what?" Miranda said.

Her father mimed clicking a mouse. It was an old family joke. Click 'print' to download your diploma.

Miranda realised with an even-further sinking heart that she'd left it too late to escape, because the street doors had been closed and everyone was moving to the pews to be seated. As predicted, the seats around the radiators filled up first.

Her father ushered her to a side-bench. From here they could observe while sitting some way apart from the others.

"It's a clairvoyance evening," he said as the babble was quietening down. "They have them every now and again to raise funds."

She was still eyeing the exit as the service began, but one of the elderly men had set a chair beside it. Someone started to sing an unaccompanied hymn and, after a bar or so, thirty reedy voices all joined in. It wasn't any tune that she knew.

Then Doctor Arthur Anderson, the man in the flood-salvage suit, took the floor and began to speak. He didn't use the pulpit, and he didn't use notes. This was clearly a speech that he'd made many times on similar occasions.

He said, "The spirits are all around us, they say. Well, it's true. And I know that because when the moment's right and the will is there, I can see them as plainly as I can see you. And people say to me, Arthur, they say, you've described them to me just as they were in life, but how does that work? How come uncle Bert's still got his glass eye on the other side? How come mum's still in her favourite cardigan, did that pass over too? Because I thought we gave it to Oxfam. And what I say to them is this. I don't know. Because I don't. I just see what I see."

He paused for a moment and looked aside at the floor, as if to gather his thoughts, and then he went on, "Do I see the spirits? I believe I do, but I don't *know* that I do. It's a much-abused word, is spirit. We can't hear it without thinking of ghosts and spooks. The whole point of a spirit is, it isn't a thing. It's the essence of something without the form it comes in. But that's a bit deep for most of us, which is why we can't think of God the Father without making him into an old man. And in the same way, we can't think of the dead without making them into the people we knew. So what I think happens is, the spirits decide, I think I'll go and talk to old Arthur. And what Arthur's going to see will be something that looks like the form that spirit left behind, because poor Arthur's only human and his mind needs something to fasten onto."

Miranda cast another look in the direction of the exit, where the elderly man on the chair was nodding in agreement.

"Daisy," the visiting speaker said with a sudden change of tone. "Who's Daisy? Whoever you are it's not your real name, it's your nickname, I know. I know you're here somewhere, put your hand up, love."

Nothing happened for a few moments but then, almost masked to Miranda by one of the church pillars, a tentative hand was raised.

"Someone used to call you Daisy, didn't he?" Anderson said. "And it's a name you've not heard for a long time. We're talking about someone who's passed over."

Miranda couldn't quite hear the response but it sounded like, "My brother." She tried to lean out a little way to see more, but it didn't help.

She knew how these things worked. He'd start fishing now, building on the woman's responses, shaking plausible-sounding information out of the tiny cues she'd be giving him.

"Just a minute, love... " Anderson said, and then he turned and spoke to the empty air beside him. Spoke to it as if there was a person standing there.

And Miranda thought, *Oh, come on.*

She thought, *They may be old and they may be credulous, but don't treat them as if they're stupid.*

"What are you telling me?" Anderson was asking the air. "It wasn't just Daisy, it was Daisy May?" He turned his attention back to the woman in the audience. "Is that right?"

"I had an Auntie May," the woman said, her voice barely audible even though she'd raised it.

"*That's* what he's trying to tell you," Anderson said with the triumph of a hard-won discovery. "That's who he's bringing the message from."

The message was something about the fears surrounding a medical procedure. The drift of it was that all would be well in the end. He went on like this, working his way through the audience, picking people out and talking to the spirits that he insisted were at their shoulders, some-times bantering or making a friendly argument out of his dialogue with the invisibles.

It was fascinating, in its way. Even though she found it ludicrous, Miranda didn't move or try to escape. She didn't want to do anything that might draw the speaker's attention. She sat tight, like someone scared of making an erroneous bid at an auction.

When she caught a movement from the corner of her eye, she looked and saw that her father was studying the handheld device that he'd been using the previous night. It was about the size of a TV remote and showed its information on a liquid crystal screen. He was holding it low, so it would be concealed from the—what could she call them? Congregation? Audience?—by the empty bench in front.

It didn't end until more than two hours later. Anderson had talked himself hoarse, but looked as if he was game to go on indefinitely. The man who'd introduced him moved a vote of thanks, and everyone applauded. Miranda joined in, enthused by the prospect of unpeeling her rear end from the woodwork. After the time she'd spent seated, it was as if she had nothing beneath her but thin flesh pinned to the bench by the pointed ends of her pelvic bones.

There was a bucket collection for the roof fund, and then there was an announcement of a small spread in the vestry consisting of tea and packet cakes and buttered malt bread.

"I'm not staying," Miranda warned her father.

"Neither am I," he said. "Just give me one minute."

She was assuming that her father wanted to talk to the speaker, but Hood ignored him and exchanged words with some of the others. They crowded around him, all but neglecting their guest. One woman had brought along a magazine that she produced and now pressed on him.

"I saved this for you, Doctor Hood," Miranda heard her say.

"*Did* you, Mrs Lord?" Hood said. "Thank you."

"They've got a psychic's page where people write in. One of the letters is just like the experience you told us about."

"I shall read it. Thank you."

And even though Miranda was trying her best to find it all too ridiculous for words, she couldn't help feeling a twinge of envy at the genuine warmth that surrounded her father in this unlikely place.

He'd promised her a minute. They were out in just under twenty.

They walked some of the way home in silence. But then Miranda couldn't help herself.

"Please don't tell me you were taken in by any of that," she said.

"Not the slightest danger," he told her. "Don't worry."

"He was a total fraud."

"Ah," Hood said. "You can be wrong without being a fraud. Just as you can be sincere without being right."

"What were you measuring?"

He showed her the instrument. "It's called a tri-field natural EM meter. They were developed to measure the activity in electromagnetic storms. Ghosthunters use them."

"And what did you pick up tonight?"

"Nothing at all."

The main road was ahead. There were no cars to be seen, but the traffic lights changed and then changed back.

As they crossed, Miranda said, "They treated you like one of the family."

"I'm their pet sceptic," her father said. "They appreciate me. I give them open-minded attention without prejudice."

As they made the turn through the gateway that led into the private lane, she said, "I don't know where I stand with you. One minute I'm convinced you're off your trolley. Then I can see a kind of sense in what you're doing. Then suddenly I'm in the middle of a freak show and I don't know *what* to think."

"Don't think, then," he told her. "Just observe. I'm not going insane, however it looks. You could say that I'm just finding ways of preserving my sanity in the face of pressure. You should leave me to it."

"Don't think I wouldn't, if I could."

"Miranda, my problems are not your problems. I'm bright enough and old enough and ugly enough to sort them out for myself."

"Well," she said, "two out of three isn't bad."

When they got near to the house, she paused in the lane to check on her car. She couldn't remember locking it earlier, but it turned out that she had. Looking up from the vehicle, she saw that her father had gone ahead and was at the top of the house steps with his key already in the door. He seemed to hesitate, and then he pushed the door open and went inside.

It had only been a moment, but in that hesitation she believed that she could read him exactly. It wasn't as if he'd paused in apprehension of what he might find.

It was more as if he was bracing himself for the disappointment of finding nothing.

The next morning Miranda slept late, but was still up and about before her father. She'd spoken to Dan for half an hour the night before and given him a list of people to call. She could get away with a week's absence, she reckoned. In one week, she'd lose only money. More than a week, and she might begin to lose students. Two cancelled lessons in a row might not bother her less committed pupils, but with the more competitive ones it would start to count against her.

She filled a dish with boiling water to steam her vocal cords, and made a pot of tea with the rest. Then she poured herself a mug without milk and took it into the dining room, ready to run her voice exercises.

She'd always found this room a little bit intimidating. It had a clubby, Edwardian billiards-hall look, dark and high-ceilinged, done out in maroons and greens with dado rails and panelling. A low chandelier hung over the dining table. A hundred or more family pictures hung on the walls.

And there was the piano, of course.

Her mother's upright Bechstein. Her father had offered to let her take it, but where would it go? The most that her own tiny lounge could run to was a Yamaha keyboard stowed off its legs in the space behind the sofa. And besides… moving in with Dan had been one of those try-it-and-see decisions, not the whole starry-eyed hog. She suspected that moving in and bringing a piano would have been rather more than their tentative relationship could take.

She raised the lid to play herself a starting note, and was appalled at the thickness of the dust that had been allowed to gather on it. There was more on the lid than on anywhere else, and her fingers left marks where she touched it. The sooner he found a replacement for Mrs Llewellyn, the better.

Then she frowned. She rubbed her fingers together and felt the texture of the powder that clung to them. Silky. Then she sniffed. Lavender.

Lavender?

It wasn't dust at all. It was talcum powder.

He'd dusted the piano lid with her mother's talc.

For what? Ghost prints?

She felt helpless.

Fortunately he hadn't dusted the keys as well, possibly out of a scientist's respect for their underlying machinery. She struck a C and began her scales.

Few people had any idea of the sheer physical technique involved in producing vocal sound. After all, they probably reckoned, who taught the birds to sing? She heard plenty who believed that you just stood there and did it, and who stood there and did it down their noses, in whiny fake accents, off-key, off-note, off the beat and with their voices full of breath and strain.

Miranda's mother had taught her in this very room. She'd coaxed her through the grades and driven her to the festivals. Miranda could remember running up to her father's study to show him her prizes; second, third in the class, the occasional first... and always the same reaction. He'd look over his reading glasses and say something along the lines of, *That's very good, Miranda. You'll have to sing something for me later.*

Always later. And somehow he was always occupied elsewhere when she sang.

Miranda sensed that she was not alone.

She became aware of him standing there in the doorway. She didn't have to turn. She saw his reflection move in the glass of the photo frames, broken up and repeated like an image in an insect's eye.

"This is where it happened to me," he said.

She looked at him. He'd drawn a mug of tea from the pot and was there with it in his hand.

"How?" she said.

"The piano lid was open. I tried to pick out a scale. You know how much musical ability I've got. For once, it just came. And I had an overwhelming certainty that I wasn't alone."

"But you didn't actually see her."

"I saw nothing. I'm talking about awareness. Something I realised I had no definition for. Utter conviction without sensory evidence. I took my own pulse, and it was racing for no reason."

Mug in hand, he moved around the room. This side of the house got the worst of the morning light, and was often gloomy. As now.

He said, "I looked for some kind of explanation. Because something here required one. It's said that sometimes you can get a sense of presence or foreboding caused by a low-frequency standing wave from a fan or a vibrating object. But I tested the entire room and found nothing. Or stimulation of a certain part of the brain can induce a sense of formless apprehension, like there's someone standing uncomfortably close to you." He stopped by the enormous fireplace. There was a firescreen in the empty grate and a basket of dried, dead flowers before it.

He said, "I had an encephalogram check over at the psych department and there's nothing to that, either. All I know… is that for a moment I knew she was here. It happened again a week later, in one of the rooms upstairs. I don't know what triggered it that time. Something did, I'm sure. Something must."

He was behind her now. He leaned past her to reach the dusty piano, and started to pick out a scale with one finger.

Five notes into it, he went wrong.

The bad note jarred, and a mood was broken.

"Don't hang around here," he said. "Time's not for wasting. Get on with your life."

She hoped he wouldn't look at her. But of course, he did.

He seemed bewildered. "What did I say?"

But all she could do by way of an answer was to turn away from him and run from the room.

Later that morning, she met up with Peter Lee in the University library. He'd told her that with his own work on hold, he was making a little extra money researching old science journals for one of the other professors.

The library was an 'eighties addition, and such a monolith of a building that it looked as if it ought to have Stalin's picture hanging down the side of it. From there they walked across the campus to the visitor parking where Miranda had left her car. She'd asked Peter Lee to go to the house with her see how much of the borrowed equipment could be spirited back to its rightful place. She was hoping that her father would be out when they got there. But he wasn't.

They could hear voices coming from the kitchen. When Miranda went through she found her father sitting at the kitchen table with a woman that she didn't immediately recognise. Both looked up at her. Peter Lee hung back in the hallway, but Hood spotted him and called him in and then made the introductions.

The woman's name was Yvonne. Yvonne Lord. She was the woman who'd saved a magazine to give to Miranda's father the previous evening.

"Yvonne's been describing her experience for me," Hood explained. "It makes quite a story."

"I'm sure it does," Miranda said.

"Tell it again," he suggested, and at that point he cast a look in Miranda's direction. "We're all open minded, here," he said. "Aren't we?"

"Well, I don't know what you'll make of it," Yvonne Lord said. "I'm afraid it might sound stupid." She was a broad-shouldered, blonde-rinsed, quite handsome-looking woman of around fifty or fifty-five.

Peter Lee was pulling out a chair and sitting down, so Miranda reluctantly did likewise as the visitor began.

"It's happened to me five times in the past three weeks," she said. "Always when I'm just drifting off to sleep."

Yvonne Lord was a widow. Her husband, much older than her, had been dead for almost three years. Even though she was a believer, she'd had no paranormal experience during most of that time. It was only when she'd had the bedroom redecorated that the apparitions had started.

"I see him in the room with me, over by the wall," she said. It didn't matter whether the light was on or not, she could see him whatever. He seemed to be calling to her but making no sound, reaching for her but making no progress. It was as if he was pulling against something, like a man harnessed to a big sled with weights that he could barely move.

The first couple of times it had happened, she'd been unable to react or speak. The third time, she said his name and believed that he responded by renewing his efforts. It was then that she became aware of other presences. These were much vaguer, and without faces, and they came right out of the wall. These, she realised, were the forces that were holding him back. As she watched, their strength overcame his and they pulled him away. Though he fought them every inch he eventually vanished, silently screaming, into the new Sanderson vinyl that she'd picked out to match the carpet.

She was doing fine until the screaming part. Then her voice betrayed an unsteadiness that gave Miranda a moment's feeling of guilt.

After that, she fell silent. Doctor Hood, who'd been taking notes, laid down his pen and said, "Is that everything?"

Yvonne Lord nodded.

"Right," Hood said, "Thank you. I think we can dismiss the idea of a poltergeist outbreak because it has none of the features. And it's not a crisis apparition because they only happen once, at a time closely related to the moment of death. Which leaves us with a residual or an intelligent haunting."

Peter Lee said, "What's the difference?"

"A residual haunting is just imprinted, usually on a location. Something triggers it and it plays back without variations. There's no life or actual presence involved. An intelligent haunting is more interesting because it implies the existence of life after death. The apparition can vary its behaviour and interact with the observer. On what I've heard so far, this could make a claim to fall into either category. Everything depends on whether the apparition was merely following a pattern, or whether it really did alter its actions when you called your husband's name."

Peter Lee looked at the woman. "What do you think, Mrs Lord?" he said. "Can you say for sure that there was a response involved?"

Yvonne Lord spoke carefully. "I think there's some part of my husband that's still with us," she said. "I think he's aware and in distress. The very thought of that is very hard for me to bear. I'll do whatever it takes to get him out of it."

"Dad... " Miranda said then. "There's something I need to ask you. Can we... ?"

She left the question hanging, and Hood got to his feet. Leaving the graduate student and Yvonne Lord together, they moved through into the dining room.

Hood got in first, saying, "Where did you meet Peter Lee?"

"He's helping me to sort out the mess you've got into. I bring him home, and what do I find? Tales from the Frigging Crypt in our own frigging kitchen! How embarrassing is that?"

She couldn't help her voice escalating in intensity, but she did manage to keep its volume down. The effect was that she could barely prevent it from turning into an indignant squeak.

"Separate this out," Hood said, dropping his voice and almost matching her tone. "There's what she saw, and what she thought she saw. The distinction between the two is exactly the area I'm interested in."

"Yeah, well give some thought to what *she* might be interested in."

"Oh, for God's *sake*, Miranda!"

"You were quick enough to spot the glad eye from Mrs Llewellyn when there was no hocus-pocus involved!"

"Do you really not know someone's genuine pain when you see it?"

She wanted to say that the reality of the pain didn't prove the authenticity of its supposed cause, that maybe the mind just cut and shaped its own expression where the distress had no ready form... until she realised that she was getting perilously close to quoting the dubious wisdom of Doctor Arthur Anderson, at which point she broke off the argument and went to haul Peter Lee out of the kitchen. He and Yvonne Lord were making polite conversation, but he got to his feet and came at her command.

"We're going out," she called back over her shoulder.

She took Peter Lee to a corner pub a couple of streets away.

"Sorry about that," she said as they walked towards it. "Had to get away. I've heard more intelligent noises coming out of a colostomy bag."

The pub was city-centre cod-Victorian in an authentic Victorian shell, open at both ends and filled with a lunchtime business crowd. She managed to catch someone's eye and got herself a pint of Jennings and the grapefruit juice that Peter Lee had asked for.

"Is that all you drink?" she said as she put the glasses down on the half-a-table that he'd managed to bag while she was at the bar.

"In the middle of the day, it is," he said. "Anything stronger puts me to sleep."

"Me too," she said, and knocked back a third of the beer in one go. "God," she said when she'd set the glass down again, "I just don't know what to do with him. All those years, he was like a giant to me. Now it's like… "

Whoa. She was beginning to hear how she must be sounding.

"I'm sorry," she said. "You've got your career on the line. You don't want to be hearing my problems."

Peter Lee shrugged.

"'Sokay," he said.

"What do you make of all that, though? How can an educated person even start to entertain such a notion?"

"Sometimes it takes an educated person to know enough to say, 'I don't know.'"

She looked at him, eyebrows raised. "That's deep," she said, suddenly realising that thanks to the beer she was getting the first warning signals from a low-down and dangerous-feeling belch.

Peter Lee started picking the ice out of his grapefruit juice and dropping it into the ashtray.

"I had a strange experience of my own, once," he said.

Which he then went on to tell her about.

Miranda woke up on the sofa in the ballroom-sized lounge a few hours later, living proof that she and daytime drinking were necessary strangers. Her head felt bad, in the way that fruit goes bad. Soft, rotten, ready to split.

She went up to the bathroom to look for some aspirin. It was a room that she rarely saw when she visited, having a bathroom of her own on the attic level. When she opened the door of the wall cabinet, it was to find all of her mother's toiletries lined up on the shelves. The bottles, the lotions, the perfumed bath cubes that people bought each other as presents but no-one ever used. The home colour kit, the highlighting shampoo, the lavender talcum powder.

She knew that most of her mother's clothes were in the wardrobes, still. He'd told her as much. He was waiting until the time felt right to let them go, he said.

She found some soluble aspirin, but nothing to dissolve them in. On her way down to the kitchen she was vaguely aware that something was different, without immediately being certain of what… and then she realised that not only was the enormous speaker gone from the landing, but also the wiring that had hung down the stairwell. All removed. Various cameras and other ghostbusting items appeared to have been stripped out as well.

That brightened her, a little.

In the kitchen, sipping from a clean glass out of the dishwasher, she picked up Yvonne Lord's magazine and leafed through it until she found the page of readers' letters to Rita the Psychic. The first was from a woman whose husband had died and who was now being visited regularly by a pigeon that stood on her bedroom windowsill and tapped at the glass with its beak. Could this be my husband, Rita, the reader wanted to know, returning with a message for me? Yes, replied Psychic Rita, I believe it almost certainly is, which caused Miranda to blow soluble aspirin down her nose.

The phone started ringing then, and she was still choking when she picked up the receiver. It was a real effort just to manage, "Hello?"

"You're awake, then," she heard Peter Lee's voice say.

"What makes you think I was asleep?"

"The sounds you were making when I left you at the house."

"Did you move some of the gear back to the lab?"

"We're not at the lab," he said. "Are you fit to drive? There's something going on here that you maybe need to see."

It was a suburban close of modern houses, none of them more than ten years old. They'd been crammed onto the available land like penguins on a rock. Each had a one-car garage and a driveway and an immaculate Brazilian strip of garden, and the convenience of being able to step straight out of your front door and into your neighbour's face.

The horseshoe-end of the close had turning space for one car, and there were seven non-resident vehicles in it with their wheels up on the pavement. The biggest of these was a white University service van. There was no mistaking the house Miranda needed; the kids from the department were all over it.

She parked the car as near as she could. Two of them were up ladders, fixing plastic blackout sheeting over the upper story windows. Down below them she recognised one of the graduate students hooking up a heavy-duty generator cable between the house and the van. Others were stepping over it with boxes, taking care not to trip. Some of the boxes looked familiar.

Miranda followed the students in. No-one challenged her. The front door was pinned back, the house opened up to the world as if for surgery. A boy in the hallway was fixing up an array of six Pentax cameras in a framework. She heard her father's voice somewhere upstairs saying, *Check the walls for buried wires. Anything that conducts. Start at the manifestation point and work outwards.*

Hard to tell for sure from down here, but it sounded as if he was enjoying his evening.

The stairs were impassable for the moment and so she made her way through the house, looking for someone that she could recognise. She found Peter Lee in the glazed conservatory on the back of the building. The invading party had taken over the space, and Peter Lee was setting up a command centre here. At this moment he was down on the floor trying to link up four portable TVs with the outputs of four separate video recorders, which in turn had to be matched with switchable input from somewhere near a dozen cameras.

She stood over him for a while, watching without being noticed, and then to get his attention said, "When did all this get under way?"

He looked up, squinting with one eye because of the bright tungsten working light behind her shoulder.

"While you were sleeping," he said. "We brought all the gear from the house and a vanload more from the lab." Then he grinned. "Duncan Dalby's going to hit the roof."

"Nobody seems worried."

"It's a ghost hunt!" he said.

She gave up on Peter Lee and moved back into the main part of the house, where her father was now in the hallway. As soon as he spotted her, he broke off his conversation and said, "Miranda! Don't just stand there, make yourself useful."

Someone bumped past her with a laser printer.

"Doing what?" she said.

"Help Mrs Lord with the coffee."

As she took a breath to tell him what she thought of that idea, there was an approving chorus of voices from all the rooms around her. So instead of responding, she clamped her lips shut and went through into the kitchen.

By late evening, everything was in place. Video cameras were tested and running. The house had a complete new nervous system and a brain room to drive it. Devices in the upstairs rooms ranged from a state-of-the-art ion cloud detector to an array of cheap motion sensors from the home security section of a DIY store. Spot-temperature observation, infra-red profiling, electro-magnetic field detection... in the midst of directing the installation, Doctor Hood had taken the time to liaise with anxious or indignant neighbours out in the Close. She'd heard him soothe them, reassure them, convince them that the work here was crucial and without any attendant dangers to the surrounding property...

And all without ever once mentioning the 'g' word.

Everyone gathered in the sitting room to hear Mrs Lord tell her story once again and to discuss a strategy for the evening's observations. It had been impossible for Miranda to get a head-count before this, because every-one had been constantly on the move and there had been some people who'd turned up with gear, worked for a while and then hadn't been seen again.

Now she counted nine, including Peter Lee and three of the graduate students she'd met back at the Physics department. All listened intently as Yvonne Lord went through the story that Miranda had heard earlier on in the day. Miranda had the worst spot, right at the back of the crowd, almost pushed out into the hallway, trying to see over everybody's heads.

When Yvonne Lord's story was done, Hood sent her upstairs to take a Valium and get herself ready for bed before the cameras went live. Once she was out of earshot, he opened the matter up for discussion.

Someone said, "What if we're looking at something purely psychological?"

"You mean, is it only in her imagination?" Doctor Hood said. "That's entirely possible, but we're not going to start with a conclusion and then cherrypick our evidence to fit. I know that's a bit radical for this profession, but let's give it a try for once. As long as ghosts wear clothes I'm inclined to be convinced that the psychological is a major element. But let's not be closed to the possibility of the actual existence of some underlying physical trigger, here. So-called spirit photographs often show a ball of fog where a live observer sees a human form. That factor alone is of serious interest to me."

Everyone was assigned to a post. Nobody said as much out loud, but Miranda's role was to keep out of the way. Yasmin the medical technician went up to attach a pulse monitor to Mrs Lord, and on returning gave Doctor Hood the go-ahead to send all the cameras and monitoring equipment live.

Miranda felt herself prickle all over as the ghost house went on-line.

Everyone fell silent, and tried to settle. There was no way of knowing how long they'd have to wait for something to happen. Maybe nothing would. Maybe their presence would be enough to upset the conditions that had caused the phenomenon. Or maybe ghosts just didn't like a crowd. As far as was possible, they'd confined their wiring and mess to the downstairs rooms and kept the upstairs looking normal. That meant a lot of gear hidden behind furniture, in the loft, and even in the wall cavity.

Under these bizarre conditions, artificially relaxed by the Valium, Yvonne Lord had undertaken to lie in her own bed with a pulse meter taped to one hand and a signalling device adapted from a Playstation joystick in the other, and in that unnatural state to wait for her dead husband to make his nightly appearance.

In a creaky cane chair at the back of the conservatory, Miranda let out a long breath and felt much of her energy following it. Her main view was of the backs of her father and Peter Lee, watching over all the monitors and readouts, observing, tweaking, calibrating, swapping theories in the lowest of low voices.

Looked at from any angle, it was a joke, wasn't it? Spookhunting was for the oddball, the damaged, the credulous. Bobble-hat people. Not bright kids like these.

And yet...

Under more normal academic circumstances, under the tutelage of the world-famous Doctor Hood, these same bright kids would be exercising their intellects in the search for and study of Dark Matter. And what was Dark Matter? Miranda was no scientist but she was a scientist's daughter, and knew that her father's regular field of study involved a material of unknown composition that had never been seen, measured, nor even proven to exist, and yet was reckoned to comprise more than ninety per cent of the known universe. The strongest argument for its existence was that without it, the heavens would fall. Spiral galaxies would fly apart and the light from distant stars would bend without reason.

Despite nobody knowing what it was or what it was made of, Dark Matter had to exist in *some* form, because otherwise certain phenomena lacked any rationale.

Which of course had no parallel in anything that was going on here.

She could hear Yvonne Lord's breathing over an intercom-sized speaker on the main desk. Every now and again there'd be a rustle of sheets as the woman shifted her position.

Everyone waited, and nothing much happened.

Miranda was looking at Peter Lee.

*I had a strange experience of my own, once.*

He'd been walking home late one night, he'd told her. This had been some years before, when he'd been a second-year student. He'd had a lot on his mind and had only been vaguely aware of a figure walking ahead of him. When he thought about it later he realised that the figure had been dressed in very old-fashioned garb, gaslight-era clothing, but the fact hadn't struck him as anything remarkable at that moment. All that he'd registered was the presence of a man in front of him, heading in the same direction as himself.

When the man reached the house where Peter Lee was living at the time, he stopped as if to enter. Peter Lee registered this, and took an interest. The gap between them was closing as Peter Lee approached. The man met his eyes, smiled… and then walked right through the closed and locked door.

That was it, and that was how he'd told it. His only such experience, ever. The significant element to Peter Lee's mind was not that he'd seen a ghost, but that the ghost had so obviously seen him.

Miranda's father was looking pensive.

"Nothing much happening here," he said. "Let's run some juice through the wall. See if we can start something rolling."

Peter Lee got up and moved out of the conservatory and into the main part of the house. Yasmin the medic, half-hidden by monitor screens, said, "How do you record an observation when your observer's asleep on the job?"

"Already?" Doctor Hood said. "Are you sure?"

"I'm on sound. Her pulse has slowed and she's making z's."

Miranda turned her attention toward the intercom speaker and, yes, she could hear a faint snoring coming out of it as well.

"I don't want her *that* relaxed," Doctor Hood said.

"Does she do Valium every night?" Miranda ventured. "Maybe the whole thing's no more than a recurring dream."

"Ion surge," someone said then, with an edge of excitement that everyone immediately picked up on. Other voices chipped in with further observations, some called through from the adjacent room.

"I'm picking up an EM field by the wall."

"Temperature down two degrees."

Doctor Hood looked at all the TV monitors and switched cameras on a couple of them. Miranda looked over his shoulder and saw the same thing that he did. Nothing. Empty stairs, empty landing, empty bedroom apart from the half-visible figure of Yvonne Lord in one corner of a screen, nothing happening in the boxroom on the other side of the bedroom wall. All in grainy digicam nightshot vision, images magically pulled out of the darkness.

"How closely did that coincide with the voltage?" Hood said.

Peter Lee stuck his head around the door.

"I hadn't started the voltage yet," he said.

"High, high activity," said the boy who'd reported the ion surge. "I've got levels jumping all over the place."

"Sound?"

"Woman in a room breathing," the girl said. "Slow breathing, slow pulse, same as before."

"Is she reacting to anything?"

"Nope."

"Is she even aware?"

"Doesn't look like it. We've got an independent phenomenon. It isn't coming from her."

Then there was a sound that made everybody gasp and jump at the same time, as six Pentax cameras fired off all at once and only inches from the room microphone. The switchblade sound of the shutters was followed by a chorus of motor drives as the film rolls advanced.

On the monitors, there was nothing to see. Yvonne Lord stirred a little.

Responding to movement within the range of their infrared trigger, the reset cameras fired off yet again.

And still, in the room, there was nothing.

Doctor Hood was on his feet. "For God's sake, woman! What do you think we're here for? Wake up and look!"

"Live body on the stairs," somebody said then. "Moving."

There was a whimper from one of the students nearby. A few heads turned in the direction of the hallway. Miranda realised that her fists were bunched up so tight that her nails were hurting her hands. Those all around her were focused on the work they had to do, but she could sense without looking that in this little chintzy house, on its quick-build middle-income suburban dormitory estate, there was a sudden and shared terror in the air. The theoretical had suddenly become all too real.

She glanced at those students she could see from where she was seated. One was flushed, another bloodless, one was actually shaking.

"Moving up or down?" Hood said.

"Up."

Miranda said, "It's Peter Lee."

She'd just spotted him on one of the screens, crossing the upper landing. As he entered the bedroom, he passed from one screen and onto another in a different part of the array. Greyed-out, featureless, and leaving a streaky trail of fading pixels as he moved, on the screens he looked as convincing a ghost as any spirit footage.

"He's compromising the experiment," someone said.

"Quiet, there," Doctor Hood said. "Stick with your observations."

She saw Peter Lee cross the room and crouch by the bed, just his shoulder in shot and nothing visible at the wall where the apparitions were supposed to take place.

"He's talking," the girl on sound reported.

"Put it on the speaker?"

"He's on it," she said. "The mike's barely picking him up. I don't know why. He ought to be coming through loud and clear."

Doctor Hood bent to listen more closely. But most of what Miranda could hear was just loud static hiss with the odd, formless surge of sound pushing up through it without actually breaking into clarity, like bad shortwave after midnight. And on that same soundtrack the cameras kept firing, winding, firing again…

"Whoever's there, he can see them," Hood said.

… and still the video monitors showed an all-but-empty view of a suburban bedroom where Peter Lee, seen from above and behind, stood and faced a cleared space before a blank and newly-decorated wall.

And yes, he seemed to be talking to someone that the cameras couldn't see.

"The needles are dancing off the scale," someone said and then, "Oh my God, I think they're answering him."

And someone else said, "She's waking up."

And then there was a real, honest-to-God, first-hand sound as a muffled cry was heard through the fabric of the house; the awakened Yvonne Lord had sat up in bed and was shouting out her husband's name at the top of her voice.

Scientific discipline finally cracked. Everyone rose to their feet. Someone screamed and it sounded as if someone else in the next room was throwing up. In the turmoil, Doctor Hood pushed his way through the clutter of people and equipment and disappeared into the hallway. Miranda could see him on the monitor then, making his way up the stairs two at a time.

"Temperature up two degrees," called a lone, conscientious voice, but no-one else was paying any attention. At least one person was in tears. Everyone was talking at once and somebody was saying, over and over, *I want to go, I want to go...*

Miranda followed her father.

When she reached the upper landing she could still hear the racket going on downstairs, like a noisy party where the music suddenly stops. No-one had tried to come after her.

The room lights were on. They were so bright, they hurt. Yvonne Lord was sitting up and crying uncontrollably, and her father was at the side of the bed with his arm around her shoulders. Peter Lee stood a few feet away, his features drained and shocked-looking, his stance a little unsteady. The cameras were silent now, their rolls of film all used up.

Miranda said, "What did you see?"

Peter Lee said. "It's not what she thinks."

"Did you interact with the manifestation?" Hood said. "Did he answer you?"

"He wasn't aware of me. All he can see is her. He doesn't even know he's died, yet. The others answered for him."

"What others?"

"I don't know who they are. They're trying to help him over." He looked at Yvonne Lord. "But it's her. She won't let him go. Every night she keeps on calling him back. Every night he tries to reach her, and every night they have to pull him away. He fights them. Sometimes she sees what's happening. Whether she sees it or not, it still goes on."

Miranda looked at her father. He was still holding Yvonne Lord, rocking her for comfort, but absently. He didn't appear to be listening.

"You'll see nothing on the film," Peter Lee said, and wiped his dry lips with the back of a shaking hand. "It's not like he's haunting her. It's more like, *she* won't stop haunting *him*."

She drove her father home. He sat beside her in the car and said almost nothing.

Yvonne Lord had gone to relatives and a couple of the more iron-nerved of the graduate students had made the equipment secure in the house for the night. They'd done it on the condition that all the others waited right outside, and they worked with all the lights on. Angry neighbours tried to make a scene, but nobody would talk to them. The Close was silent now. The vehicles were gone and the house stood empty.

It was well after midnight when they turned into the quiet lane of big houses behind the cathedral. Someone was walking a dog, pausing under a streetlamp down at the far end while the animal stopped to sniff and pee, but that was the only life around.

She followed her father into the house. There was a vague sense of *deja vu* about the moment, and she knew why.

This was exactly the way that it had felt, coming back to the house from the hospital on the night that her mother had finally died.

She'd always had the guilty feeling that her mother's death had never hit her as hard as it should. She'd rationalised this in various ways, telling herself that she'd channelled her own grief into concern for her father. But she wondered if instead she'd merely used him as a buffer, hiding behind him while he took the full brunt of the hurt.

Just as they'd done that night, he switched on lights and she went to make tea. Little rituals. Little comforts.

As she was swilling out the pot, she heard him in the dining room.

She heard the sound of the piano lid being raised and then she heard him playing a halting scale on the keys.

Just a simple one. Do, re, me, fa...

And then a wrong note.

He didn't try again. She heard him close the lid and then she heard him going upstairs. Slowly, as if in defeat.

She felt her heart lurch, momentarily overcome with a weight of love mixed with self-pity. He'd always been able to lessen her sorrows just by being there, but she felt that she could offer nothing that would lessen his. And she could no longer pretend or imagine that he'd be there forever. When he was gone for good, who would she hide behind then?

The night beyond the kitchen window was blacker than black. There was a blind, but they never drew it down. Her reflection looked back at her, a creature drawn with a neon wand in liquid crude. The water on the hob made a sound like a jetliner streaming ice vapour from its wings. It was as if all of her senses had edges. This was how she could remember feeling sometimes as a little girl, when she'd stayed up too long and too late but wouldn't admit that she was tired.

A thought crossed her mind, and made her skin prickle.

She went through into the dining room and, gently so as not to announce it with a sound, lifted the lid on the piano. As she settled onto the stool, she inhaled the deep scent of lavender and it was as if she felt her heart flood.

Delicately, walking her hand up the keyboard, she played a chromatic scale. Then triads in various keys. Then a melodic and a harmonic minor. Though she played them softly, they broke the silence like pistol shots. These were the patterns of notes underlying the vocal exercises that her mother had taught her to warm up with. How many times must they have been heard in this room?

Not often, of late. But once, long ago...

But nothing.

It wasn't working.

The notes were just notes. They brought no sense of presence. Not beyond anything she might be imagining, anyway. For a moment she'd thought that it might have been within reach, but already she could feel the magic leaking away.

Until she heard her father's voice upstairs.

They were alone in the house. But that wasn't how it sounded.

She couldn't hear words, just the low rumble of his speech. She held her breath, the better to hear. Held it for so long that she was getting light-headed. Although she couldn't be sure of exactly what was being said, it sounded like some kind of a question or perhaps an entreaty. Was he on the phone? Could it be something as stupid and obvious as that?

But in the moment that Miranda finally let go of her breath and exhaled, she could almost have sworn that she heard a woman's voice replying.

Her head snapped up and she looked at the ceiling, as if by sheer intensity of will she might be able to look right through it and on into the rooms above. She could have cursed herself for her timing. She listened even harder, but now she heard nothing.

If there had been a response, it had been a brief one. One word, two words, no more. Maybe just an echo in her head. Maybe just the blood pounding in her brain.

She wanted to run upstairs. But her finger was still holding down the last key on the piano. Even though the note had long faded, the action was not yet closed.

Close it, and the moment would be over.

Which it was anyway, as she heard the heavy tread of her father descending the house stairs.

She found him in the kitchen, finishing what she'd started. Steam from the kettle had fogged the kitchen window. His back was to her and as he sensed her, he turned his head to look over his shoulder.

Something was different.

Miranda said, "Was it her?"

He winked at her and smiled, as fathers do at their little girls when life's in order and much as it should be, and returned to his task.

He didn't acknowledge her again.

Back in the dining room, she lowered the lid on the piano. What had originally been an even dusting of talc had become well messed-up. Any apparition that now cared to leave its mark would have to take its chances at passing unseen.

Miranda paused, staring at something she hadn't noticed before. Had her father done this? She was certain it hadn't been her.

Scrawled in the powder, lightly drawn with an idle fingertip, all but faded and blurred, there were two words.

*Release me.*

Nothing else.

Miranda leaned forward, her face only inches from the lid. She could see every trace, contour and swirl of the letters, every grain of the powder. The grains on the lacquer like stars in empty space. She took a deep breath, pursed her lips, and blew. Not hard like someone trying to blow out a flame, but gently, steadily, like someone cooling an angry patch of skin.

As she blew, the words faded. After only a few seconds they were all but gone. And when they really were gone, gone for good, she sat back and felt a peace like nothing she'd ever experienced before.

From the kitchen, she heard her father call her name.

Nothing here was anything that she could explain.

"Coming, dad," she said.

Knowing that, for this moment at least, all was well. ❧

# Jailbird for Jesus

§ "So," he said to me. "What does an honest week's work feel like?"

"You should give it a try sometime," I said, looking out of the car window as tattoo parlor followed titty bar on the way down Airline Drive.

"Yeah," he said, slowing for a bakery truck that had just pulled out ahead of us. "Make four dollars an hour and join you back there in the Ozone Motel. Like that's gonna happen. How about I set you down at this corner?"

"Anyone sees that, it's going to look weird," I said. "Let me out right in front."

So when we reached the gas station he turned onto the concrete apron, and as we slowed to a stop by one of the fuel islands he said, "Watch yourself. Look respectful when you get out."

"What are you staring at?"

"That shirt," he said. "Jesus. Talk about playing the part."

I opened the door and stepped down and looked back into the Cherokee to say, "Thank you for the ride, sir."

"Just keep your nose clean," he said, and he was starting to move off even before I'd got the door closed. Like this was a place you might pass through if you had to, but where you'd never choose to linger. He made a big loop around the islands and then rejoined Airline Drive to head back the way he'd come.

He wasn't necessarily wrong. Airline Drive ran through an end of town that had seen great days, and these weren't them. You'd find no family restaurants or miniature golf here. This was the bargain-basement retail zone for fast food, fireworks and fornication. And soon it would start getting dark.

I crossed the gas station's forecourt to enter the store. Half a dozen automobiles were lined up outside the repair shop that operated around the back, mostly fitting discount tires and mufflers. Some of those vehicles were top-of-the-range, collected from their owners in smart downtown offices and delivered back to them at the end of the working day.

The store was the usual three aisles of late-night needs plus a donut display and a coffee machine. The whole thing was run from the far end by a solitary employee. Behind the counter right now was a shaven-headed black man of brick-wall bulk, wearing the yellow Penry's uniform shirt unbuttoned over a singlet. I hadn't seen him before, but even before I could open my mouth he said, "You the new guy?"

"John Lafcadio," I said.

"Oberon Luce," he said, and stuck out his hand. I shook it.

"Oberon?" I said, not sure that I'd heard it right.

"What of it, *Lafcadio*?" he said.

"Nothing," I said.

"Least I don't got my parole officer drivin me to my job."

I glanced at the desk. Not only were there three cameras covering the forecourt, there was a microphone pickup out there as well. "Who says he's my parole officer?" I said.

"You one of the Jailbirds for Jesus or not?"

"I guess," I said.

"Well, there you go."

I joined him behind the counter for the handover. As I was signing in I said, "How's it been?"

"Quiet," he said. "Coffee machine's on the spazz and the donuts are still yesterday's. The man from the magazine place came to fill up the racks and left some free dirty books. Don't let Old Jake see them less you want to watch your new boss having a coronary."

There wasn't much more to the handover than that. The takings from Luce's shift went into the back office, where he dropped them through a one-way slot into a safe set in the concrete floor. Most of the sales were on charge accounts and credit cards, so there wasn't a lot of cash business. The owner called by twice a day to collect the money and check it against the record. Any shortfall came out of the cashier's wages. Two shortfalls, and you were out.

I'd be starting my shift with a clean roll and a twenty-five dollar float. Old Jake Penry might be a businessman and lay preacher willing to offer ex-convicts a job and a measure of trust to help them get rehabilitated, but Old Jake Penry wasn't stupid with it.

Oberon Luce disappeared around the side of the building and re-appeared a couple of minutes later behind the wheel of an ageing Ford Fairlane. Less than a minute after that he was gone, carried away in the steady Airline Drive traffic.

Over the next half-hour I kept an eye on forecourt sales and tidied up some of the stock in the store. I tapped one of the donuts against the glass in the case; any staler, and it could have been rinsed off and sold as a bagel. A couple of people came in and bought phone cards. A beer truck driver asked for directions. Someone out at the pumps was having trouble with the card swiper and I had to get on the mike and tell him how to do it. Then I had to tell him where to find his receipt slip because he was looking in the wrong place.

While that was happening I heard the connecting door to the repair shop swing open, and looked at the in-store surveillance monitor to see one of the mechanics heading for the coffee machine. I saw him stop and read the handwritten notice on the front of it, and then from over the shelving I heard him curse.

I called out, "Don't you have your own supply back there?"

"We got our own hot water, but that's no good when the coffee can's empty," he said, emerging into sight from the end of one of the aisles.

"I can sell you a jar."

"Not at Old Jake's prices." He was young, with a shock of dark curly hair that sat on top of his head like alfalfa spilling out of a wrap.

The embroidered name on his coverall read *Dave* in scarlet thread. He took a coke from the chiller cabinet and slapped coins down on the counter.

"Just remember," he said with a glance up at the camera. "Wherever you are, whatever you're doing, God is always watching you."

Then he hooked a finger under the ringpull, lifted one foot from the floor, and cut a rasping fart in the same instant that he popped the tab.

"That sure scratched the inner itch," he said, and strolled back through into the workshop.

Business was steady through the evening, and in the first lull I went and took the front panel off the coffee machine to see if there was anything I might be able to do with it. Someone came in while I was getting the wingnuts unscrewed.

"Right with you," I called out, and I set the panel down and went back to the counter. There was a tall man waiting for me, straight-backed, slight paunch over his belt, shock of white hair. It was Jake Penry. He must have reached over the counter because he was holding about a hundred dollar's worth of cheap single-use cameras that had been packaged as a hanging strip. If you wanted to buy one, you tore it off the bottom. He obviously meant this by way of a demonstration.

He said, "I could be out that door with all of these and the money from the cash drawer by now."

"The cash drawer's locked and you'd have found me in the way," I said.

"Think you could take me on, son?"

Well, I had at least a two-decade advantage but it didn't seem wise to be pointing it out.

"Just trying to save you some money, boss," I said. "The coffeemaker's down again. I watched the service engineer fixing the same fault on Monday. What did he bill you, fifty dollars for the callout? And all he did was clean the filter."

He narrowed his eyes in that pissed-off-amused way of people who don't like to climb down over anything and aren't used to the need for it.

"Is that right?" he said.

"Yes, sir, it is," I said.

"Is there any situation you couldn't talk your way out of?" he said.

"I had the misfortune to meet a judge who seemed to think so," I told him.

While this had been going on, Dave the mechanic had come through from the repair shop with the day's worksheets. Taking them from him, Penry said, "I want to see your time cards for last week, Dave."

"Whenever you like, Mister Penry," Dave said.

"Now sounds good to me."

Old Jake headed through to the back, and Dave gave me a meaningful look while calling after him, "I'm right behind you, sir."

Then he lowered his voice and added, "Smooching ass with the rest of them."

"I see the gratitude starts to wear a little thin with time," I said.

"Screw gratitude," Dave said. "Jailbirds for Jesus fills this place with cheap labor and gives him a ticket into heaven. For Jake that's a win-win situation."

Shortly after that, the repair shop closed down for the night. When the half-dozen mechanics had all set off for home, Dunleavy, the repair shop manager, rolled down the shutters and came through into my section to set up the night alarm. I had to look the other way as he tapped the four-number keycode into a wall panel behind the counter.

When he'd gone, that was it. I was alone. My shift would finish at six a.m., when I'd hand over to my replacement and then walk down to the bus stop for a ride back to the Ozone Motel. There I'd sleep for about four hours until the noise from housekeeping disturbed me.

When it was fully dark I brought all the loose stuff inside and made bundles of the day's unsold newspapers, and then I switched off half the store lights and locked the doors. From now on, all transactions would be through the security window. If you wanted something that wouldn't fit into my sliding drawer, you wouldn't get it.

I found where Oberon Luce had put the free dirty magazines, and took a couple of the more normal-looking ones. Then I settled in for the night. I had the security screens on my eyeline, the microphone within reach, and all the fuel reset buttons to hand; unless somebody wanted a carton of milk or a magazine I'd have no reason to move between now and the end of my shift, unless it was to scratch or pee.

From my limited experience so far, the weeknights were never too busy. They were, however, something of a weirdo parade.

It took less than half an hour to get started.

I couldn't have told you what kind of car it was, just that it was black, and riding low, and bulging with a drum-machine sound. Add-on custom parts had changed its shape beyond recognition, and the alterations had been carried out with little talent or skill. The windows were tinted, so I couldn't see who was in it.

Then the noise level rocketed as the doors opened and a couple of boys got out. One went to the fuel pump and the other walked over toward me. At this hour, for a cash sale, you paid first.

Knuckle-draggers. The boy crossing the forecourt was fat and soft with a scarf knotted on his head, a fantasy apache. He stared at me as he approached.

"I don't know you," he said.

"That's okay," I said, which stumped him for an answer and effectively ended the exchange. He put down five dollars, peeling it slowly from a thick wad of bills and watching for my reaction. I didn't give one. I just went ahead and set up the amount on the pump.

Big wad of bills. The peacock strut of the uncreditworthy.

While they were filling up I could see that there were three of them. They favored the kind of music that annoys you at stop lights. At that age, you don't think about ear damage. If it's too loud, you're too old.

When they'd got their five dollars' worth, they climbed back into the car but they didn't drive off. They just sat there with the doors open and the speakers blasting out. Someone came on in an SUV, swiped, filled up, picked up their slip and drove away, and still the boys sat there.

After a couple of minutes I pulled the mike over to me and said, "Can you take the party somewhere else, please, boys."

Nothing happened. They probably hadn't even heard. I wasn't about to go out to them; they didn't scare me, but why be stupid? I switched off the forecourt lights instead.

When they looked toward me, I pointed. *Now go.* They couldn't mistake the message. Then I switched all the lights back on.

It took a moment for the tubes to gink back into life and when they did, one of the boys—a different one—was walking over. He was doing a white boy's idea of a jungle cat stroll. It should have been funny, but it was kind of off-centered and sinister.

He stopped in front of the glass and looked past me into the store.

"Give me some of those flowers," he said, pointing, his voice crackly from the pickup mike. I looked around.

"Which kind?" I said.

"The white ones."

For his mother, or what? It was an unlikely purchase, aside from the fact that the blooms had been on sale for several days and were past their best. But I put the lock on the drawer and went to get them.

If he thought I'd open the door to hand them out, he could think again. But that wasn't his plan. When I told him the price, he said, "Now I've changed my mind."

I said nothing. Just put the flowers under the counter and out of sight. If he'd been hoping to get me running up and down for his amusement, he'd have to be disappointed.

"I'll have some of those blue things instead," he said, pointing again.

"What blue things?"

"On that shelf at the end."

"Those are baby wipes."

"I'll have two."

By now I really wasn't in the mood.

"No," I said.

He seemed genuinely surprised. This wasn't the script he had in his mind.

"What do you mean?" he said.

"You've given us the joke. I'll be laughing all night. Now quit while you're ahead and make your exit."

He opened his mouth to speak, but then he closed it again and his face set.

Then, deliberately, he drew aside his printed wool coat to reveal the handle of a 9mm automatic pistol thrust into the waistband of his pants. Letting the coat fall back, he stuck up his thumb and pointed his forefinger, mimicking the shape of a gun and pointing it at my face before making a pretend-pow, grinning, and turning to walk away.

I let him go. Watched him get into the car. Saw the ostentatious, rubber-squealing departure that I knew had to be coming.

Then I got out from behind the counter and went to the store's pay phone.

The first number I called was transferred to a service after seven rings. So then I called the police switchboard.

"I need the officer of the watch," I told the woman who answered. "It's an urgent operational matter."

"Is it an emergency?"

"It could develop into one."

"Please hang up and dial 911."

"I'm a police officer," I said. "Just put me through."

"Your name, sir."

"I'm working under cover. I don't want to give you my name on an open line."

"One moment, please."

I waited. After a few moments I heard, "Major Devereaux speaking. How can I help you?"

I told him where I was, and gave him a description of the car and its license number.

I said, "When it left here it was heading east on Airline Drive. Three white males in their early twenties. One of them's carrying a concealed weapon and an attitude. He made a point of showing me the gun. I got the impression they may be intending to use it tonight. And judging from how coked-up they were, probably soon."

"Can you stay on the line, please?"

"I don't think I can. I'm in a situation, here. I explained it to your operator."

I didn't think they'd be back, but you never knew. I'd messed up the movie in their heads. Bit players like me were supposed to lie stunned and humiliated in their wake, and I'd failed to play along.

The moment I hung up the phone, it rang.

I hadn't been expecting this. I hesitated, and then I picked it up.

"Hey," said a voice from what sounded like a cellular phone in a moving car.

"Who's this?"

"You've got a short memory. Turn off the workshop alarms."

"What?"

"You heard me. Turn off the alarms and have the door open ready. I'll explain when I get there. You see anything more of Old Jake?"

I had him now. It was Dave the Mechanic. My memory was fine, I just needed a little more than 'Hey' for it to work on.

I said, "Not since the start of my shift. What's this about?" and as I was saying this I could hear a voice in the background at the other end saying, *There it is.*

"Gotta go now," he said. "Don't forget what I told you."

"I don't know the code."

"Everybody knows the code," he said, "it's obvious," and then the signal broke up and I didn't get whatever came next, just the words *Dunleavy* and *favorite movie.*

Once again, I hung up the phone. It didn't ring this time.

The forecourt was empty right now, but something seemed to hang over the place and it wasn't good.

All the same, this was the kind of development I'd been sent in to wait for.

I went to the alarm panel. It was a piece of old crap. Three of the keypad buttons were grimy and the rest were clean. The 1, the 2, the zero.

Three digits for a four-digit code. I could only think of one movie that fit and so I tried the obvious, *2001.* The configuration of the panel lights changed for about a second, and then went back the way they'd been.

Was that it? Had I done it? There seemed to be only one way to find out. I went over with the spare key and opened the connecting door into the workshop.

No bells rang when I switched the lights on and went through. Nothing happened at all.

Well, Dunleavy a sci-fi freak. You never can tell.

Once in the repair bays, I rolled up the shutter as instructed. As the edge of the door rose, the live night air flooded in. It had all the smells of the roadside, hot tar and exhaust and a strange static charge.

When I went outside I felt strange under the lights, like a hermit crab out of its shell. So what now, I wondered? I couldn't go back to my post and leave the bays wide open and unattended. This was an area where, like water finding its level, lowlife crept out of the shadows and eased itself in the direction of any opportunity.

I took a washcloth and went around the fuel islands wiping road grease off the glass windows on the pumps. It wasn't a necessary job, but one that let me watch over my turf without drawing attention.

Thus occupied, I waited.

Someone had been stealing expensive cars to order, and somewhere in the service history of every one of the missing vehicles was a visit to Penry's Tire and Muffler Shop. None of the visits had been recent, which had made the pattern harder to spot.

Our guess was that someone had been copying keys and using a grabber to record keyfob security codes while each car was in the workshop. But we'd no idea who or how. If we were right, the thieves waited until the visit was all but forgotten, and then set out to collect. The method meant no hotwiring, no alarms to beat, no damage to the vehicle.

Worksheets carried the owners' addresses, so the vehicles wouldn't be hard to track down. Some cars had been stolen from off the street at night. A couple had been taken from locked but otherwise unprotected garages.

Others with better security at home had been followed to parking lots and taken in daylight.

We didn't know where they went to. Some said the Far East, some even reckoned Japan. In some cases it was most likely that they'd be broken up for their parts.

All we knew for certain was that there was this one place that they'd all passed through.

I was feeling keyed-up at the prospect of a result. Even more enticing was the prospect of coming out from undercover and saying goodbye to the Ozone Motel, where every bedsheet had a readable history.

Something stroked the back of my neck when I saw a silver Mercedes coming down the road towards me. It was speeding. But it slowed before it reached the gas station, and came in without leaving the telltale rubber marks that would betray a stunt turn. It shot across the apron and entered the open workshop at such a speed that I fully expected it to come out the other side of the building in a shower of masonry.

No such thing happened, though. I'd been looking to see if Dave the mechanic had been behind the wheel, but it wasn't him. It *was* someone I recognised, though.

The driver was a soft-looking white boy with a knotted scarf covering his head.

Dave came in the following car, the knuckle-draggers' home-custom vehicle, with the other two boys. I realised with a shock something that had been staring me in the face; from the resemblance, Dave and the driver surely had to be brothers. I left the washcloth on the gas pump and went to meet them.

They'd done this before. They had a routine. The black car let Dave out on the forecourt and followed the Mercedes into the workshop, where the shutters were already beginning to descend.

Dave took me by the arm and walked me toward the lights of the store. "You did good, John," he said. "It's John, isn't it?"

"What's happening?" I said.

"You must have worked it out by now. If you haven't, there's an empty place at the retard's picnic."

"You're talking to a man on parole, here!" I said, playing the part. "What are you trying to do to me?"

"Look, John," he said. "You have to understand this. Things happen. It's the way of the world. You understand what I mean?"

"I have no idea what you're talking about."

"Let me put it another way. Nobody gave you any choices tonight. So nothing that happened here is your fault. So your conscience is clear and that means you should have no trouble keeping your mouth shut."

"That's too deep for me," I said.

"Let me explain it like this," he said. "You cause us a problem, we take you down with us. It's as simple as that. But you won't be making trouble, will you? Sit in your box and read your girlie book."

And that's what I did, or at least I pretended to. I couldn't get to the pay phone because they'd have seen me through the open door. I ran the forecourt, took in some money, sold some stuff, watched a stand-up row between a Winnebago driver and his partner that almost ended with him driving off without her. One sobbing, mad-as-hell woman with mascara like a Zorro mask. Now, *there* was a complication that I didn't need.

All the while, I kept glancing toward the open doorway and trying to get some clue as to what they were doing through there. I didn't think they were chopping the Mercedes, that was too big a job to have done before morning. And it's mainly the newer vehicles that get broken up for their parts, in some cases bringing almost double the car's intact value. The most blatant scam I'd ever seen had involved a repair shop that would offer you a great deal to fix up your stolen, stripped and abandoned car when you got it back from the pound… as well they might, since the parts they put in were the same ones they'd taken out of it a few nights before.

No, I reckoned they were probably retagging this one… changing the number, switching the license plates, disguising it for resale. A re-tagged car can be hard to detect. You don't have to send them as far as Japan—I've even known of car dealerships that have been taken in. With a computer and a scanner you can fake all kinds of ownership certificates and registration documents.

After a while, Dave appeared in the doorway.

"Hey," he said. "John."

"What?"

"Need you for something."

"Can't leave the window."

He looked toward the forecourt. "Nobody's out there right now," he said. "Come on. What's the matter with you? I ain't gonna bite."

Something wasn't quite right in his attitude. I'd sensed it, and he'd picked that up. I came out from behind my counter and followed him into the repair shop, wondering what I was going to find.

The Mercedes was on the hoist, about four feet off the ground and having its new plates fitted. The black car was in the next bay with its doors open and a radio playing. It wasn't playing music, though.

I said, "Hey. You got a police scanner. They legal?"

Then two of them got hold of me and threw me against the shelves that lined the wall.

"Yeah," one of them said as they picked me up off the floor, "we got a scanner. And guess what it told us."

Dave's brother, the one with the gun in his belt, didn't wait for me to answer but said, "Everybody look out for three white guys in a black car, one with a concealed weapon. Reported from an undisclosed location by an undercover cop."

"That could have been anyone," I managed.

"An undisclosed location in the vicinity of Airline Drive."

*Oh, thanks a bunch, people,* I thought.

"Okay," I said. "Don't make it worse for yourselves than it already is."

One of them punched me and Dave said, "Take him out."

Dave's brother pulled the gun out of his belt and levelled it at my forehead, and I involuntarily screwed up my eyes.

"Whoa, whoa!" Dave called out quickly. "I meant, take him outside. You do it here and they've got a crime scene. You know what that means. Someone shines a magic light and your name as good as shows up, written in brains."

The one changing the plates stepped back from the car and pressed the control to lower the hoist.

"All done here," he said as it descended.

"Okay," Dave told the others. "You heard me. Lose the cop."

"You're too late," I said. "I already called this in."

"No you didn't," Dave said, and walked away from me as the others grabbed me by the arms and sped me over to the black car.

"You're dead," one of them said close to my ear. "What does it feel like?"

And I didn't get to answer because they thrust my head down and boosted me into the back, and then one jumped in on either side and held me in that awkward can't-breathe position while Dave's brother got behind the wheel and reversed us out of the bay. Dave had hit the red button to raise the shutters, and I heard our antenna twang as it caught on the way out.

They let me sit up after a while, but there wasn't much advantage to it. Nobody was going to see me through those tinted windows, and I didn't dare make a bid for attention because I could feel that one of them was holding a blade on me. It was pushing right into my side, threatening to cut me with every bump and turn.

We were still on Airline Drive, but this was no longer the lively part. This section was farther out of town, and all but deserted. Keep on going and you join the railroad tracks and pass factory after factory, each one visible through razor wire across an empty lot with parking for a thousand cars. All of them built in the boom years after the war, and most of them finished off by the recession.

Awfully quiet.

As these places went.

The boy with the knife leaned closer to me so that I could smell his stale breath, and he jabbed me with the point as he spoke.

"Feel it?" he said, and got some pleasure out of my involuntary jump.

Between them they had me pinned. My arms were behind me and my knees were jammed up against the seats in front. Dave's brother at the wheel glanced back over his shoulder and said, "Get his clothes off."

"There's no room," the knuckledragger without the knife said.

"I don't mean like, undress Barbie," Dave's brother said. "Just cut them. I'm gonna find some gravel."

"Why?"

"I saw this biker once, okay? It was hotter than hot and he was riding with no shirt on. He wiped out on a bend and hit the dirt on this gravel road. You could see his skin all flayed out on the ground where he'd gone along. He was like meat."

"Did he die?"

"He wanted to."

I started to speak and got chopped in the throat, which silenced me pretty well. I was thrust forward so that my face slammed into the seats, and the shirt was cut off my back. They dropped the window a few inches to stuff it out, and the wind ripped it away. They stamped on my feet to lever my shoes off. My socks went with them and everything followed my shirt.

"He's panting like a dog, back here," one of them commented in a voice of wonder.

When my head came up again we were no longer on Airline Drive, but some back road that I didn't recognise.

"Where are we heading?" the kid with the knife said.

"Other side of the railroad tracks," Dave's brother said. "There's a dirt road I remember. It's long and straight. Hard clay topped off with black cinders. The track workers and linesmen use it. If throwing him out doesn't do the job, we can always drag him a little."

There was nothing I could hang onto. Nothing apart from the short end of the seat belt that I could feel underneath me. It was just a few inches of webbing with a buckle on it but I managed to loop it around my wrist a couple of times. But what was I thinking of? I was sitting right next to a boy with a knife. One stroke of the blade and he'd have me cut loose in a second or less.

"Get him ready," Dave's brother said.

"He's ready now."

I could see the railroad. We were going to go under it. The street narrowed to a single car's width and passed under a trestle that sat on big stone blocks, one massive column to either side. The blocks had been painted with yellow and black diagonal stripes. Dave's brother had his foot right down, and wasn't slowing.

"Hey," one of the others said nervously.

"Don't distract the driver," Dave's brother said, and he leaned back in his seat and started to steer one-handed just to make a point.

Right then it was as if someone pulled a flare in the car.

It was blindingly bright. The boys screamed curses for about one full second. I felt the knife go in about half an centimeter as my captor flinched, and twisting myself away from the point is probably what saved me. The screaming stopped abruptly when the car hit one of the supports.

The shock drove the breath out of me, just as it did with everyone else. I've never felt anything like it. Everyone in the car suddenly seemed to turn boneless and to bounce like a ragdoll. The boys to either side of me went face-first into the fancy custom racing headrests on the seats in front of them and then rebounded, their faces destroyed. Dave's brother slammed into the wheel and carried on over it and through the windshield, not stopping until he met the wall.

The car half-spun and then there was a second shock as its rear end hit the other support. For a moment I thought it was all over, and then we bounced off something else, and then it was.

I somehow ended up lying across the empty front seats, covered in windshield glass, my arm twisted around and stuck through the gap into the rear of the car. The belt strap was still around my wrist. My shoulder hurt and I couldn't feel my fingers.

As I levered myself up, the glass fell from me and the air sparkled. The car was still flooded with that incredible light. I thought I could hear a train passing overhead; but no, it wasn't a train.

Dave's brother was gone. He was out on the road somewhere, all messed up. Which I count as a kind of poetic justice. The boy with the knife had stuck it in himself. The other one would survive, although it would be discovered in the Emergency Room that he'd bitten off most of his tongue. They'd look for the piece at the scene and not find it.

My bruises would come later. Right now, apart from the place where I'd been stuck with the point of the knife, I seemed to be unmarked.

"Well," I rasped, as the air glittered and the roar grew louder overhead. The knife boy stared back at me, unseeing. "You wanted to know what being dead felt like? Well, now you do."

Except I don't think that I actually managed any sound.

I climbed out through the open space where the windshield had been. A hurricane wind was beating down on the neat circle of light that was being cast around the wreck. The mess was breathtaking. You could hardly even tell it had been a car.

Shirtless and barefoot, bleached in the candlepower, I screwed up my eyes and looked up into the searchlight beam from the spotter-helicopter overhead. Its beauty overwhelmed me. I couldn't take it for too long before it started to become a physical pain. Then, when I lowered my eyes, I found that I'd been all but blinded to the night.

But I could still hear. I could hear the pulsing of police sirens as they approached from the distance, guided by radioed directions from above. Responding to their sound, I started to walk toward them.

The ground cut at my feet, but I felt nothing. The cold wind of the downdraft poured over my skin but again, I felt nothing. Nothing save the sense that I had walked whole out of disaster and that I was, indisputably, blessed.

The helicopter moved and the searchlight tracked me. It swung away from me once, to check for movement back at the wreck, but it was back on me again within seconds. The sirens were louder now, and I was beginning to see the approaching headlights. Both cars stopped before me and I could see officers jumping out. One of them was my 'parole officer'. Except, of course, he was no such thing. His name was Danny Fialka and he was a fellow policeman. Some of the patrolmen were drawing their sidearms and shouting for me to get face-down on the ground, but Danny waved them away.

"Are you hurt, John?" he said.

"I think my shoulder's out," I said.

I felt a blanket being put around me. He got me into one of the cars and then he called for someone to find me something to wear. I could see the wreck from here. Our people were clustered around one side of it. They'd found the live one and were calling for assistance. I could see others over by the pillar, shining their flashlights down onto the concertina'd remains of Dave's brother.

Danny was crouching outside the open door.

I asked him how the copter found me.

"It was the shirt," he said. "Lying on the road back there like a big yellow flag. They followed the rest of your clothes till they found you."

"But who told them to come looking?" I said. "I never got a chance to call anyone."

"No, but you managed to set off the alarm," Danny said.

"What alarm?"

"The silent alarm. The one with a phone connection that puts on a light in the despatchers' room."

"I didn't trigger that," I said. "I turned it off."

That's what I'd thought, but it turned out I was wrong. I hadn't disabled the panel after all. When I'd walked into the repair shop, it had sent off a signal. Silent alarms got lower priority than emergency calls, so it had been some time before anyone realised its significance.

The cause of my salvation was a simple one. I'd got the right digits on the keypad, but the wrong movie.

Did *you* know there was a movie called *12:01*? I didn't. But you can bet I do now. ☙

# Hunter, Killer

§ FRANK waited until the patrol had gone by, and then he ran for the wire.

Patrol? From what he'd been able to see, it had hardly warranted the name. More like goons in badly-fitting uniforms taking a stroll around the perimeter, the three of them bearing more than a passing resemblance to Curly, Larry and Moe; if the official word was that security around here was supposed to be as good as it could ever get, the reality seemed to be more a matter of the lowest bidder and the crappiest service. There was supposed to be a vehicle check every fifteen minutes and a foot patrol of the fencing every hour, but Frank seemed to have been waiting for an awfully long time with nothing happening. And then when they'd finally arrived, they'd ambled on by without even shining a light in his direction.

He felt almost let down. Here he was, high on his own adrenalin, and they couldn't even make a stab at discovery. He'd heard a rumour that at least twelve people had made it past them in the last two years; he'd thought it impossible, but with security like this he was beginning to see how it could have happened.

The fence was even less of a problem than he'd expected. It stood ten feet high but it had been thrown up in a hurry, by men who had been looking over their shoulders constantly as they worked. No cutting would be required; he could simply prise out some of the staples that held the wire to the post and then roll it up far enough to squeeze under. Crouched at the foot of it, he took a crowbar from his tote bag. It clinked against the sawn-off barrel of the shotgun and he froze, but nothing happened. Nobody seemed to have heard.

Dogs would have made a difference, of course. But dogs couldn't be worked so close to the complex; within a few hundred yards they began to panic, and at this distance they'd be uncontrollable. It was as if they sensed the unseen presence in the building, and had to respond. So instead it all fell on the shoulders of the night shift, and the night shift obviously shrugged a little under the weight and looked around for some way to make life easier. Frank had done security work himself, somewhere in amongst the dozens of jobs that he'd held down for varying lengths of time, and he reckoned he knew the score; in his own brief stint as nightwatchman with an engineering firm he'd counted on getting at least four hours' sleep on an average shift in order to keep his energies up for the day job. He couldn't remember what his day job had been at the time, but it was probably something best forgotten.

Yes, he knew the score. But given the circumstances here, he'd expected better. These people had contracts on power stations and air bases, after all, and yet they couldn't stuff the holes around one piece of industrial plant.

Not even when the general understanding was that almost certain death awaited anyone who got in.

*But not me*, he told himself as he levered on his screwdriver and felt the staple easing out of the wood. Not you, Frank.

It sprang free, and flew off into the darkness.

He began to work on the next.

The so-called lucky ones had been the three who'd been spotted and pulled out before they'd covered any distance. None of the others had ever been seen again. But they were losers, this much Frank understood; they'd gone walking in with the mark upon their foreheads and simply collected whatever destiny they'd been assigned. Frank was up for more than that. Ever since he'd been a child, he'd sensed that he was special. He was going to be somebody.

And he was starting to get a little tired of waiting.

The wire came up, and he pushed his tote bag through. Then after it he slid the plank with the nails, and then he put his face down into the dirt and started to crawl. The ground was cold, colder than the night itself. And the space wasn't as big as he'd thought, so that the links along the bottom of the wire plucked at his back. He felt the material of his jacket catch, and then spring free.

And then he was through.

He scrambled to his knees. He was inside the perimeter now, but he'd hardly begun. Across the fifty yards of cleared space ahead of him was an eight-foot wall topped with razor wire, the actual boundary of the complex itself. He slung the tote bag over his shoulder, picked up the plank, and headed across.

He didn't want to waste any time. He was too exposed, here, and even the Three Stooges couldn't miss him if they decided to turn and come around again. This had been part of a road, once; when the authorities had thrown up the containment fence, they'd gone ahead and taken a measurement and hadn't paid too much attention to where it had run. Like the old Berlin wall which it so much resembled, the new perimeter crossed roads and pavements and parking lots and the gardens of a few nearby houses, and on the side by the old docks at least one entire warehouse block had been bulldozed to take it through.

The wall looked so much higher close-to. And the razor wire... the razor wire was positively frightening. Even the name made him want to pucker up inside. He laid the plank at an angle against the wall, and he wished it was a ladder. It would have been, if the man who'd promised him one hadn't messed him around and asked for more money. He'd hocked everything that he owned for the gun, so what did the bastard expect? Blood? He'd taken the plank from a fence over a derelict railway siding, and he'd pounded in nails to form makeshift treads. He'd had to carry it through the streets, hoping that he wouldn't be stopped and wondering how he'd explain it if he was. Now, as it leaned against the outer wall of the newspaper printing plant, he could see that it really needed to be about a foot longer.

Well, tough, he told himself, and pulled the fire blanket out of his tote bag and unrolled it.

He wondered if they'd miss it, back in the hostel kitchen. He wondered, but he didn't exactly care very much. The hostel was a dismal place, full of old unshaven men who'd lost all of their teeth and whose faces seemed to fold in on themselves, and of younger men with glazed eyes and permanent facial displays of half-healed scabs that might equally have come from drunken fights or drunken falls. They lived on soup and handouts, they slept in tiny fleabag rooms subdivided from what had once been an assembly hall. For half a year now he'd lived amongst them in a permanent state of dismay, studying his face in every mirror that he passed for the signs that he might be coming to resemble them. All right, say there was a fire, and there was no blanket to put it out. Who'd mourn any of them?

Who'd mourn *him*?

The plank bowed in the middle as he climbed it. He was scared that it would break, and that he'd fall onto the nails; he couldn't windmill his arms for balance because he had the fire blanket in both hands, and the tote bag across his back didn't help his sense of stability. It only held the gun and a flashlight and the few tools for the fence that he'd been able to gather, but it was enough to worry him. He could feel himself starting to overbalance sideways even as he threw the blanket over the wire, but then the blanket caught and he was able to hold on.

He clung there for a few moments, almost poised for a drop. Another inch or so, and the plank was going to slide away from underneath him.

But then, moving slowly and deliberately, he was able to reach up and get a footing on the wall.

The plank fell. He heard it go. But never mind, there was all kinds of crap down there. They wouldn't spot it before morning.

The fire blanket was of a heavy weave with some kind of a metallised coating on one side, and the razor wire didn't pierce it. He felt it bounce under his weight as he scrambled over, felt the points through the thickness of the material, but none of them broke through. Once on the inside, the idea was to lower himself down until he'd only have two or three feet to drop, and then to kind of jiggle around in the hope of tearing the blanket free so that he could pull it down after.

But so much for forward planning. He couldn't keep a hold on the material, and he fell like a sack of shit.

Landed like one, too.

All that he could think of as he lay there on the asphalt gasping for wind, was that he was going to have to leave the blanket up there flapping away like a flag. It was an unmistakable sign of entry. Once they found it, they'd send in one of the armoured cars that was the only safe way to manoeuvre around inside the more accessible areas of the plant. Without knowing the layout, he didn't know how much of the complex that would cover. They might catch him. They might drag him out.

Just like one of the losers.

For a while, now, this day had been all that he'd had to look forward to. And if they took this away from him, what then?

He started to get to his feet. He'd been winded, but that was all. He unzipped the tote bag, and he took out the gun and the flashlight; they were all that he'd need now, and the rest he could leave behind. As he was crouched over the bag, busily sorting himself out, the realisation hit him. He was inside; this was the danger zone, right here, it had already started and he was fussing around with his bits and pieces like some halfwitted old gimmer. He looked about him quickly, wildly, but he saw nothing. He didn't know what he ought to be expecting, but of one thing he was certain—when it came it would come fast, and it would take no prisoners.

The gun in his right hand, the flashlight in his left, he straightened with the wall at his back. He'd no experience with firearms but the gun felt balanced and secure, and he knew that he'd been right to saw it down. Anything longer would have been too awkward; he'd have caught the barrel in every doorway, and probably blown off his own foot in a panic when the time came to swing around and take aim. As it was he could rely on an operating distance of about ten yards, according to the man who'd sold it to him. Beyond that, the shot would quickly lose its pattern and become far too dispersed.

Ten yards. Ten strides. He had to hit it within ten strides of it reaching him.

And he didn't even know what it would look like.

He did what he always did when the thought of the danger threatened to overwhelm him. He thought of the rewards, instead. Not just the cash that had been offered by the proprietor and by the developers of the adjoining docklands—an offer which had enraged the authorities and been opposed by the police, amounting as it did to an inducement to suicide—but also the prospect of seeing the boy again. It had been nearly a year, and Frank couldn't even imagine what he'd look like by now. But as soon as he was rich, his ex would almost certainly come out of hiding and bring their kid with her. After that, they'd see. Let her try to pass him off as nothing then, when he was famous.

He was in a yard of some kind. It looked like a prison yard, or the back of a modern brewery. The wall of the complex had no doors or windows around here, just a blank facade of brick and then an upper storey of some kind of moulded cladding. Some way further on down the yard was lit, but here it was dark. His choice was deliberate; the lights came from hastily-erected watchtowers outside the perimeter and covered areas that were supposedly under constant observation, but their coverage was patchy and seemed to be distributed without much sense of purpose. He'd heard a rumour that certain of the entrances to the complex were continually spotlit with infra-red and targeted by automatic machine guns that would fire as soon as anything moved within their field of view. This was in case of an escape attempt by whatever still roamed inside; for it to break through into the outside world…

(Was something moving over there, on the edge between the light and the shadows?)

… would be a true disaster on an epic scale. No survivor had ever actually seen it in action—or seen it at all, in fact, unless you counted what were probably the most famous eight seconds of out-of-focus home video in history, retrieved from a still-running Panasonic camcorder amidst the bloody remains of what had been the paper's assistant features editor—but it had left plenty of mess behind it to give everyone a fair idea. In the days that it had taken to seal off the entire plant, close to a million people had grabbed their essentials and jammed the roads in an attempt to be somewhere else. They'd been filtering back ever since as it had gradually become clear that the apocalypse had been postponed even if it hadn't altogether been cancelled, but most of the property in the immediate area stood empty and was likely to remain that way. Finding buyers? A sick joke. The docklands redevelopment boom of the decade had suddenly become a financial disaster; housing inside a leper colony would have been easier to move. Apartments that had carried a six-figure premium now couldn't even be rented off as warehouse space—which was an irony, since most of them had been exactly that before conversion.

Nothing was moving along the edge of the lit area. It was his imagination. He'd always had a vivid imagination. He'd read hundreds of comics, dozens of books; but that had all been a long time ago.

He started to move, following the wall away from the light.

Not knowing, that was what made it so scary. The video had been so blurry that it had shown movement and nothing more; he'd seen on TV how they'd run it through space computers that were supposed to bring out the picture better, but it was like starting with a smudge of exhaust smoke and trying to work up a detailed image of the car that had made it. Frank trusted the reality of most things that he'd seen on TV, but even he couldn't swallow that. His personal opinion was that the camera had simply been pointing at furniture as it fell. He'd seen some ugly furniture in his time, but none of it had ever killed anybody.

He turned a corner.

A big articulated flatbed truck stood in the yard, its trailer half-unloaded of its newsprint. The paper was on big spools like toilet rolls, each of which probably weighed a ton or more; they'd been out here in the weather ever since the day of shutdown, and would almost certainly be ruined by now. The forklift that was presumably meant to have unloaded them appeared to have careered off on its own and run points-first into the wall some way down. Frank shone his flashlight around but there was no evidence of the truck's driver, or of the forklift's operator. The loading bay stood open and Frank, nervously hefting the weight of his sawn-off shotgun, went inside.

The feeling of danger intensified. He shone the light around into every corner of the bay. The most commonplace objects cast looming shadows like gargoyles. Around the sides of the bay was a platform about four feet above ground level. At the back was a door, which stood open. He climbed a short iron stairway to the platform's level, and then he crossed to the door. There was no light at all beyond it.

He went in.

He could hear his own breathing, feel the beat of his heart like a demented prisoner in his chest. But as far as he could tell, he moved in silence. He went through one set of fire doors and then another, easing through and holding onto the doors so that they closed without noise behind him. The loading bay had been bare and functional, but he emerged into something quite different. He'd come through the back way into the building's entrance foyer.

There was some light coming in from the towers outside, but not enough. The power supply to the complex hadn't been cut—he'd been able to study its lights from a distance for several nights running, ultimately learning nothing—but the supply in certain areas seemed to have failed, and this was one of them.

He ran his beam around. The entranceway was a glass revolving door, with push-doors to either side for the nervous and obese. The palms around the visitors' seating area had died in their pots, now resembling limp dune grasses with no green in them at all. At the unmanned security point, a telephone hung abandoned on its wire. There was a big modern-art mural on the wall beyond the desk.

Frank stopped. It looked pretty weird, even by modern art standards. It was a big airbrushed stain covering half the wall, and it had a stencil-cut silhouette of a running man at its centre. The image was intensely realistic, everything in his outline being charged with energy. You could read the terror in him.

And then Frank realised.

It was no mural. The spray wasn't paint. It was a preserved image, not unlike those blast shadows that they'd found on a wall at Hiroshima. What he was seeing was the last moment of a man's life, flash-photographed onto the white plaster in the violently exploding bodily fluids of another.

He swallowed hard, and looked at the floor.

There were stains, the contract carpeting all ripped-up and burned in one spot. That was all. No signs of anything arriving, no signs of anything leaving. Even a slime trail would have been better than nothing, because it would at least have been a starting-point for some picture in his mind; the sheer unknowability of the enemy was probably its worst and most terrifying feature. So far, he now realised, he'd been tending to think of it like a big dog or a bear. In the scenarios that he ran in his mind, a big dog or a bear fell easily before the blast of his shotgun; but the image would no longer hold up in the light of this first evidence that he'd found, and he had nothing to put in its place.

For the first time seriously, he began to think about backing out.

And then he closed his eyes. He knew that he shouldn't, but he closed his eyes just for one moment and tried to summon it all up before him. The pattern of his life. The depth of his loss, and the awesome zero of his achievements.

Then he went on.

He could see lights here and there, ahead of him down the main corridor. He could hear the constant background whisper of air conditioning. Apart from the dead plants, the place could have been deserted only ten minutes ago instead of two years before. At least he'd now passed the point at which he could have been pulled out against his will; they couldn't get their armoured carrier this far inside the building, and they sure as hell were unlikely to venture in without it. The corridor looked familiar. This had been on the TV news as well, back when they'd sent in one of those little robots that looked like an anglepoise lamp mounted on a toy tractor. They'd borrowed it from a bomb disposal unit, and the unit had been mightily pissed off when they didn't get it back. Everything had been fine until it had reached the big newsroom at the corridor's end, at which point it had passed beyond the range of the operator's radio signals and ploughed onward alone. TV pictures had faded with the on-board batteries a few hours later.

On the way, they'd featured nothing that was at all unusual.

Frank checked each office as he passed. Jackets still hung on the backs of chairs. Cups of long-congealed tea and coffee stood untouched on a number of desks; it had all happened just after eleven in the morning. One room was empty apart from a big Xerox machine with its lid raised and a last, forgotten page still in place on the glass.

And on just about every desk stood little framed photographs of the yet-to-be-bereaved.

The corridor's end opened into the big, empty newsroom, just the way that he'd seen it. This was where the lights still burned, bright as day and, for a moment, painful to his dark-attuned eyes. He turned off the flashlight to save the batteries, and stuck it inside his jacket. Then he switched the shotgun from one hand to the other, wiped his palm on his pants, and switched it back as he moved through the double-doors.

He'd never been in a newsroom before. It was no big deal. It was like a big modern barn with about a hundred desks and a computer on every one of them, and more mess than he'd ever seen in his life. Books and papers and old newspapers were piled everywhere, hanging from the tables like so much foliage and overflowing the wastebins like popcorn. The computer screens flickered like sentinels, just a few of them darkened like the dead spots in a honeycomb.

There was the robot that they'd sent in, slewed nose-first into a filing cabinet. It gave him a slight buzz, having seen it on TV and now seeing it—well, not in the flesh, perhaps, but in the hardware. The video camera sat on top of the arm like a single eye, staring fixedly at the teak-effect front of the drawer as if studying it for defects.

Frank prowled the length of the room, tensed for anything that might pop up from behind one of the desks. He glanced at one of the screens in passing. There was a half-written piece on the display, frozen in time and never to be finished. He didn't stop to read it all, but he flickered a smile at the headline. *Bros.* Talk about yesterday's news...

He stepped around a chair that had been flung back as if in panic. Had it prowled through here, sweeping them all before it? If it had, then it had allowed none of them to get away in the end. God, it had to be fast.

Well, he thought… I'm fast, too. He'd been running every day, and he'd practiced his gunplay in the bathroom of the hostel at dead of night after studying the greats. Alan Ladd, in *Shane*. And the Duke, when he'd played Rooster Cogburn. Not to mention Peter Weller in *Robocop*. He could do the fast draws and trigger spins and everything. When it came for him, he'd be ready.

It hadn't come for him by the time he got to the end of the newsroom.

As before, the corridor beyond the newsroom was dark. But again as before, there was light further along. He pulled out the flashlight again and clicked on the beam.

And then, staying close to the wall, he started to make his way down.

He wondered how many of the other wire-jumpers had been along this way. And of course, he wondered what had happened to them. From what he'd heard about the first ones, back in the days when an intruder was still big enough news to be worth the coverage, they sounded like the kinds of people who'd have been leaping off bridges anyway if this more spectacular opportunity hadn't presented itself. Breaking into the plant was almost like Russian Roulette for the already-committed, with five loaded chambers and the last, longest-odds chamber primed with a jack-pot big enough to make you forget why you'd ever considered suicide in the first place. Frank had never considered suicide, ever; it simply wasn't an option. But he was bright enough to acknowledge that he was down and dropping fast, and the scale of the reward had grown more and more attractive as his days had grown darker. In the end it had all come down to one straight question; how much did he have left to lose?

He carried on with his tour of the floor. He'd once held down a job with a firm of City windowcleaners, during which he'd looked in on places like this every day. They'd let him go in the end, because he couldn't take the heights in the outside cradle. But this was more than any of those places, because along with the hi-tech offices there was just about everything needed to produce a major national newspaper under the one roof. Editorial, archives, financial, typesetting and design, the whole works in a single integrated plant. It hadn't been running for more than six months when disaster had struck.

At first—and this could only be pieced together from the immediate reactions of those who'd been in mid-conversation on the telephone when it happened, since none of them had survived to write their memoirs—it had been assumed that a light aircraft had crashed onto the plant on its way to an emergency landing at the new City airport some way down river. But the fact was, nobody really knew what had hit the place. Police and striking print workers on the picket line outside the gates said that they'd heard a shriek and a bang like one of those pistol-launched distress flares, but they'd actually seen nothing. Aerial photographs had later shown a hole punched into the roof at one end of the complex, and that was it.

The police had gone in, and hadn't come out. After hearing the screams over their radios a Tactical Support Unit had gone in, and they hadn't come out either. So then the army had been called and a crack, battle-hardened team went in, and... for a while there it had been like Flanders fields, wave after wave of men being sent to their deaths while their commanders puzzled over how this could be, until finally some-one had conceded that the only reasonable bet for safety would be to make limited forays from a heavily-armed and protected vehicle. It lacked glamour, but it might actually work. Even then two more men had been lost, and nobody was quite sure how... but enough had been learned for everyone to realise that something unprecedented was on the loose, some-thing that moved fast, struck hard, and was devoid of mercy.

The decision had been taken to close the place down, sealing in what-ever roamed there until a more definite plan of action could be formed. In the course of planning the shutdown, it had taken another three men.

That had been enough.

They'd pulled back, they'd locked the gates, they'd thrown up the outer perimeter fence for a further level of containment and then they'd backed off to consider the problem. Considering would cost nothing. Everything else had seemed to cost lives by the bucketful, plummeting straight down into the well without even the sound of a splash.

The proprietor, of course, was furious. He'd have started a campaign over it, if he'd still had a newspaper in which to conduct one. From his point of view the timing couldn't have been worse. He'd just emerged as the victor-by-default in a labour dispute over new technology after locking out his printworkers at the old city-centre plant and then telling them that no jobs waited for them at the new. It had been ugly for a while, and he'd been ready for it; hence the walls, hence the razor wire... those same features that had been so useful in holding-in the presence before its dangers had been fully realised. In the preceding weeks there had been a near-riot every night outside with police on horseback, water cannon, TV crews getting beaten up, the whole works. Meanwhile the proprietor, secure in the success of his coup, had been— in the words of informed sources—happier than a dog with two dicks. He couldn't have been slapping himself any harder on the back if he'd taken a course in yoga.

But then, quite literally, the roof had fallen in on his triumph.

It was the news story of the decade, and all his rivals had the best of it; at least until after a few more weeks had passed and seen a humiliating climbdown and a renegotiation with the unions to open up the old plant and resume production. By which time the containment had been in place, and the surrounding area had spontaneously cleared of much of its population, and the writs had been starting to fly in earnest.

The man was rich. He'd survive. But others, mostly tied into local waterfront development, had found themselves facing losses on the scale of the Nicaraguan national debt. The various interests had put their heads together, and the reward had been announced. It gave no consideration to the indecisiveness of the authorities, or to those who called for isolation and a programme of intensive scientific study; it simply meant that whoever could sneak into the danger zone and come out with the intruder's head—whatever it might happen to look like—could begin to number his or her assets in the millions.

Millions.

Frank could hardly even begin to imagine a million of anything. All that he could think of were big cars and huge houses and yachts moored in places where the trash weren't allowed. There on the yacht were Frank and his boy, best pals. Frank was drinking champagne. The boy had a Coke. They were talking about football.

She wouldn't even tell him the boy's legal name.

He'd thought about this venture for weeks. In his mind's eye, he always went in like Bruce Willis or Big Arnie and the worst thing that could ever happen was that he'd be seen entering and the armoured squad would dive in and bring him out before he'd managed to get anywhere. That would be too much. Beneath dignity. And if his failure were to make it onto the TV news then he might as well put the gun to his head right there and then, because she'd see it and there he'd be, confirmed in her opinion as the flop of the century. The way she talked about him, he'd never done a thing right in his life. Sometimes he wished that he'd strangled her when he'd had the chance, instead of exercising restraint and just knocking her backwards over the sofa. Even then she'd blown it up out of all proportion in court, as if she hadn't been asking for it.

He stopped, holding the flashlight beam steady.

Here was the first real evidence of damage.

The false ceiling had buckled down and all of the doors along this small side-passageway had sprung open. He wasn't exactly sure where he was. One room was full of office stationery and the rest of them comprised some kind of library or storage area, at a guess. He could see rows and rows of shelves, and more boxes than he could count. Those on the uppermost shelves had burst under the downward pressure of the dropped ceiling, spewing out clippings and cuttings and, in one of the rooms, sleeves of microfiche like so many playing cards. Ahead of him the passageway made a right-angled turn, with no clue of what might lie beyond.

He stopped, and listened.

Nothing.

So then, cautiously, he went on.

He sensed it before he saw it. A feeling of open space, of walls breached and the outside world let in. The torchbeam tracked along the floor and then suddenly it was shooting off down into nowhere.

He shone the beam upward. The entire ceiling had been punched down like the roof of a straw hut under the impact of a falling safe which had then carried on, taking the floor with it. He was looking up at the stars. Trailing wires and burned insulation hung around the edges like tatters of flesh around an exit wound.

Testing the floor with each step, he inched forward to the edge and looked down. The hole wasn't as big as he might have expected. Twenty feet across, not much more; the passageway continued over on the far side. He was looking down through at least two more floors, and there were probably more of them beyond the range of the flashlight. The falling object had crashed on as if through so many layers in a Pavlova, leaving the bared and bent ends of steel reinforcing rods to stick out of the concrete on every level. Two floors down he could see the wreckage of half a car, chomped neatly in two because it had stood in the way. So the basement levels were a parking garage.

*What was that?* He spun around.

Nothing there.

Maybe it had died. From its performance just after its arrival, it appeared to have chomped through a mountain of living flesh like the Tasmanian Devil in the Bugs Bunny cartoons, leaving nothing but scraps and stains. Since then, almost nothing. Only nine intruders in all this time, barely a snack by those early standards. It might have starved.

In which case, he'd claim it anyway. The best scenario would be to find it alive but too enfeebled to attack, in which case he could simply put it down like a mad dog. No-one need ever know. He sure as hell wouldn't let them barter him down on the reward, just because he hadn't had quite the tussle that they had in mind.

It might be weak.

Or equally, just very, very hungry.

He looked into the hole again. He'd checked out nearly all of this floor, but he'd found nothing. So the chances were that it was lurking down below. Weakened, dead, whatever, he was going to have to go down into the parking basement and find out.

He went back, looking for stairs.

Frank was wishing that he could have more faith in his own theory. But he couldn't help thinking of that sequence of holes, and how tough anything would have to be in order to survive that kind of impact. There was a special kind of ammunition that he'd been offered but hadn't been able to afford. French-made, his supplier had said, and very hard to get hold of. The round consisted of a number of buckshot pellets threaded onto a wire; it was called a necklace round and, discharged at close range, was supposedly devastating in its effect. It had been tested on beef carcases, and had cut them in two. Frank had weighed it up and thought about it, but the decision in the end had been one purely of economy. This was before he'd known about the impending problems with the man who was supposed to be selling him a ladder. In retrospect he wished he'd gone out and stolen a ladder from someone's backyard, which was probably what the man had been planning to do anyway, and then gone ahead and bought the necklace rounds… even only as insurance. The phrase *out of one's depth* came up into his mind as he pushed open the stairway door on its pneumatic damper, but he turned it aside.

He edged through, tensed for any surprise. The stairway was bare and functional. The walls were of painted cinderblock and the stairs of cast concrete. Frank shone his light down the centre of the well, probing around the limited area that he was able to cover and watching for any response—a flinch, a darting shape, any flicker of movement at all. He kept at it for quite a while, even though it had quickly become clear that he was going to learn nothing this way. The fact of it was, he was putting off the moment of descent; and as soon as he'd realised this and admitted it to himself, he'd no further excuse for delay.

You're a hunter, he told himself. A killer. So get the fuck down those stairs and start acting like one.

He started to descend.

First turning, no problem.

Second turning...

He missed his footing as something leapt up into the air before him. It was bone-white and knobbly, that was all he could tell; he was scrambling back and trying to get it all together the way he'd rehearsed it in his mind a hundred times over, but somehow it wouldn't fall into place. He was panicking. A part of him knew it, and that part of him also knew with utter certainty that he was done for already. He was swinging up the shotgun but he was also losing his balance, and he was slow... his mind was firing off these commands in every direction, and his limbs were responding like so much ballast. The shotgun caught on something as he tried to bring it to bear. The flashlight was gone, spinning away across the landing between flights. He was falling. His finger was pulling on the shotgun trigger...

*Oh, Christ*, he thought, *not that, not yet...*

And there was a kick like a car door being thrown back against him, and an explosion in the stairwell that made the delicate structures of his ears feel as if they'd been turned to so much pulp, and a hot and bitter wind fanned his leg as an entire chunk of the balustrade was taken away in a single bite...

And when he hit the floor, he immediately scrabbled backwards into the angle where the walls met, and he stayed there.

The echoes seemed to go on for a long time, all the way up the stairwell and then back down again. The flashlight came to rest.

Frank was still in the corner. And still, as far as he was able to tell, in one piece.

Nothing moved.

Gingerly, he looked at the gun. His finger was still white on the trigger. He'd given it both barrels and he hadn't even got it up level, let alone taken aim; in fact, he'd come pretty close to blowing the front of his own leg off. His ammunition wasn't unlimited. He could reload, and then he could reload again; and then after that he could maybe think of using the shotgun as a club, because he'd be out of cartridges.

So, what had he seen?

Stiffly, he levered himself out of his corner and got to his feet. He was feeling stupid, the way he'd once felt when he'd come home late one night and a neighbour's cat had jumped out of the doorway and made him yell out loud. First he reloaded, leaving the spent cartridges where they fell. Then he picked up the flashlight and moved to the top of the stairs to look down. The beam appeared weaker than before. He didn't think that it was just his imagination.

There it was, lying at the bottom. He'd kicked a stick. A white, carved, knobbly stick that had been lying on the second stair and which had flipped up into the air when he'd stepped onto the end of it.

But no. Not a stick, exactly.

A human bone.

He went down to where it lay, and crouched before it with a sick kind of fascination. It was definitely a bone, and it wasn't spotless. There was old black meat sticking to it like shreds of pasted-on leather, the way it might look if it had been buried in somebody's garden for a month or so. One of the few quiz questions that he could answer concerned the longest bone in the human body; and here it was, the thighbone, looking like some elegant piece of ivory carving. He didn't touch it. Once had been enough. But he looked all around that small area of the stairwell, and he found nothing more.

It must have heard him. Surely, wherever it was, it must have heard the shotgun blast. If it hadn't known of his presence before, it would know of him now.

Think positive, he told himself. Look for the bonuses.

Well, the dress rehearsal was out of the way. He didn't think that he'd react quite so blindly a second time.

And that was about it.

He was half-expecting to see more human traces further down the stairwell, but there were none. Maybe there was something unspeakable right down at the bottom, but he didn't plan to descend that far. What he did find was a big grey electrical junction box behind the car park's upper-level access door, and when he opened up the box he found that it carried the fuses for no less than twenty circuits and that every one of the breaker switches had popped out. He started to push them back in, and with the third of them the stairwell lights came on.

When he put his nose out into the parking area, the place seemed almost to have been returned to life again.

Parked cars shone under the striplighting, looking as if they'd been abandoned only for hours instead of months. He saw Mercedes, BMWs, a scattering of Saabs and Volvos; these were the reserved spaces closest to the elevator and beyond them, in the unreserved slots, stood a scattering of mid-market family saloons and the odd, halfheartedly-restored old banger. Way down at the far end of the level was the big hole; he could have gone along to it and looked up to the spot where he'd been standing only a few minutes before, but he didn't. The ceiling was low, the aisles narrow, and just across the way he could see a car ramp which angled down to the next level. Down there a striplight was flickering, spasming, trying to ignite but not quite making it. Frank eased out onto the parking floor, and held onto the door behind him so that it closed without noise.

It didn't matter where you were, these places always looked the same. A ramp at either end, painted arrows on the floor, oilstains, yellow zones, all the usual fire hazard notices, and all the atmosphere of a freightyard. He moved out as quietly as he could, scanning all around him; the malfunctioning light was putting out a zizz and crackle that made the silence less than total.

Now, he thought, come for me now. Now, when I'm ready; now, when I can see you coming; now, before my nerve finally deserts me for good and I turn to run into the arms of the pickup squad.

But nothing came.

He walked down the ramp, in the direction of the strobing light. Close to the foot of the ramp lay a motorcycle, keys in and looking as if its rider had laid it down on its side and then walked away as if from a fallen horse. It was a big Honda, its expensive-looking paintwork the colour of crushed berries and its brightwork shining through a layer of dust like liquid mercury. The mirror down against the ground was broken, otherwise it appeared to be undamaged. After looking it over, he looked around. Elsewhere on this level there were other signs of attempted flight; a couple of cars that had been run out of their spaces only to crash in the middle of the aisle, and one that had simply run along a wall for a number of yards and then stopped, one complete side ripped and destroyed while the other was untouched.

Frank moved on. He gave a start at one point, thinking that he'd seen something out of the corner of his eye. But it was only a fire hose, coiled over against the wall. He saw no signs of any living presence, except for the complete handful of human hair that he spied trapped in the closed rear door of a Microbus.

He dropped another level. He stayed out in the middle of the ramps and the aisles, keeping space around him all the time. *Now*, he kept thinking, *Come now*, but still nothing came.

Maybe it was afraid of the gun. Or maybe it liked a waiting game. If that was the case, its patience had to be phenomenal.

Perhaps he was right. Perhaps it had starved and was dead, after all.

At the furthest point of the very lowest level, he found the resting-place of the object that had rammed its way down through the layers of the building like so much paper.

Rock bottom.

Even after punching through a roof and four reinforced floors, it had still carried enough energy to make a hole of about twenty feet deep or more. He had to get the flashlight out and shine it down into the crater. What he saw didn't impress him much.

It looked like nothing more than a big rubber ball with its outside layers flaked and scorched away. And there was no way of telling whether it had happened because of the impact or afterwards, but somewhere along the line it had split from one side to the other and the contents had oozed from the gap in the manner of matter from a septic wound. Now the ooze seemed to have hardened, like candlewax or lava. He directed the torchbeam onto the inside, as well as he could, but the ball seemed to be empty. The inner surface might have been scaly, it was hard to say.

And that was it.

As far as Frank was concerned, the whole thing was a big let-down. He'd been hyping himself up for weeks, and for what? Nothing. Now even this was unimpressive. He'd been expecting a chunk of a flying saucer or maybe a Star Wars-type escape pod. It just looked like a shitball.

A sound echoed down from somewhere above. Not an animal sound, nor the sound of anything that might be stalking him, but an engine. He listened for a while longer, and he heard it again. He knew what it had to be; it was the pickup squad, on its way down to round him up and drag him out.

He turned to face the rest of the empty parking level.

"*What's the matter with you?*" he yelled, and his voice sounded shockingly loud in his own ears. "*Scared to come out? What is it, you only like to pick on them when they're running away?*" He stopped for a moment, but all that he could hear was the distant revving of the armoured truck's engine. It sounded as if it was stuck somewhere, or at the very least having to attempt some kind of a tight manoeuvre.

"Well," he said, "*I'll tell you what I think of that. I'll tell you what I think of you, and it isn't much. Are you listening? You're FULL OF SHIT!*"

Silence.

He spun around and looked behind him. He'd suddenly had the premonition of something rising out of the hole, rearing up over him as it spread itself wide and then falling on him like a tidal wave.

But there was nothing.

Frank turned from the hole again. He used his sleeve to rub the tears from his face. He couldn't have said whether they were of disappointment, or of rage, or relief. There had been no beast. There would be no reward. There would be no glory. The dreary downward spiral of his life would continue unchanged.

Or would it?

Could life really be the same, when you'd almost literally been to hell and back? Could it? The experience had to count for something in terms of self-respect, if nothing else. To have been tested, and to have gone the course without ever once turning to run... he'd at least done that, hadn't he?

He felt his heart beginning to lift, as the realisation came over him. Frank was no deep thinker, and had never pretended to be. But something important had happened to him down here, and he knew that he would leave this place like one reborn. He'd raised the nerve to face this demon, and he'd held on without flinching. Perhaps now, he might have the strength to face his own.

Although he'd still have preferred to get his hands on the money.

It was time to go. All that was left for him now was to get away from the complex without being caught, and he'd an idea of how he might do it. Dropping low so that he had less chance of being seen over the waist-high concrete barriers, he scampered up to the level above and then doubled back up the next ramp to the one above that. The revving of the security wagon's engine grew louder and more immediate as he ascended, and on the second level from the top he was able to see it.

He stayed low, watching. It was a big, heavily-armoured transit van of the kind used to move around large amounts of cash. There was wire over the windows and about half a ton extra of add-on plating, with bumpers and vent covers. The glass was tinted so that he couldn't see inside; and it was a fair bet that those inside couldn't see much of the world beyond the windshield, either. It looked big and mean and ponderous, and it couldn't make the turn onto the down-ramp.

At least, not in one. That was the reason for all the manoeuvering. The van was shuffling back and forth, over-revving and crashing its gears, and with every move it gained at best only a few inches on the angle. As Frank watched, there was a screech of metal as some part of it kissed the barrier. He could almost sense the pressure-cooker frustration of those inside. It rocked on its wheels as the brakes went on and off, on and off, and the level was filled with the choking stink of its exhaust.

At last, the armoured van was aligned with the ramp. It bumped its way down to the level below.

And there, after less than a dozen yards of progress, it began the tortu-ous business of getting itself out of the end of the ramp and into the aisle.

No wonder they'd only managed to pull out three of the twelve, Frank was thinking. The other wire-jumpers probably died of old age while they were waiting.

He watched from hiding for a while longer. And then after they'd taken a few more shots at it and got themselves well and truly committed, he leaped up and ran.

Somebody saw him. It hardly seemed possible, but they did. He heard the brakes slam on, and then the horn started to sound with some urgency.

The armoured van began to reverse, but without much danger of immediate success. Frank was running hard for the upper level now. Compared to the van, he was a bird.

The big Honda motorcycle lay almost where he'd seen it last; there were new scrape-marks on the concrete alongside it, indicating that the armoured van had nudged it out of the way in order to get past. Frank was hoping that this hadn't caused any damage because the way he had it planned in his mind, the bike was his ticket back to freedom.

Laying down the shotgun, he took hold of the handlebars and righted it. This took all of his strength, and then some. For a moment he almost thought that he wasn't going to manage it, but then the bike rocked upright and he kicked down the stand to hold it in place.

Two years. It hadn't been run in two years. But it was an almost-new, top-of-the range model, and the storage conditions down here weren't exactly adverse, so Frank's hopes of getting it started were pretty high. He turned over the starter, and the sound of it reverberated under the concrete ceiling; it didn't catch, but it *did* sound healthy enough.

He'd go out the way that the armoured van had come in. All that stuff about infra-red beams and machine guns, they'd have to have them turned off out of a fear of killing their own. On a bike like this, he could be out and through their defences before they knew what had hit them. Nobody would stop him. Nobody would get in his way, ever again. He'd been to hell and back; he could do anything. He tried the starter once more.

The bike started with a roar.

He was away.

The sound of its engine in the confined space was tremendous. He took off up the ramp like a demon, and had to use his foot like a speedway rider to get him around the narrow turn at the top. Only a few yards ahead was the entrance ramp; shuttered before, it now stood open to the big night sky and the air. God, he felt elated; he could taste it already. He opened the throttle wide, and went head-down for freedom.

The bike slammed on the brakes.

Frank didn't know what he'd done. He wasn't aware of doing anything at all. But the bike was slowing, and had almost come to a stop. He twisted the throttle hard over all the way, but nothing happened. He could feel his balance starting to go.

What the hell. He was almost there. He'd run for it.

But before he could start to dismount something weird started to happen, and it happened fast. The chrome safety bars on the sides of the bike wrenched themselves free and wrapped around his legs, effectively clamping them into place. Then the entire bike began to topple sideways, taking him with it. He fought to keep it upright, but there was nothing he could do. He was slammed down onto the ground, bike and everything, and a wrench of agony shot up from his leg as it was crunched between metal and concrete.

He wriggled, he squirmed. But now the bike was starting to rev again all on its own, and still it held him in a grip. The engine revved harder and harder as if gathering its power and then, in a sequence of rapid-action moves, the entire machine seemed to spring apart under him and then, spreading itself, to close around him again like a hand. It all happened so fast, he could hardly make out what was going on... and then he saw that the fork had dropped the front wheel and inverted itself over the handlebar and was pointing its twin prongs at his chest. Even as he looked, the painted metal seemed to skin back and a long, toothlike hook protruded from each.

The fork struck him like a snake, at the same moment that a number of other components and cables and widgets took a grab at the various available soft parts of his body. Frank tried to scream, but something flipped over his face from behind and got a sudden hold on his upper teeth and started to bend his head back hard, and then harder, and then far too hard.

With one tremendous surge of engine power, the bike re-inverted itself. Frank, at the centre of the process, burst like a depressurised egg as the hand became a bike again. The shell of him was crunched up into the structure of the machine, his face mashed into the manifold so that his last sensation in life was the smell of frying sweetbreads. The rest of him flew out in shreds or splashed down onto the ground beneath. The entire process had taken less than eight seconds, at the end of which the machine landed on its two wheels and flipped down its stand, put-putting away at the centre of a widening pool of blood and offal.

And then, just as the armoured truck came inching backwards up the ramp, it threw out a snout and sucked up all of the mess like a high-pressure vacuum, leaving little more than a fresh stain on the concrete.

The van went by. The only difference in the scene was that where previously the bike had been lying on its side, now it stood upright... but nobody seemed to notice it. As the truck was making its final withdrawal into the world again, the bike retched a little as a piece of bone stuck somewhere inside its digestive process. It flexed, and then it lengthened and narrowed slightly, and there was a crushing sound as the bone was powdered by the increased internal pressure.

The outside shutter-door rolled down, ending with a crash. The lights stayed on. There was silence through the plant, and silence in the parking garage.

Except for one discreet belch.

And later, when all the reports had been written and the fire blanket retrieved from the wire and the night shift had handed over to the day crew, there was a movement in the plant that went undetected by anyone as the big Honda flipped up its stand and motored alone to a new position.

Then nothing much happened for a while.

And then, having given the matter some consideration, the beast opted for a change. It puffed out its cheeks, arched its back, and became a Volkswagen.

And then it continued the waiting game. ❧

# My Repeater

§ WHAT can I say? It was a job, and I was glad to get it. The money wasn't great, but I had no skills and nothing to offer beyond a vague feeling that I was meant for something better. My mother knew someone who knew the owner, and I got a message to go along and show myself. I started two days later. Training was minimal. Customers were few in number.

I'd been there six weeks when I saw my first returnee.

He must have got off the bus at the far end of town, and it had started to rain on him as he'd been walking through the centre. I saw him coming up the road. The road was called Technology Drive, and it had been built to run north out of town and into the hills. Ours was the only building on it. You walked about two hundred yards to get to us, with open scrub on either side. If you wanted to follow the road further you could, but there was nothing much to look at unless you wanted to see how the weeds had broken up the concrete.

He walked with his head down, and with his hands in the pockets of his brown overcoat. The rain was light but he walked as if he was taking a beating.

He looked vaguely familiar. But at that point I hadn't considered the possibility that any of the people I'd been dealing with might ever come back.

He came in and went straight to the ledge under the window where we kept the boxes of forms. He didn't have to ask for any help. When he brought the paperwork over to the counter, the boxes had been filled in and the waivers were all in order and I'd little more to do than run through the questionnaire and then take it all through to my boss for his approval.

Morley was in his little back office, where he spent most of the days reading old magazines. He had a desk, a chair, and an anglepoise lamp that couldn't hold a pose without slowly collapsing. I think he had a framed picture on the wall but I can't for the life of me remember what it was of.

"Customer, boss," I told him, and showed him the papers.

He looked them over, and then tilted his chair back a couple of extra degrees so that he could see through the doorway to the main part of the shop. He stared at the waiting man for a moment, then gave me a nod and returned his attention to his reading. Most of his magazines were old technical publications, filled with page after page of fine print. They carried long lists of obsolete gear and they looked about as much fun as telephone directories.

I went back to the counter, and worked out the charges on the spread-sheet. The further back in time you wanted to go, the more it cost. Then there were other complicating factors, like bodyweight and geography.

When we'd sorted out the payment, I gave him a keycard to put in the machine.

"Booth five," I told him.

He went inside and closed the door. I made all the settings and locked off the switches, and then there was nothing else to do but press the big red button.

"Are you ready, sir?" I called out to him.

"Get on with it," I heard him say.

So I got on with it. It was no thrill, just a routine—any buzz had gone out of it very quickly. But something jolted me in that moment as I realised why he'd seemed just a little bit familiar. It was the target settings that I recognised. I'd set them before. He'd been in about twelve days previously and he'd specified exactly the same destination.

But he'd been at least ten years older then.

It was a nothing job in a run-down travel bureau in a town in the middle of nowhere. I could have been stacking shelves in a supermarket or earning merit stars in a fast-food franchise, but instead I was sending a small group of losers back in time to relive their mistakes. I know that's what they did, because the same bunch of people brought us so much in the way of repeat business.

There must have been hundreds of bureaux like ours, small-town operations all scraping by as the last of their investors' capital dwindled. They'd been set up as a franchise network when the technology had first become available. They were like those long-distance phone places where you buy time at a counter and they assign you a booth while they set up the call; only here, you paid your money to be sent back to a date and a place of your choice.

Anyone could walk in and do it.

But only a strange few ever did.

The predicted boom had been a bust. I suppose it was like space travel. Full of romance and possibilities until it became achievable, and a matter of doubtful value ever after.

Here's what I learned when I talked it over with Morley:

He laid his magazine face-down on the desk and said, "I bet there's something in your life that you'd change, if you could."

"That's got to be true of everybody," I said. "Hasn't it?"

"So why don't you consider going back?"

I suppose the correct answer was that it would be a huge and scary one-way trip, and to make it would involve abandoning the life I now had. And for what? No certain outcome.

But what I said was, "You don't pay me enough."

"I'm not talking about the cost of it," Morley said. "Say I offered you a free one. Would you consider it then?"

"That would depend if you were serious."

"I'm serious. You're hesitating. Why?"

"I haven't thought about it that much."

"Think about it now. It sounds like a great idea. But why doesn't it *feel* like a great idea?"

"I don't know," I said. "It just doesn't."

But the more I thought about it, the more I thought I understood. It was obvious that I would never successfully go back and fix everything with Caroline Pocock, the proof being that she despised me so thoroughly in the here and now. Whatever I might try to amend, that was the known outcome.

I said, "Does that explain why the only people I see coming through that door seem to be life's born losers?"

"That's exactly what they are," Morley said. "They're the ones who can't accept what became common knowledge after the first few years. Which is that you gamble everything, and nothing changes. Nothing significant, anyway. The status quo is like one big self-regulating ecology. All that happens is that the balance shifts and whatever you do to try to upset it, it just sets itself right."

"How does that work?"

"Nobody knows. The rules are beyond grasping. If you go back to meet yourself, you won't be there. The past that you return to may not even be the past you left behind. Whatever you try to alter, somehow it all still comes out the same. Or else it's different in a way that suits you no better. There's a whole new branch of fractal mathematics that tries to explain it and what it all comes down to is, there's an infinite number of ways for something to go wrong and only one way for it to go right."

I said, "So the overall effect is like, when you pee in the swimming pool and nobody notices."

Clearly this was an analogy that had never occurred to him, because he stopped and gave me a very strange look before carrying on. He wasn't a healthy-looking man. He had pale eyes and grey-looking skin. His hair had lost most of its colour, as well. He dressed as if he didn't care about his appearance, in clothes that most people would have bagged up and sent to a charity shop.

He said, "The people who set these places up thought they'd make a fortune. Most of them went bust within ten years. The rest of us squeeze a living from the same bunch of hopeless romantics who think they're the ones who'll beat the system." He gestured toward the public area beyond his office door. "You've seen enough of them by now," he said. "They keep coming back. They're older, they're younger, they're just in a loop thinking, *I almost did it then, I'll do it for sure next time*. Next time, next time. They scrape up the money and they come limping back. They can't even see how they've thrown away the lives that they set out to fix."

That first returnee of mine was back within the week.

This time, he was much older. I mean, seriously. He was recognisable but he looked as if he'd spent the last couple of decades scavenging for his life in a war zone. Maybe I exaggerate. But not by much. He didn't seem to have washed or shaved in ages. I could smell him from across the room. He just stood there holding onto the wall by the door, as if that last long walk up the road had taken everything out of him.

I said, "Hi."

He fixed on me. I wondered if he was drunk, but when he spoke I was fairly sure that he wasn't. The messages were just taking their time to get through.

He said, "I'm sorry. I've come a long way."

"Can I get you anything?"

He shook his head, and then moved over to where the forms were and pulled out a chair. I made a mental note to tell Morley that the whole area would need a scrub-down with disinfectant and then I realised, with gloom, that the job would fall to me.

I watched the man. The one I now thought of as My Repeater. I'd seen other returnees by now, but he'd been my first. It wasn't so much that he was now old, more that he'd become old before his time. He looked as if he'd been sleeping rough, and I wondered how he'd managed to get his latest stake together. By years of begging and spending nothing, by the look of him.

He brought the paperwork over. I held my breath.

"Just a few last details to get," I said.

"I know," he said.

I went through the usual questionnaire as quickly as I could and when he emptied the money from his pockets onto the counter, I had to force myself to pick it up. The grubby notes were in bundles, and there was a lot of small change. I felt as if I wanted to scrub the coins before touching them.

It always had to be cash. Travellers weren't creditworthy. They walked away from their futures when the Big Red Button was pressed, leaving no one to pay off the debts.

I said, "Do you want to take a seat while I count this?"

"I'll just wait here," he said.

And he did, too. He leaned on the counter and watched, with me breathing as shallowly as I could and trying not to rush it so much that I'd make a mistake and have to do it again.

Only days before, I'd seen him in good health. Now he was a shocking wreck. I couldn't imagine what he'd been through and I didn't want to ask. The part that I couldn't get my head around was that although the change seemed like a magical stroke that had happened in a matter of days, it wasn't. While his younger self had been standing before me, this older version had been somewhere out there, probably heading my way. They were *all* out there, at more or less the same time—every one of his repeated selves, going over and over the same piece of ground. Never meeting, never overlapping, co-existing in some elaborate choreography managed by forces unknown. Causing no ripples, accomplishing nothing, scraping up their cash and heading right back here. The person he was, and all of the people he would ever be. Fixed. Determined. Tripping over the same moment, again and again and again.

I felt a sudden and unaccountable sympathy. It bordered on tenderness, and it was an awkward and unfamiliar feeling; doubly hard to deal with, considering the scent and the state of him.

Lowering my voice so that Morley wouldn't overhear, I said, "Second chances don't come cheap, do they?"

"You give it whatever it takes," he said.

He looked so bleak and downcast that it made me sorry I'd spoken at all.

⌒◊⌒

I had an idea, and I pitched it to Morley.

I said, "If we kept one file on each repeater, it would save us having to cover the same ground every time."

"You lazy little bugger," he said.

"I'm not being lazy," I protested. "I thought I was being efficient."

"So somebody comes in here and we face him with a file that shows half a dozen returns that he doesn't even know he's going to make yet. What's that going to do to him?"

"Stop him from wasting his life?"

Morley said, "Watch my lips. It's already happened. Nothing's going to change it. All you can do is add to his misery."

And that was the last of my employee suggestions.

⌒◊⌒

I got an hour for lunch, and some days my old school friend Dominic would turn up and we'd walk out along Technology Drive until we reached its lonely end way up in the hills. There we'd sit on a rock and throw stones at bottles until it was time for me to go back.

I must have seemed down that day, because Dominic said, "What's the matter with you?"

"Morley," I said.

"What about him?"

"He's depressing me."

Dominic knew Morley. Partly because it was a small town and everybody knew everybody, if only indirectly, but also because in my first week Morley had made one of his few front-of-house appearances to tell Dominic to stop hanging around the shop and making conversation with me.

He said, "Morley depresses everybody. Even his daughter took her own life rather than listen to his conversation."

This was a surprise. "Seriously?" I said.

"Far as I know."

"When?"

"Years back. When Dinosaurs Ruled the Earth."

I didn't know what to say to this, so I pitched a few more stones at the bottle we'd set up. One of them caught it a glancing blow, and knocked it over. It didn't break, but it fell amongst the remains of countless others that had.

"Who says so?" I wondered aloud as I went over to set it up again.

"My mum," Dominic said. "She used to know him, in the days when he was a human being."

On the walk down, he told me what he knew of the story, which was very little… just that Morley's daughter had written a note and then opened her wrists while stretched out fully-clothed in the bath. She'd cut them lengthways rather than across which, according to Dominic, was proof that she'd meant it. She'd been nineteen. No-one knew for certain what her reasons were. Morley had burned the note.

Technology Drive was like an abandoned airstrip. Just being there made you feel guilty and excited with the thrill of trespass, and for no reason at all. It was as wrecked and overgrown as any Inca road, and in its time had served far less purpose. We picked our way down it, stepping from one tilted block to another. The drains had fallen in and all of the roadside wiring had been dug up and stolen. There was also about seven miles of buried fibreoptic cable that no thief had yet been able to think of a use for.

They talked of it as the Boulevard of failed business plans. The cargo-cultists' landing strip for a prosperous future that never came. Crap like that.

Nineteen years old.

I wondered what she'd looked like.

The afternoon was uneventful. That evening, I borrowed the car and went out with Dominic. We spent most of it in the Net cafe attached to the local Indian restaurant, and then after I'd dropped him off at home I contrived to drive past Caroline Pocock's house a few times, which is no mean trick for a place down a cul-de-sac. Then I parked and watched for a while. I didn't know which window was hers, but long ago I'd picked one at random and by now I'd convinced myself that it was her bedroom. I stayed there until her father came out in his pyjamas and stared at the car and then I took off.

It was after one in the morning when I passed the end of Technology Drive and saw lights in the Bureau's windows. I stopped the car and walked back to the junction. Someone was moving around inside.

Burglars? Looking for what? There was nothing in the place worth stealing. I didn't get too close because I didn't want to be seen. I stayed back in the darkness and waited for another movement. After about a minute, I saw who was in there. It was Morley. He wasn't doing anything much. He was just mooching around.

I saw him polish the glass panel in one of the booth doors with his sleeve, I saw him straighten one of the disclaimer signs on the wall. He mostly looked as if he couldn't quite bring himself to go home.

I couldn't imagine why. He lived on his own. There'd be no one waiting there that he might want to avoid.

I didn't get to bed until after two o'clock. I had a restless night. My thinking kept going around in the same circles. If life is lousy and you go back to change it, all that happens is that you fulfil the pattern that delivered your lousy life. Your choices are no choices at all. It seemed all wrong but think about it long enough, and you'd be scared even to breathe.

After all of that, I overslept and had to scramble.

I was late getting in. Morley was there already. I don't *think* he'd been there all night. He muttered something sarcastic and went off into the back office. The fact of it was that he could have run the place single-handed and saved himself the cost of my miserable wages, if he'd chosen to. What he had me doing was mostly dogsbody work. When I wasn't behind the counter I pushed a mop or answered the phone. The technology, though it was getting pretty old, was maintenance-free and the operation of it was idiot-proof.

I think it was just that he didn't like to go out there and face the clientele any more.

Around ten-thirty that morning, a taxi drew up outside and this young male of around my own age got out. He was well-dressed and had a sharp-looking haircut. You could tell just by looking at him that here was someone from a good family with money, and that he'd been favoured by the education system. Almost everyone from my school slouched, and their mouths hung open in repose. He stood looking the building over as the taxi pulled away, and then he came inside.

He spent twenty minutes or more reading through the forms before he brought them over to the counter.

He said, apologetically, "You'll have to help me with these. I can't work out what I'm supposed to do."

"Sure," I said, and I started to go through everything with him. He'd filled in some of the stuff, and he'd left blank the parts he wasn't clear about.

This time, I knew it way before I saw the name.

"You've never done this before?" I said.

"Nope," he said. I tried not to stare at him. Here, in the midst of his pattern of recycling visits, was the visit that began it all. He was bright, springy, full of confidence. The only giveaway was a dangerous-looking light in his eyes, but it was like the nerve of a bungee-jumper getting ready to go. In his own mind he knew exactly what had to be done, and he was about to step out and do it.

I went to get Morley's approval on the paperwork. My thoughts were racing.

Back at the counter, the young man was waiting. He was tapping out a drumbeat on the counter's edge with the fingernails of both hands.

"Everything all right?" he said.

"Everything's fine," I said with forced brightness.

"When do I go? Do I go right now?"

I lowered my voice and said, "Can I say something to you first?"

My repeater stopped his nervous drumming and looked at me; polite, puzzled, curious.

I said, "Walk away from this. Get on with your life. Whatever you think you're going to change, I can tell you for certain it won't work."

"Thanks for the advice," he said. "But I know exactly what I've got to do."

So then I did what I'd been warned against. "Just one moment," I said.

Then I went and got the records of his last few visits. The ones that I'd witnessed, but that he'd yet to live through.

I laid them on the counter for him to see.

He looked at them. Then he looked at me. The light in his eyes was still there, but it had changed. He wasn't so certain any more, and I could see that he was scared.

"What's all this?" he said.

"That's you," I said. "That's your entire life if you don't walk away."

He stared down at the papers again. They all carried his signature.

*I've got him*, I was thinking. *It was a risk, but it's working.*

"Fuck you," he said. "Do what I've paid for, or get me your supervisor."

But Morley was already coming out of the back office. "All right," I started to say, "forget I even spoke." I could hear the desperation in my voice as I started to backtrack, but it was too late.

Morley said, "What's the problem?"

"I thought you people gave a service," my repeater said, and he pointed toward me. "Since when was it his job to interfere in my private business?"

Morley looked down, and saw the files on the counter.

"There's been a misunderstanding, sir," he said then, raking them toward him and dropping them under the counter without giving them a second glance. Then he looked at me and said, with a considerable chill factor, "Go and wait in my office."

I went into the back, but I could still hear them talking.

*"Booth four, sir,"* I heard Morley say. *"I hope it works out for you."*

*"I reckon it will,"* I heard the young man say.

A couple of minutes later, the young man was on his journey and I was on the carpet.

"What do you think you're playing at?" Morley said.

"I was just trying to save him a load of grief."

"He's *got* a load of grief. Sometimes it's just a person's lot to live it out."

"You didn't see his face when he looked at his file."

"I told you, *no* files. Didn't you hear me?" He rammed the point home with his forefinger in my chest, stabbing me with every word. "You don't... show... the clients... their... fucking... files."

"If you'd only stayed out of it," I pressed on, "I'll bet you anything I could have convinced him. I was almost there. I could have rescued a wasted life."

"You know nothing," Morley said, but I was warming to my theme now; now that there was no chance of being proved wrong, I was starting to believe that I'd had control of the situation prior to Morley's interference.

"I bet he was just about to turn," I said, "and then you had to come wading in."

"He's on rails," Morley said dismissively. "We're all on rails. Knowing it won't make any difference."

"But what if things *do* change?" I argued, and suddenly the doubts that I'd been unable to articulate all fell into place like jointed plates.

"What are you talking about?"

I said, "Maybe things change all the time and we just don't know it. Maybe your daughter wouldn't be dead now if you weren't too pigheaded to go back and fix what went wrong."

Bad move.

I knew then that I'd gone too far. I also knew that it was too late to take it back.

Morley just stood there and closed his eyes. I could see the whites flickering where the lids didn't quite meet. He took a shuddering breath and swayed a little. I thought for a moment that he was starting a fit, but it was just that I'd never seen anyone in the grip of such bone-shaking, overwhelming anger before.

He said, "Get out of my place."

He was barely audible. My hands were shaking as I gathered my stuff together and as I was going out of the door that he held open for me, I couldn't bring myself to look back at him.

I heard him say, "I've forgiven you an awful lot since you came to work here. I can see now I let you get away with too much."

"Sorry," I said.

"Not sorry enough," were his last words to me.

I couldn't eat that night, and I felt so sick about it all that I couldn't tell anyone why. It wasn't just that I'd never been fired from a job before. And it wasn't because I'd failed with my repeater, because I'd been onto a loser there from the beginning—the very evidence that I'd tried to show him had been proof in my hands that he'd continue. I just wished I could have taken back what I'd said to Morley about his daughter.

But there it was. You can't change what's passed.

Unless.

Unless I was right. For some odd reason I kept thinking about the spreadsheet we used to work out the charges. When you changed one little thing deep down, everything shifted around as a result. It made a whole new picture.

Maybe we're just talking about the spreadsheet of everything. There's no past as such, there's just the big 'is'. No final, bottom line, just an endless middle. Updating all the time, undergoing constant changes in the always-has-been. Our certainties rewriting themselves from one instant to the next. For every miserable repeater, maybe there are a thousand happy and successful travellers whose journey simply vanished from the record once their misery was removed and the journey became unnecessary.

Not a bad leap. For someone so young, naïve and stupid.

I know that there are brain-damaged people who live entirely in the moment, whose memories fade in the instant they're formed. They need a notebook so they can keep checking on who they are, where they live and where they're from, who all these strangers around them might be.

Maybe this whole time thing's just a magic notebook.

And we're just the readers who believe all we see.

The next morning, I confessed to my mother about losing the job. It was that, or go through the pretence of getting dressed and going out early with no reason. She wasn't as surprised as I thought she'd be, but she asked about my unpaid wages. I hadn't even thought about them, and I really didn't feel like facing Morley again. But then when she started to talk about going with me to make sure that I got what I was due, I made hasty arrangements to go back alone.

The building on Technology Drive was all closed up. I looked in through all the windows but nobody was there.

So I went away, and returned late in the afternoon. By then someone had called the police out. Two uniformed officers had turned up in a van, along with a man that I recognised as the owner of a big womenswear shop in the middle of town. I mean it was a big shop, not that it sold stuff to big women. It was called "Enrico et Nora" and he was Enrico. I didn't know it at the time but he was Morley's sleeping partner in the business. The policemen were getting ready to break the door in.

I said, "Can I ask what's going on?"

"It's bolted on the inside," Enrico said. "Who are you?" The police wanted to know who I was as well, so I told them.

Then they brought this heavy thing on handles out of the van, and used it to batter the door in.

Nobody said I couldn't follow them inside, so I did.

I'd walked through the same door every working day for the past couple of months, but now it didn't feel right. All the lights were on, even though it was daytime. I was tensed for something awful. I know it may sound melodramatic, but it felt like the kind of scenario that precedes the discovery of a lonely death.

One of the officers had his head inside one of the booths. He pulled it out and said, "How do those things work?"

"It takes two people," I explained. "One to travel and one to operate from the outside. There's a system so one person can't do both."

They started looking in each of the booths, I'd guess in case Morley was lying in one of them.

But I was looking over at the counter.

The anglepoise lamp from Morley's office was standing on it. When I glanced over into booth five, I could see that there was one of our key-cards in the activating slot. Back on the counter, the lamp was positioned in such a way that the edge of its metal shade rested squarely on the Big Red Button.

He'd have had maybe a minute to get himself into the booth as the lamp slowly descended.

The settings on the machine meant nothing to me, but I could imagine where they'd led. I don't know if he'd aimed to get there hours before, to prevent the child from killing herself, or months before, to divert her from wanting to.

I told them all about it.

And even as I was telling them, I looked out through the window.

I knew that he couldn't have succeeded, of course. I knew it because I lived in a world where Morley's daughter lay long-dead in her grave and I'd seen the damaged plaything that loss had made of her father. If he'd gone back and saved her, then none of that could ever have happened. But it had.

I could see a figure heading up Technology Drive, walking from where the bus had dropped him off. I couldn't see his features yet, but I could read the determination in his stride.

*Next time,* his attitude seemed to say. *I almost did it then, I'll do it for sure next time.*

The police went into the back to look through the papers in Morley's desk. Enrico went looking for a phone to call his lawyer. I moved around to my usual place behind the counter.

And there I waited, to see which of my repeaters it would be. ℰ

# The Wishing Ball

GILLIAN'S first sight of the man called Rick O'Neill was across a deck of white tabletops and through a forest of umbrellas that had never been touched by rain. His hand was on her mother's arm, and even at this distance Gillian could sense that Janice was all frozen up as if the hand of a leper was on her and she didn't want anybody to see or know how it felt. The man was smiling and talking, and Janice wasn't doing either. But she was listening.

Gillian went over. They couldn't have been together more than five minutes, because that was how long she'd spent amongst the junior paperbacks in the Dalton's bookstore. This was the recreational end of the shopping mall, a wide plaza with four movie theatres and a handful of fast-food concessions, all of them doing slow early-evening business. The plaza had been set with tables and sunshade umbrellas under a ceiling so high that you could almost kid yourself that you were out in the open air as you sucked on an Orange Julius. The two adults were by a donut stand, which had its shutters down.

The man saw her first. "Hey," he said to Janice, "is this your kid?"

"Yes," Janice said stiffly.

"She's lucky, she got your looks." He turned to Gillian, and bent to put his face at her level. This was the moment at which she decided for sure that she wasn't going to like him. He said, "What's your name?"

"Gillian. What's yours?"

But if he'd heard the question, he obviously didn't intend to respond to it. "Tell you what, Gillian," he said, and he dug around in his pants pocket and brought out a crumpled bill which he opened up before her. "Here's a five. Go to the gift shop over there and pick yourself out something nice."

Gillian looked at her mother, unsure of what to do. But Janice nodded, barely, and so she took the bill.

"Thank you," she said.

She glanced back at them once as she headed over toward the gift shop. There were empty chairs close to hand, but neither of them seemed inclined to sit. The man was wearing an expensive-looking lightweight suit, but his haircut looked cheap and his skin was as pale as that of a new-born baby mouse. When he'd stooped to face her, she'd looked into the kind of hard little black-button eyes which would always seem friendly even though most of the time they probably weren't. Janice was ruler-straight before him. At least he wasn't touching her now.

The gift shop was full of crap; of all the places that he could have sent her, this was probably the worst. She couldn't see anything on any of the shelves that wasn't an embarrassment; executive puzzles with blobs of mercury sliding around mazes, transistor radios disguised as Coke cans, toilet paper with a joke or a crossword puzzle on every sheet, a porcelain sneaker, barbecue aprons with belly-dancer tassels… the soft toys at the back of the store seemed decent enough, but they were also priced way beyond the five-dollar bracket. Besides, Gillian had more or less decided on the way across the mall that she was going to spend the money on a present for Tom. Her father's birthday was coming up in a couple of days' time, but she'd only got to hear about it that morning when they'd dropped him at the airport. Even then, it had only been something that had been mentioned in passing. Gillian's birthdays were big occasions but her parents never seemed to make much fuss about their own, so a present from her would be a real surprise. And being surrounded by so much junk made it easy to feel selfless.

Maybe adults saw this kind of stuff differently. Who was to say? She picked up a head of Elvis Presley which started to play *Love me tender, Love me true* like a music box as she held it, but she set it down again quickly at the sight of the fifteen-dollar label. From where she was standing, she could look right out through the shelves and the open front of the store. Her mother and the stranger made a subtly different picture now, one that Gillian could read even over the distance. The one-sided chill had developed into a one-sided argument, Janice coming up to the boil but with the lid still tightly on; she looked briefly toward the gift store and Gillian knew then that she'd better be heading back, if only for the sake of the stranger's future health. From a shelf at eye level she took a glass paperweight with a tag that was just within her price range, and carried this out to the counter by the entrance.

The boy who took her money was tall and good-looking, and he didn't bend down to talk to her. Turning the paperweight in his hand as if to inspect it for flaws, he said, "Have you ever seen one of these before?"

Gillian shook her head.

"Watch," he said, and then he shook the globe twice before setting it down on the counter.

What Gillian had taken to be solid glass now proved to be hollow, and filled with a swirling blizzard that gradually settled to reveal the village scene inside. For a moment she stared, caught up in the effect, and for that moment it was touch and go whether Tom would get his hands on it after all.

"Now what you do is," the young man said, "you make a wish while the snow's still falling."

He wrapped it in tissue and put it into a paper bag with a picture of Snoopy on the side. Gillian was thinking that it was going to make a perfect present, because Tom was always wishing out loud for more of what he called The Slippery Green Stuff. Gillian had gone queasy just thinking about it, until Janice had explained that her dad was talking about money.

This time, neither of them saw her coming until she was well within earshot. "I'm warning you, Rick," Janice was saying, "you're getting way out of your depth," and the man—Rick?—said, "A warning for what? For old times' sake?" But then suddenly their radar seemed to sense her, and they both clammed up at the same time and turned at her approach.

She took the paperweight out of the tissue and held it out to show him. "This is what I bought," she said. "There's five cents' change."

"Keep the change," he said. "You can owe it to me."

But Janice had been rummaging around in her bag, and now she brought out something which she stuffed into the man's breast pocket. She did it so quickly that she was finished before he'd realised what was happening.

"Here's a ten," she said. "Now nobody owes you anything." And then she put her hand on Gillian's shoulder to turn and steer her away. "Come on, tiger," she said, and they walked away from the man without even saying goodbye. Gillian glanced back once before the stairs and the fountain came between them, and the man was just standing there with his hands in his pockets as he watched them go.

Out in the parking lot, you knew that it was November; a lot of the women were in those long quilted coats and the men were in sleeveless body jackets, loading all the stuff that they'd bought into their open hatchbacks. There was still some light in the sky, but it was getting grey and weak compared to the glare of the elevated Interstate which passed so close that the lot was almost in its shadow. Janice couldn't remember where she'd left their yellow Pinto, as usual, and Gillian had to lead her to it.

They waited as a blue pickup reversed out of its slot. Gillian saw Janice take a quick look back at the mall entrance.

Gillian said, "Was he one of your friends?"

"Not a friend," Janice said, her gaze lingering on the glass doors as if willing them to fuse and lock together. "Just somebody I used to know. We won't be seeing him again."

The pickup accelerated suddenly, making a too-showy turn at the far end of the row. Gillian waited to hear Janice's usual under-the-breath muttering of *asshole*, but it didn't come; instead she walked across to the Pinto, weighed down more by the things on her mind than by the few store bags that she carried.

The bags went on the back seat, the two of them got in. Gillian held onto the paperweight, thinking that it might roll around and break if she left it. The more she thought about it, the neater a gift it seemed likely to make. Tom was always working at home, really late into the evenings sometimes, and his desk was always a mess. Even if the wishing part was only so much bull, as she strongly suspected, it would still be something that he could use. It might even help in the pursuit of The Slippery Green Stuff. She was tempted to take it out of its bag again for another look at the way the snow inside shook up into a blizzard, but thought it maybe wouldn't be tactful while Janice was watching.

Janice hadn't started the car yet. She was sitting with her eyes closed and her head bowed forward, forehead almost touching the rim of the steering wheel.

"What's wrong?" Gillian said.

"Nothing's wrong," Janice said, opening her eyes and straightening slowly. "Just a slight headache, that's all."

It was properly dark by the time that they reached the house, a half-hour later. Gillian got to operate the remote control to open the garage door, and once they were inside she ran through the kitchen to switch off the beeping alarm control box before all the bells and howlers could let loose. The house felt dead with nobody in it, but that feeling went away as the room lights came on. Then, as Gillian brought the shopping bags through and set them on the kitchen table, she could hear that Janice was on the phone out in the hall; she seemed to get halfway through dialling a number before changing her mind and abruptly hanging up. The next thing that Gillian heard was Janice climbing the stairs.

It was wrong, all wrong. The best part of shopping was always when you got your new stuff home and took it out for the very first time, but here the bags lay unopened and with all the excitement slowly leaking out of them. There were some dungarees for Gillian, two pairs of Gloria Vanderbilts for Janice ("the only kind of jeans I can get my ass into these days," she called them), some knitwear, and some ski gloves that had been marked down in a sale; but the only bag that Gillian felt able to open on her own was the Snoopy bag, crumpled around the top now from the way she'd been holding it. She drew out the shapeless lump of tissue, and from the tissue uncovered Tom's present-to-be.

Her fingermarks had clouded up the glass a little, like pawprints, but the tissue cleaned them off. She gave the paperweight a good long shake and then set it down so that she could watch, and make a wish.

The snowstorm swirled, flurried, began to settle. It seemed ungenerous to think it of the man who'd given her the money to buy the thing, but she wished for him to leave their lives as completely and as abruptly as they way in which he'd made his appearance.

Rick O'Neill drove on past the lighted Haddon house, and turned his car around in the next cul-de-sac. He hadn't seen anything to change the impression that he'd formed when he'd first located the property that same morning. Not poverty row, he'd thought, but a long way from rich. It was a disappointment, but it didn't deter him. Having made the turn, he headed back in toward Arlington with the idea of finding somewhere to eat and to kill a couple of hours. Now that Janice and her kid were home, he wanted to give them time to get settled before he came back.

And he would be going back, only they wouldn't know of his visit until some time after he'd gone. Rick O'Neill had once made a reasonable living out of his ability to slip un-noticed through other people's houses, leaving behind rather less than the full inventory of valuables; his career had suffered a recent interruption of more than nine years' duration, all of them spent in the state penitentiary over in Pinal County, Arizona, but he had no doubt that the old skills would come back to him as easily as the driving had. He'd been out of jail for nearly four days now, and already he was starting to feel back on top of it all. His first act—apart from buying himself a beer which he found he'd lost the taste for—had been to bus out to Sky Harbor airport from where he'd returned with someone else's luggage from the terminal building and some distant stranger's wheels from the parking lot. His second act had been to make like an arrow across three states to get himself to this spot.

His third would be to pass through the Haddon house without taking anything, leaving some small but unmistakable sign for Janice to see. This was to be the opening shot in his planned campaign of psychological warfare—more effective and harder to pin you down for than any other kind, if he understood the experts on these matters. He'd taken out every psychology book in the prison library at one time or another, and at least two of them he'd read all of the way through. He'd take money from them if they had it, although by the look of their second-hand car and their second-rate house they probably wouldn't have much, but the main object of this exercise was going to be to give the Haddon household a lesson in fear. Fear of the unknown, fear of exposure. Fear of what the future might turn out to be like for them.

And more than anything else, fear of what a one-time housebreaker named Rick O'Neill could do to their lives.

The diner that he found had all the looks and character of a cinder-block shoebox, but it was dark and it was quiet. He sat at the back of the room at a table from where he could watch the door, and when the waitress came over he ordered the all-day breakfast. "Anything else?" she said, and he thought about a beer.

"Make it a glass of milk," he said.

Sometime over the next couple of days he was going to have to give some close consideration to his finances. There had been about fifteen hundred in travellers' checks in the luggage that he'd boosted, and if he could make the right contacts he could probably get back about half of their face value. He was no bad-check specialist himself, he didn't even want to think about trying to pass them on his own; that was the kind of move that could put him back in jail and it wouldn't be through bad luck, it would be through stupidity. Stupidity, he thought, was when you failed to organise things that should rightly be within your control; bad luck was when you gave a screaming householder a little tap to silence her and the bones of her skull caved in like a stale piecrust. That kind of luck, in Rick O'Neill's case, had translated into a murder charge which his sharp and eager lawyer had bargained down with the help of the testimony of Rick's girl.

Tom Haddon had been sharp in the courtroom, all right. But he hadn't been sharp enough to see through Rick's girl at her most calculating, had he?

Rick had grown weary of hearing the story again and again. Every new face on the block seemed to have something to add to it, right up to the point where Haddon and Janice—Janice Frick, in those days—had been married in a quick and quiet ceremony across the county line before moving out of state altogether. And after a while, when everything had quietened down, Rick began to wonder... could the two of them really have been doing their best for him? He'd heard of people in worse spots getting away with it altogether.

"Heading West?" the waitress said from by his shoulder, snapping him out of it. She put his order before him, and his milk on a coaster to the side.

Rick said, "Why?"

"Radio says to keep off the I-thirty for the next hour. A big truck turned over, or something."

She was a big girl, bleached-blonde, and kind of interesting to have leaning over him so close. But it didn't last for more than a moment. He said, "I'll be staying around here for a while."

"What line of business you in?"

"These days I'm into debt collection," he said.

The meal was about as enticing as the architecture, but with a slice of anaemic-looking cherry pie to follow it passed an hour. He kept checking his watch, but the time wouldn't move any faster. The watch belonged to the same poor sap who'd a) been unlucky enough to be around the same height and build as Rick, and b) had left his baggage trolley unattended outside the men's room back at Sky Harbor. It was a fancy little digital job on an expanding bracelet, brand-new and with lots of push-button features. There hadn't been anything like it around before he'd gone away, but fortunately Rick had managed to keep in touch with the real world through the TV and the advertisements in the slick magazines.

He spun it out for as long as he could, but eventually he became aware that the bleached-blonde was shooting him curious looks down the length of the counter. He paid up, left her a small tip. Maybe if he'd told her that he was an airline pilot instead of that debt-collector business, she might have been sitting on his lap by now.

Once in the car, he headed back into town and picked up the Forest Park road. Within twenty minutes he was making the turn, and five minutes after that he was cruising slowly past the Haddon house for the third time that day. There was still a light on in what he took to be one of the bedrooms. He passed on by and, less than a mile further along, found a little spur where he could leave the car without it being visible from the road.

Walking back in the dark? No problem, he was a professional. If you were a professional you weren't deterred by jail years, they simply beat the pity out of you so that the same mistakes wouldn't be made again.

The light had gone out by the time that he reached the house; it was after eleven, now. It was a split-level place built into the hillside, rambling and not too well-maintained. When he'd first come by he'd been expecting something newer, far more chic and high-profile; this place didn't even run to a swimming pool, and wouldn't have been hurt by a lick of paint here and there. Cheap, cheap, cheap, he thought as he squatted in the bushes upslope and studied the angles of the house by moonlight. Janice had hooked herself to a rising lawyer, but obviously the shakeup that their marriage had given to his career had stopped that rise dead. Rick would probably have to forget about squeezing them for money... but then, this wasn't really about money at all, was it?

He went down, and hopped over the fence into the yard. The easiest access looked to be via a set of flimsy-looking french-windows reached across a patio that was halfway through being relaid and which had been in that state for some time. Rick bridged a plank over the gravelbed and stepped silently across it. Within two minutes he'd cheated the simple alarm contacts on the frame and was inside the house.

He crossed the sitting room without a sound; born to burgle, that was Rick O'Neill. All of the internal doors on this level stood open. He could hardly have asked for an easier time of it. Through the open hallway and over into the kitchen, reading the grey tones of the night like a cat; he glanced up once at the high rail of the upper landing as he passed beneath, but there was no sound from any of the bedrooms beyond. Tom Haddon wasn't a problem to be worried about right now, Rick knew because he'd followed them out to the airport that same morning. This had also been his first sight of the kid, a big surprise for him because such a thing had never even crossed his mind. Janice, a mother? And, in a strange kind of way, he'd thought as he'd watched them coming out of the house, the child was more like the bright and hungry Janice that he'd known than the well-padded stranger who'd been squeezing herself behind the wheel of the yellow Pinto.

Once in the kitchen, he opened the refrigerator door to give himself a working light. After a few seconds the appliance's motor kicked in, a shivering rumble that took the hard edge out of the surrounding silence. He looked around; there, on the wall opposite, was exactly the kind of thing that he was looking for. It was a wipe-off memory board with a grease-pencil hanging on a string alongside; a homely feature, something belonging to a world where the Rick O'Neills were never more than just predators passing through.

He went over, his shadow scaling-down to meet him as he reached for the pencil in the weak illumination from the refrigerator. There were already the beginnings of a list on the board, *salt, scourer, Shake 'n Bake*. All that he needed now was to add a couple of words of his own, something completely innocuous but enough to start the ball rolling. Some hint at an IOU maybe, to get her thinking and to make her sweat for a while.

Then he had it, something simple but meaningful. He'd leave her the date on which his sentence had begun.

"I could blow your brains out," Janice said as the room light came on and almost blinded him. "But who'd notice the difference?"

It wasn't the sound of voices from downstairs that woke Gillian; that had been accomplished by the creaky board on the landing just outside her room, the one that she'd learned to listen for around midnight every Christmas Eve. But this time nobody came in even though she held her breath, and after a few moments she'd heard the faint shuffling of Janice descending the stairs.

No, the voices didn't wake her. But it was the voices that got her out of bed.

She went to the landing rail and looked down into the hall. "You're an even bigger fool than I thought," she heard, "and that's really saying something." It was her mother's voice, and it was coming from the kitchen. A broad fan of light spread from the kitchen doorway across the floor of the darkened hall, and in the fan a shadow moved.

"Now, wait a minute," a man's voice said. No, not a man; *the* man, here in their house.

"Get wise, Rick," Janice said. "You walked straight into this."

"Just give me one minute to tell you why you don't want to use that."

"You're a known housebreaker, it's nearly midnight, and nobody invited you in. You went into jail a loser and you've obviously learned nothing."

Gillian looked down at her hand. Her small fingers were curled around the snow-scene globe; she'd fallen asleep clutching it, wishing this same man away and out of their lives again before he could push his way in too deep. Now it caught the light with a dull gleam, and she shook it and wished again and tried to make out the blizzard as it swirled around the little houses on the hill.

"You know what's going to happen, don't you?" the man was saying. "I'm talking about all your new friends in this town getting to find out that the lawyer's wife used to be a teenage whore. You got close neighbours, Janice, I checked the area. Somebody hears a gunshot, and the police'll be here before you've dragged me five yards. So why don't we calm down and talk?"

Gillian looked up from the globe as a silhouette filled the kitchen doorway, making a small mental note someday to check up on what a *hoar* might be.

"Talk about what?" Janice said, and Gillian saw that the man was backing out of the kitchen with his hands raised in the air as if to push away something that he couldn't quite touch.

"About how little it would take to make me go away," he was saying, but now he was sounding nervous. "One thing I did learn, it's not to shake the tree too hard."

"There's no money, Rick. But I think you must have known that anyway before you broke in here."

Janice was emerging now, preceded by something that Gillian recognised as the ugly little handgun that her father kept high on a shelf in his closet where Gillian wouldn't be able to reach even if she should ever get it into her head to try. The man seemed scared, quite different to the way that he'd been in the mall, and he kept on backing away from her mother as if from some intense kind of heat. He glanced behind him, briefly, but he didn't look up to where Gillian stood. He seemed to be making for the sitting room.

He said, "Now, you don't want to do anything you're going to regret. I've written some letters."

He was almost directly below Gillian now; she had to lean out over the rail a little in order not to lose sight of him. He had a balding spot on the back of his head, where he'd tried to comb his hair across to cover it.

Janice said, "You, writing letters? You could never even write your name without sticking your tongue out the corner of your mouth. Tell me something I might believe."

But then everything seemed to change.

"You're not going to use that," the man said, and there was a note of wonder and discovery in his voice.

"You really think not?" Janice said, but there was uncertainty in hers.

"I know it. I can see it from here. You've changed too much, Janice. You lost your edge. Now you're just another fat Texas housewife, and you know it too. You spent too long thinking about stuff like what color toilet paper you ought to be buying. So I'm going to turn around now, and I'm going to walk straight out of here."

"I'm warning you, Rick... "

"I can hear you, Janice. It just don't worry me as much as it might, that's all." And he started to turn as he'd said that he would, slowly so that he wouldn't startle Janice into anything.

Here comes the wish now, Gillian thought.

The globe took forever to drop; one moment it was hard and warm in her hand like a newly-forged steel bearing, the next it was toppling into the long fall with its base turning upward as the main centre of its mass led the way.

It seemed to punch Rick's head down into his shoulders as it burst in a coronet of thick fluid and broken jewels. His hands made sudden fists but the only sound from him was a far-off squeak, as if everything had been instantly clenched-up and bottled-in. His legs gave way and he took a couple of uncertain steps sideways before dropping like an old sack. Janice stood aghast and open-mouthed, unable to take it all in as Rick lay on the hall floor and shuddered and twitched and trembled like a dog in the worst of all bad dog-dreams.

He kicked, and he bucked. And finally, he stopped.

And when the last of the life had finally rattled out of him, Janice belatedly turned her face upward to the landing, where Gillian stood at the rail in her night-dress.

"Where are we going to put him?" Gillian said.

Three days felt like too long for Tom Haddon to have been away from home, even on expenses. And then they'd messed around with his return flight so that he couldn't be sure of his arrival time, which meant that there had been no point in him phoning ahead to arrange to be met. So instead he took a cab from the airport, and had to be set down at the end of his own drive with his travelling-bag like some visitor.

The first thing that he saw as he turned from paying off the cabbie was Janice standing in the doorway; and then the second was Gillian, squeezing out around her mother's legs to come running down the drive toward him. For a moment he got that strange sensation of seeing the utterly familiar as if for the first time, something that always happened when he'd been away and which never lasted for more than a few seconds. It was already fading as, with his bag shifted to his left hand, he scooped Gillian up in his free arm and hitched her onto his hip in order to carry her back to the house.

Janice said, "How was it?"

"It went okay," Tom said as Janice stepped aside to let him and his double-burden come sideways into the hall. "The first meeting got pushed back a day, but I got the rest of it through in record time. Mostly because I didn't want to spend my birthday in a hotel on my own. I don't suppose I got any cards?"

"Sure you got cards," Janice said with a smile. "You got something else, as well."

"What?"

"Come and see."

He set his bag down, but Gillian was hanging on like a monkey and so she stayed in place as he followed Janice through into the sitting room. The french-windows stood open, and for a moment he wasn't sure exactly what he was supposed to be looking at; but then it clicked into place, and he said, 'I don't believe it.'

"They really worked fast," Gillian added. "I watched."

"I can imagine," Tom said, and he went over to the windows to look out at the newly-laid patio. The concrete base looked as if it had more or less set already, and the stone paving that he'd said that he wanted was stacked ready to one side. He wondered if it was solid enough to step out onto yet.

"Careful!" his wife and daughter said in sudden unison, as if they'd both read his mind, and Janice added, "They said not to disturb it for a couple of days."

He said, "When did they do it?"

"I charmed them into coming over yesterday. It's not your main present, but I thought you'd be pleased."

"You must really have charmed them. They told me they were backed up a month."

"Yeah, well… " she put on one of her mysterious smiles. "That was you, and this was me."

Gillian said, "I got you a present, too. Want to see it?"

She wriggled free and slid down to the floor, and Tom said, "Another present? Now I *know* it's my birthday."

Gillian ran out across the hall and thundered up the stairs to her bedroom. Tom looked at Janice, but this seemed to have taken her by surprise as well. She gave a shrug, and said, "Don't ask me."

He glanced at the patio and, lowering his voice so that Gillian wouldn't hear, said, "You sure we can afford this right now?"

"I'll juggle the books. We'll get by."

He put his hands in his pockets and looked out again at the newly-smoothed concrete. He said, "Anything else happen while I was gone?"

"Yeah, we had some excitement. The police found a car with out-of-state plates hidden about a mile down the road. Turned out it was stolen about a week ago, they don't know who by. They towed it away."

Gillian was back. "You'd better like this," she said sternly. "I've been saving up forever." And as he stepped back into the house she thrust at him a red paper bag with a picture of Snoopy on its side.

Tom opened it and took out a wad of tissue paper. The paper unfolded to reveal a digital wristwatch on an expanding bracelet.

"Like it?" he said. "I love it." He glanced quickly at Janice, suspecting some kind of conspiracy here. But if her expression was anything to go by, she was as surprised as anybody; in fact, she appeared to be faintly stunned at the sight of the gift.

"You press those little buttons and it does all kinds of things," Gillian explained as he slipped off his gold Rolex, a graduation present from his parents, and put it into his pocket. The watch that took its place must have cost his daughter all of twenty-five dollars—probably less, since it wasn't quite new. The band was a little loose, but he could take out a couple of the links. As he held out his arm to admire it, she added, "You'll have to work it all out for yourself, because I lost the instructions."

"Hey, thanks," he said. "And now if you'll go and bring my bag through from the hall, maybe I'll find something in there for each of you."

Gillian ran to get the bag. Janice was smiling, and her smile was a little glassy.

She was obviously as touched by the unexpected gift as he was himself, he thought.

The two of them could be so alike, in so many ways.

Gillian lay on her bed a couple of hours later, the conversation of her parents a comforting buzz that filtered up through the floorboards. She was inspecting the turquoise pendant that Tom had brought for her. Real Indian workmanship, he'd said. Hand-crafted. She wondered how much she'd be able to get for it at the pawnshop down by the stockyards, and how long she'd have to wait before she could take it along without Janice noticing that it had gone. Janice was probably going to be watching her for a while. Gillian had readily agreed that the entire incident with Rick O'Neill was a bad dream that had never really happened and that there was no need for it to be mentioned ever again, but still she'd seen the wariness in the looks that Janice had been giving her whenever Tom's back had been turned that evening.

She wondered if the pawnshop would go as high as twenty dollars. She already had thirty in a savings account that she could get her hands onto without either of her parents having to be present; twenty plus thirty made ten of the wishing globes, plus change. She'd have to buy them one at a time and never from the same place twice, or at least not when the same person was handling counter sales.

She thought about Mrs Turner the English teacher, who'd slapped her hand in front of everybody one time because she didn't write her A's in quite the way that Mrs Turner wanted. Mrs Turner cycled into school every day, dismounting and pushing her Schwinn the last few yards along a path that took her directly beneath the chemistry lab windows. Very handy. She thought about the plumber who'd once said a rude thing to Janice, which Tom knew nothing about. She thought about the drugstore owner who'd accused her of stealing when she hadn't, and an old man she'd heard of who told kids he'd pay them a dollar for mowing his lawn and then gave them nothing when they'd finished.

Gillian did a lot of thinking.

You never realised how many enemies you had, until you started trying to count them all. ❦

# Like Clockwork

$\mathcal{S}$ I WAS down at the end of my drive, listening to George telling me all about the new house extension that he was going to build, when we saw the ambulance go by. Our street goes nowhere, just kind of turns around on itself in a crescent of five houses at the end, and so we knew that the ambulance had to be news for somebody. Besides, it had the logo of one of the alien franchises on the side, and this was only five years after the corporate wars.

Interested? I suppose we were. But you know what it's like out in the suburbs, most people do their watching from behind the curtains. It's bad form to stand out in the open and stare.

Even so, I couldn't help looking when George said, "It's stopping at Jimmy's place." I saw the ambulance glide to a halt and then turn about its own centre before settling. It was, as George had said, outside the Hirasaki house, a white stuccoed villa on a corner plot with a low picket fence around it that wouldn't even stop a fat dachsund. The back of the ambulance opened up and I saw that two young men were helping somebody out. It might have been Jimmy himself, but it was difficult to see; the front door opened and Gloria Hirasaki came down to meet the three of them, generally getting in the way as the two men helped their patient to walk up the drive. He was weak, but he was managing.

"Was that Jimmy?" George said. "I couldn't really make him out."

"Me neither," I said. "And I didn't hear anything about him being ill."

The reason for this being that he wasn't, and hadn't been; but I didn't get to discover the real explanation behind it until two days later, when George came knocking on my back door. I was in the kitchen stuffing trash bags—an all-day job, some weeks—when I heard the knock and looked up to see his shady figure on the other side of the bug screen. When I let him in, he seemed nervous.

"I just heard something today," he said, "and I'm not sure what to make of it."

I sat him down, offered him coffee. We had a new coffeemaker which did away with beans and grinders and filters, you just shovelled garden dirt in at one end and the machine pulled out the trace elements that it needed and did everything from there. It had used up most of our consumer points for a month, and given us a few weeks in which we could breathe easy. Half the problem that I always find is in making the space to store the stuff before we're allowed to throw it out.

But George didn't want coffee, he wanted to talk.

"I found out about Jimmy," he said. "He didn't go into hospital because he was ill or anything. He went in because he got a yellow form."

"A yellow form for what?" I said. "I don't get it."

"Me neither. So, what do you say we go around there and find out?"

To understand the significance of a yellow form you have to understand all about the corporate wars, and I'm not sure that I can explain them properly—I was just a ground-gunner down at a base station in Grenada, and the nearest that we ever got to action was seeing a stricken alien cruiser shedding its bomb-load into the sea about five miles offshore in an attempt to regain height. It didn't make it, and we saw some real fireworks when it ditched some way further on and the sea got into the drive unit. The evening sky was lit up by the flash, and nobody could hear a damn thing for about half an hour.

The first thing that you have to know about the corporate wars is that we lost. In fact we lost earlier than we were supposed to, we later found out, and gave the aliens something of an economic crisis back home because of the way we'd messed up their long-term war plan for finance and resources. Not that we were ready to apologise—we were just waiting with our teeth gritted and our eyes screwed shut and our entire arsenal blown off into space, waiting for that final hammer to fall.

When the coup de grace didn't come and we finally opened our eyes, it was to find our bombed cities being rebuilt and our entire economy in the process of being restructured. Here, it seemed, was the reason why the aliens had never gone nuclear; they wanted us intact, and they wanted us to function. They never actually made any public appearances, preferring to work through human franchise operations. When I collected my discharge papers, they were accompanied by the first yellow form I ever saw; it told me where to find my new home, and contained a list of thinly-veiled threats about what would happen if I didn't move in. I hitch-hiked there expecting to find some squalid billet, and found instead the kind of place that I couldn't have afforded on my before-the-war salary even if I'd lived on bread and water for twenty years. It had eight rooms, a big yard, and space for a pool. Gabrielle was already inside and waiting for me; I hadn't seen her since the start of the conflict, and somehow our reunion seemed unreal. We lay on blankets on the floor that night, looking out at the moon through uncurtained windows and trying to make sense of it all. The next morning we found another yellow form lying on the mat, instructing us to go out and choose furniture. We hitched out to the new warehouses that had been built in the rubble on the old outskirts of town, and found ourselves wandering around amongst crowds of similarly dazed and uncomprehending couples. That was almost the last time we had to hitch anywhere, because the next day two yellow forms sent us out to look for a car each.

And that was it, the fate of the losers; we simply had to sit tight and receive gifts, lots of them. We got a certain number of credit points every month that we could spend as we chose, unless another yellow form came and directed us to a purchase over which we had no choice. Some of the yellow-form goods were really weird, alien artefacts that we could find no earthly use for, but we still had to go and pick them up. We could throw them out after a specified length of time; the one thing that we couldn't do was refuse them. It was a strange way to find yourself living, in the shadow of all-out war, but after that stunned and confusing first year it seemed that most people were finding their pride an awfully small stone to swallow, and seizing their new lifestyle with both hands and no questions asked.

Me, I had no complaints either. As former active service personnel people like me were right up there at the head of the line. After two years they moved us into an even bigger house, twelve rooms and no problem in filling them all. We weren't allowed to move our stuff, we had to junk everything and start all over again. Gabrielle cried a little as we watched some of the pieces burn, but it wasn't like anything was irreplaceable.

And when a yellow form came, you didn't argue.

Now, I didn't know the Hirasakis well; I didn't even know George all that well, when it really came down to it. We lived close and we were friendly, but that isn't the same as real friendship. I'd never seen George worried in the way that he was now, and I suppose that helped it to get to me, too. A yellow form and an ambulance made a disturbing combination.

One of the alien skimmers passed overhead as we walked towards the Hirasaki house. Their patrols are frequent but they're not regular, or at least I've never been able to make out any pattern in them. This one came by low and cruised on out of sight beyond the roof tops, and then a few seconds later it popped back into sight in the middle distance heading out across the bay towards the middle of town. They'd no windows and they never landed, so the chances of actually seeing an alien were nil; but everybody knew by now how they could find you and burn you up inside your own home without even scorching the wallpaper, and that made them a potent tool of enforcement. George and I watched it until it was right out over the Transliner tracks and unlikely to swing around and come back, and then we crossed the street and walked up Jimmy Hirasaki's driveway.

I didn't know how Gloria Hirasaki was going to react to the two of us turning up like this, but when she opened the door it was almost as if she'd been half-expecting a visit. She seemed pleased and nervous at the same time. "Jimmy's getting stronger every day," she said. "He came downstairs on his own this morning. He'll be really happy to see you."

And then she led the way into the house, which was like walking from day into night. All the blinds in the place had been drawn and no lights had been switched on, and as she closed the door behind us I had a panicky few seconds of total blindness until my eyes began to adjust and perceive that the blackout wasn't quite as complete as it had first seemed. There was a yellow glimmer ahead in the lounge.

It came from a small shaded lamp on the table beside Jimmy Hirasaki, who was sitting in a big wing-chair. My first guess, that he had some kind of eye problem, seemed to be proved wrong by the presence of an open comic book on his knees. But that was about all that I could see of him, because the light from the lamp had been cut down with a towel draped over the shade and his face was lost in the even deeper shadows of the chair.

"Jimmy?" George said doubtfully, peering into the gloom. "Hello, George," Jimmy said. "I'm glad you came over. Both of you."

"What happened?" I said. "We saw the ambulance. Did you have an accident, or what?"

"No accident," Jimmy said. He sounded hoarse, but he didn't sound weak. "I'm sorry about the lights, they're more for Gloria's benefit than anything else. I don't look quite the way I used to. It's not easy for her to adjust."

George said, "We heard about you getting a yellow form. You know what it's like, we're starting to wonder what's ahead for the rest of us. What did you have to buy, Jimmy?"

"A little surgery," Jimmy said, and I felt something down in my gut start to flicker and tremble.

"Surgery for what?" George persisted, and I sensed, rather than saw, that Jimmy was starting to move.

"One or two improvements that they decided we need," he said, and he drew away the towel that was covering the lamp.

⚭

Jimmy came out onto the street for the first time about a week later, by which time the story had broken everywhere. The appearance of a so-called convert was still news, but it was no longer hot news. They were coming out all over the city, and to everybody except the people who knew them well they looked reassuringly normal. Jimmy wasn't self-conscious about it, but I could see Gloria looking around with that nervous half-smile as if she couldn't trust herself to be able to tell a gesture of friendship from a threat of attack. The changes were disconcerting to see, but the shock of that first impression when he'd taken the cover from the lamp began to fade from me at the first touch of daylight.

Jimmy was half-Japanese, as you might expect, and he'd never actually been tall or brawny, but now he had a good four or five inches on me and moved with the quiet power of a professional athlete, without the injuries. His voice, now that the hoarseness was gone, gave you a little thrill when you heard it; standing next to him was what a lot of people imagine being in the presence of a big movie star must be like. You felt awed and nervous, somehow privileged just to be so close.

Inferior, I think is the word that best describes it.

That had to be the reason why so many simply picked up their yellow forms and went in without complaint. A few kicked and screamed, but then a skimmer would hover overhead and ensure docility as the police brought them out of their homes. Others didn't wait around, but booked themselves in without even waiting to be yellow-carded. I saw little of the panic and fear that I'd have expected, and I suspect that the reason was a simple one. I glimpsed some of its truth one evening as I watched Gabrielle through the open bedroom door. She was sitting in front of the dressing-table mirror, and I don't think she even knew that I was there. She was gazing into her own eyes and pinching thoughtfully at the skin of her neck. She'd read somewhere that this was a way to break up any fat that might be starting to form, and I remember once telling her that if she wasn't careful she'd end up looking like a turkey in a dog-collar. She'd laughed at this, but not too hard. What should have been some of our best years had been lost to the war; but now it seemed that our conquerors had devised a way of giving them back to us.

I'd asked Jimmy what the process entailed, and if there was any pain involved. He told me that he hadn't known a thing about it until it had all been over. All that he knew about the procedure was something that he'd overheard from one of the surgical franchise technicians, something about a 'first-stage peel and rewire job'. It was a phrase that I somehow couldn't get out of my mind as I waited out the following weeks.

The way that it worked out, Gabrielle went first. My call came a few days later, and to a different franchise. From the way I understood the small print the cost in consumer points would be phenomenal, but monthly payments would still leave us with a decent margin to live on. And, what the hell, it was all imaginary anyway; they sold us the stuff and they also gave us the wherewithal to pay for it, and if that was how you had to behave when you won a war, perhaps it was better to be a loser any day.

They didn't have to send a skimmer for me, or anything. I put some clean underwear and a paperback book into a little bag, and presented myself at the Foresight Building.

"I'm giving you a couple of shots," Foresight told me. "They'll kill any pain and they'll also get you over the initial weakness."

"I'm not in any pain," I said, hearing my new voice for the first time.

"You get the shots anyway," the doc said.

I'd been expecting something high-tech and sterile and impressive, but I'd been wrong. I was lying on a mean little cot in a windowless brick chamber that I shared with four others; the ceiling was vaulted, and my guess was that I was in some corner of the cellar. Sounds echoed when somebody coughed or groaned, and light was from a single naked bulb.

I wanted to see myself, but really all that I could see were my hands, and then not too well because of the low wattage of the overhead light. The shots made me feel dull and happy, and after an hour or so two attendants came and helped me up from the cot and took me outside to walk up and down the corridor. This was just as dark and as grim as the room that I'd left, the floor plain stone and the walls all soot-stained. Others were being walked as well, shambling golden giants with their unaltered supporters to either side, and as I stumbled the exhausting length of the passageway I looked in vain for a mirror.

When I was back in the dank room they ran a few checks on me and then asked if I wanted anything to help me sleep. I said I didn't need anything, that I was whacked, and again I heard the sound of my own, strangely-enhanced voice.

I think I was probably asleep before they even left me.

I couldn't remember anything of the procedure, not from the time that I'd rolled up my sleeve for the needle. When that had happened I'd still been fully dressed and out in the overcrowded reception area, so presumably I must have been walking around and co-operating for at least a while after that—but nothing of it seemed to have stayed with me, and all that I could do was to lie there and wonder. I was alert and there was a kind of tingling sensation in my mind, and I thought that perhaps I should have taken that third shot after all as there seemed to be no chance now of sleep returning. I still felt no pain; in fact, I felt pretty good. Not strong, but generally okay.

After lying there for a while longer, I decided that I felt well enough to go looking for a mirror.

The passageway was empty now, and I guessed that it was probably night. I got more than halfway along before I realised that the expedition was a mistake, and by then I didn't have the energy to make it all the way back. I supported myself on the crumbly wall and pressed on towards the lights at the end, hoping that I'd find somewhere to sit for a while. If I didn't then I'd just have to slide down and sit on the cold floor, from where I doubted that I'd be able to rise again.

The end of the passageway opened off into a whitewashed chamber that had been fixed up as an office; a barred street-level window in the far wall confirmed that we were at basement level, and that it was, indeed, after dark. Doc Foresight was sitting behind his desk, morosely contemplating a clipboard. He looked up when I came around the corner.

"You," he said.

I only had eyes for the empty chair that I could see on the other side of the desk from him. I lurched over and dropped into it gratefully. I said, "You don't look happy, doc."

"Of course I'm happy," he said bitterly. "I'm a rich man." and he tossed the clipboard over onto the desk, not caring too much whether it hit anything else.

I said, "Perhaps you can explain something to me. I've tried to make it out and I can't make any sense of it, but you're a franchise holder so maybe you'll know. They attack us and beat us. Then they set us up again and start pumping in all this investment. But they never ask for anything back."

Foresight leaned back in his chair. He was small and dark, not grey but a lot of the way towards going bald. He said, "So, what's your question?"

"I'd have thought it was obvious. What's in it for them?"

He looked up at the whitewashed ceiling and then he shrugged, delicately.

"Survival, I suppose," he said.

"Survival how?"

But then he smiled, sadly, like a teacher might at a simple question which even years of study couldn't answer, "I don't understand big money," he said, "I don't even understand lending to piss-poor little countries who've got no hope of even paying the interest, just so they can use it to buy stuff that your own factories are overproducing. I suppose if you want the true explanation, you'll find it somewhere in the gap between real life and book-keeping."

"You're kidding me," I said.

"That they needed to expand their markets so much that it was worth fighting a war and then giving the stuff away to make it happen? All right, so I'm kidding you. I'm a rich man, what do I care what you think? And what are you doing wandering around here, anyway?"

I said, "I came out to look for a mirror,"

"There aren't any,"

"Why not?"

He took a deep breath, almost a sigh. "Because people kept looking in them and then thanking me, I don't want any more of that. "

I couldn't understand his attitude, and I said so. He stared at me thoughtfully for a while, with an odd kind of half-amused expression that

I wasn't sure that I liked. Then he went over to his pharmacy cupboard and loaded up a hypodermic; the shot that he gave me seemed to wash all the tiredness out of my limbs again, but he warned me that the effect wouldn't last.

Then he said, "Come and see exactly what it is you'd be thanking me for."

Ten minutes later I was back in the same seat, wanting to be sick but finding that my new body wouldn't cough up the goods. I'm not used to seeing that kind of stuff, and it had upset me far more than I'd imagined. The process was almost fully automated, carried out by programmed franchise equipment that was working on through the night while the rest of us slept; two converts had been at the half-way stage, the worst possible stage at which to view the process. It wasn't surgery, it was butchery.

"It isn't enhancement," Foresight explained as I sat there with my head in my hands, thinking that I'd gone through the same procedures only hours before, "it's major replacement. Only the brain and maybe ten per cent of the internal body mass are carried over... and they can even scan and remodel the brain, in extreme cases."

I asked him what had happened to... well, to the rest of me.

He said, "Broken up for spares. Nothing's wasted, and it'll be a long time before converts make up any significant proportion of the population."

"Can I see them?"

"You wouldn't want to," he said, and he came over and put a sympathetic hand on my shoulder. "Would you like me to give you something to forget what you saw? I can, as long as it's done straight away."

"No," I said, "I don't want to forget," and so instead he helped me to stand so that I could go back to bed. The injected stimulant was starting to wear off, as he'd said it would.

And as I got to my feet, I saw the clipboard that he'd been studying and had tossed onto his desk when I'd arrived. On top of the bundle of invoices under the clip was a yellow form, and the yellow form had Foresight's name on it.

The change in Gabrielle was the hardest to take, because it affected me the most sharply. She looked almost the way that she had when I'd first seen her, years before at her sister's wedding and quite some time before we'd started to get serious. I don't think she'd even been quite sixteen, then. She spent a lot of those first couple of weeks before the bedroom mirror, not in sadness as she had before but with her eyes filled with tears of disbelief. I'd taken a long, hard look in that same mirror once, but now I tended to avoid it. The eyes were reassuringly my own, but the rest was... well, I don't know what it was. It wasn't me, that was for sure.

I didn't tell Gabrielle what I'd seen. She said that she'd signed for a number of extras, expensive additions to the process, and I said that it didn't matter. Which it didn't—we weren't exactly spending money of our own, and the true damage lay in the conversion itself, not in the add-ons or the extra enzymes or the built-in glands that could secrete uppers or downers at will.

The plans that I had to tell George disappeared within a couple of days of him getting home. He was totally won over. He'd always been small and kind of runty, and he'd once told me about some childhood illness he'd had which had twisted his back so that he didn't take his shirt off in public, even on a beach. It didn't show, but you couldn't tell him that. For George, it must have been like going to sleep a frog and waking up a prince. The knowledge that I had, I realised, was slowly driving a wedge between me and the rest of the converted world. "Looking good," George would call across to me when we both appeared out of doors, and I'd think of my true body split up into raw chunks and tagged in Foresight's deep freeze, waiting for a cancer case or the victim of some industrial accident amongst the workforce who carried no alien credit.

This was a side of life that I was going to see more of, when the bills for Gabrielle's 'extras' came in.

But before that I have to tell you about one afternoon when I went over to see George, the afternoon that I finally realised that my thoughts of him as a possible ally would have to be wiped from my mind forever.

Mary showed me through to the back, to their new cedar-decked sun room with its glass roof and sliding control blinds. George was lying on one of those tubular aluminium loungers, but the blinds had been drawn against the sun and instead he was under an angled lamp that washed him with a faintly greenish glow. We had one just like it at home, it had been one of the must-buys a couple of months ago and I'd been waiting the required time until I could throw it out, because I'd rigged it up and tried it and found it to be useless for any purpose that I could imagine.

I said as much to George, and he said, "No, you're wrong, just put your hand under," so I did. My hand began to tingle and to experience a feeling of deep warmth, and I drew it back quickly. My unconverted body had felt nothing in the rays, nothing at all.

"It's about five times better than sunshine," George said, and lazily turned himself over on the lounger to lie face-down like a dog in the mid-day desert. He sighed loudly and contentedly, obviously feeling so good that it didn't much matter to him whether I was there or not.

I was staring at his exposed back. I'd seen it before, only a couple of days after he'd returned from his conversion, but now it was different. Something was pushing up under the skin around either shoulder, two body-length, parallel structures that were pressing up tight like new knuckles at the top and threatening to split their way through. The skin had been stretched so thinly that I could almost make out the complexity of gristle and sinew beneath. They seemed to be causing him no discomfort at all; so sensitive before, he didn't even seem to be aware of this new disfigurement.

I didn't wait around or ask him about them, but my own shoulders were starting to itch and as soon as I got into the house I ran into the bedroom and tore off my shirt and twisted myself around so that I could get a look in the mirror. I saw nothing out of the ordinary, just a back that would have made a lifeguard's look puny; no bumps, no marks, no signs of anything growing there. Feeling foolish and troubled at the same time, I walked through the rooms where all of the useless must-buys were stacked, donning my shirt and wondering how many of these apparently useless goods would turn out to have new applications for the converted. Some of the boxes and cases had been re-opened, I noticed, and I went on through to look for Gabrielle.

I found her out on the patio, lying naked under that same design of lamp. Its glow gave her the look of some ancient bronze of a goddess, raised after centuries on a sea bed. It was a shock to find her out of doors like this, because although the patio was fairly private it wasn't particularly well-screened; it was something that I couldn't even imagine her having considered before.

But that had been before. Now, as she became aware of me, she looked up at me and smiled; and I saw the rapid blink of a milky inner eyelid, a quick flick-across that was almost too fast to make out.

It struck me as frightening, and deeply disturbing.

And—I have to say it—it struck me as something alien, in every sense of the word.

The end of the month came, and with it came the accounting. I was dismayed to find that Gabrielle hadn't only ordered extras in her conversion, but that she'd gone out and signed for quite a lot of new warehouse goods as well; dismayed, because for the first time ever our charges were in excess of our allowance. I didn't know what I was supposed to do in a case like this. Given the size of the allowance, I hadn't even thought that it would be possible.

I thought that we might ride it out for another month, cut back on our outgoings and hope that it would all balance up, but that didn't work. I'd tried to talk to Gabrielle about it, and she'd seemed to listen, but when I saw the new figures I realised that she hadn't. That was the evening that I saw Jimmy Hirasaki for the first time in a while, just a glimpse at one of his windows in the cool October night, but enough to register the gross distortion that had taken place in his body and to wonder at the strange, birdlike spread of his silhouette.

It was also the evening that I stripped off again before the bedroom mirror and reached over to run my hands over my shoulders, this time feeling the hard projections that were growing like small apples under the skin.

My new body stayed calm, and wouldn't respond to the spiritual terror that I was experiencing; others around me hardly seemed to notice the changes in themselves, and so were unlikely to react with much sympathy to mine. When I went over to talk to George, he immediately assumed that my debts were the main source of my worries.

"Don't get in a state over it," he said. He was sitting forward on the edge of his sofa, as if it was uncomfortable for him to lean back. The projections on his shoulders had grown even further and now strained at the material of his shirt, like the wings of a moth as it begins to burst from its shell, and I noticed that his hands had become longer and bonier as if the flesh was falling away to reveal claws inside. "The same thing's happening all over town. All you have to do is sign up on a work gang, put in the few days you need to make up the difference, and then quit when you're even." And then he smiled a viper's smile. "You remember work, don't you?"

Yes, I remembered work. I didn't miss it much, but I remembered it. The work gangs that George was referring to were mostly transient labourers who cleared land for the new warehouses, or else they went out along the Transliner routes to build bridges and supply depots. Sometimes it seemed that the whole world was becoming a machine, a one-way device for commerce and consumption. So far the gangs had consisted entirely of those who got no credit from the conquerors, the fringe people in their shanties on the edge of town, and I wondered how they'd react to finding a convert standing in line with them; but from the way that George was talking it sounded as if I wouldn't be the first, and my guess was that I'd be a long way from being the last.

"Just consider the alternative," he said, and for a moment I could see the old George in that resculpted face. "The alternative is a visit from one of the skimmers. We can sit here and we can talk about what's fair and what's right, but when it comes down to it that's the reality we have to deal with."

I managed to stick with it for one day.

It wasn't the work, which consisted of bending wire and pouring concrete underground for a Transliner subway; my rebuilt body coped with ease, and I was hardly even tired at the end of the shift. It was more the stark terror that I saw in the faces of the unconverted when they looked at me, their refusal to meet my eyes or even to speak to me if contact could be avoided, and when once there was a muttering of resentment that even

I could barely hear, it was answered with the sudden appearance of a skimmer at the tunnel's end. It hovered for a few seconds, cutting out the daylight to enhance its menace with darkness, and then it was gone.

I only knew that I couldn't live like this. I'd think about the days before the war and I'd want to weep, but my body wouldn't allow it.

It was then that I realised, there was a way. It meant losing everything that I had and starting again… but what did I have, really? Gabrielle was no longer Gabrielle, and was becoming even less so every day. I had no friends. I owned nothing that was truly worth having.

So one evening, when the sky was clear and the stars were pin-bright and there was nowhere for a skimmer to hide unseen, I made my way across town to the Foresight Building and broke in.

"I'm sorry," Foresight said. "I can't do it."

"You mean you won't?"

"I can't, that's all."

"Is it the money?"

"No," he said, "it isn't the money."

Getting in had been easy. I'd been able to rip an entire window of bars out of the brickwork, with barely a sound. I'd found Foresight as I had before, in his whitewashed below-ground office, sitting out the night alone. He was, as yet, still unconverted. *You*, he'd said simply when he saw me, showing no surprise but seeming to recognise me straight away, almost as if I'd been expected.

So then I'd explained what I wanted him to do, convincing myself as I spoke that it had to be possible, and then had come his flat refusal.

"But why?" I said. "Is it because you don't keep track of the pieces?"

"We keep records," he said. "And yes, the procedure's feasible. But believe me, you don't want to know why I can't help you."

*You don't want to know*; he'd said that to me once before and I'd insisted, and what I'd seen as a result had been a part of my ruin. But anything else would have meant living in the shadow of the truth without ever seeing its shape, and because I detected a trace of sympathy behind Foresight's turn-down I knew that I had to keep at him. He stalked off down one of the brick corridors to make some late checks on his clientele, and I went after.

My request? It seemed simple enough. I wanted him to rebuild me.

After what I'd seen in his surgical rooms I didn't doubt that the technique was there, all fully automated and error-free on the franchise equipment, and I could be pretty sure of being whole again except for a few scars. I'd thought it through and it didn't seem too likely, given the glut of spare parts that must have accompanied the conversion programme, that any of the pieces would be unavailable. The main difficulty as I saw it wasn't practical, it was social.

I couldn't go back, not to live as the only human being in a house in a street of monsters, but I also doubted that I'd be allowed simply to disappear. The way out, as I saw it, lay in an offhand remark of Foresight's; he'd said that in extreme cases the copying and enhancement process could also be applied to the brain, and I didn't see why my case shouldn't be considered as far-gone as any. I could duck out and find whatever new life lay ahead for me, whilst my functioning double could return to live out the old.

"Come on, Foresight," I said, "you owe me." And that stopped him, wearily, in his tracks.

"And how do you arrive at that conclusion?" he said.

"You converted me. And then, as if that wasn't enough, you let me see what I was. All I'm asking is to be restored, it's maybe four hours' work for those machines and then less to rig up a copy. I won't tell and I certainly won't be coming back. So where's your problem?"

He turned to me then. And I realised that what I'd seen in him wasn't sympathy, it was pity.

"The problem is that it's all too late," he said. "You came up with all these ideas and arguments on the night of your conversion, but you don't even remember. You want to know *why* you don't remember?"

"Tell me," I said.

"Because what you're asking for, I already did. And the reason why you don't remember is because you *are* the copy."

❦

I remember lying on my cot, alone in that narrow basement room, listening to them as they argued on the other side of the door; my doctor and my double, swapping a few hard truths but with the harshness mostly going in one direction only. I was afraid that Foresight was going to fling open the door and point to me as proof, lying there still weak and with the stitch-marks still on me, but he didn't. I'd been crawling back to strength for months, and still had some way to go; no rapid recoveries for the true flesh. Foresight came in later and said that he'd gone, and that I wasn't to worry. He said that he was going to give me something that would help me sleep, when what he really meant was that he was going to give me something that would make me sleep. I was damn sure I wasn't going to manage it on my own, that night.

Some time later, when I was walking again and the day of my leaving was coming somewhere into sight, the doc tried to explain it to me. He explained that my double was less than human, and that the anguish it seemed to experience was no more real than that of one of his lab animals. Emotional clockwork, he called it, and the phrase became a kind of talisman for me, something that I repeated to myself whenever I sensed the guilt beginning to rise again.

I had to leave town, because I couldn't take the risk of being seen by anyone who'd known me, and so I took a series of jobs before settling as one of a Transliner bridge maintenance gang right at the other end of the country. They were hard, miserable days at first, eased only by a constant exhaustion which kept me from thinking too much. I kept out of the cities now, unable to suppress the panic that I felt whenever I saw the slowly mutating forms of the converted, and got myself a more or less permanent room in a run-down building that had formerly been a bombed-out tourist hotel.

"You heard the rumours?" Eloise said to me one day at the end of the shift. Eloise was our team boss, and had been a front-line medic in the wars. Born suspicious and perhaps made a little healthily loopy by the mayhem she'd seen, she'd destroyed her unit's service records at the end of the conflict in the belief that military personnel were likely to be the first targets for alien extermination squads. Most of her people made up the team that I was working in now.

"Rumours?" I said. "What rumours?"

"They're doming the cities," she said. "Can you imagine it? Domed cities, just like in the stories, so the Masters won't have to walk in our sunshine."

"They don't anyway," I said.

I still don't know whether she was serious or not. I'd come to like Eloise, but I still wasn't sure that I had the hang of her sense of humour. As I hitched a ride with a 'liner to get home at the end of the day, I was wondering if I could get to know her better; she'd shown an interest in my scars that I sensed wasn't purely professional. When I thought of Gabrielle now, it was as you'd think of someone who no longer lived; perfect in memory, the memory being that of the first night in our unfurnished new home with the war over and a safe future assured.

But what future was there, really? Eloise said that things had to stabilise soon, to reach a liveable balance, and I believed her. But how it would happen, I honestly couldn't say.

I found out when I got home that evening.

There was an envelope lying on the bed, actually on the pillow, which annoyed me because I didn't like anybody going into the room when I wasn't there. I'd nothing worth taking, but that wasn't the point. The envelope was blank, I noticed as I tore it open.

Out came a yellow form. On the yellow form, my new name.

And as I stood at the window looking out into the cold, cold sunset, my hands in my pockets and my heart like a stone, I watched the distant lights of a skimmer as it hovered and probed and made its slow patrol of the city outskirts. I knew that it was only my imagination, but sketched out against the sky behind it I seemed to see the faint ghost-image of a rising pattern of latticework, It was curved like the beginnings of a dome, and dark like a shadow of tomorrow. ❧

# The Blackwood Oak

9 DAMIEN could see that the biker and his girlfriend had pitched their tent among the trees, about fifty yards up the hill from the picnic area. It was an orange two-man ridge job, well-used and a little faded. They'd chosen an awkward spot, away from the other campers. But with the flysheet unzipped they'd have one of the best views in the whole valley, right out across the lake to the wooded hills on the other side.

He took the keys out of the pickup and swung the door closed as the biker walked toward him.

"Damien Ryan," he said. "Ranger Service. What's your problem?"

The biker seemed embarrassed. He was about twenty-five, a couple of years older than Damien and a bigger man all round. He wore a white T-shirt, with the upper half of his motorcycle leathers peeled down to his waist. Presumably so he could wash. Certainly not so he could shave.

"It's in the tent," he said. "Thanks for coming out." His cellphone was still in his hand.

They walked up the hill together. The girlfriend was waiting alongside their big Honda Goldwing, arms folded protectively across her chest even though the day wasn't cold. She wore jeans and a tank top. She was skinny and her arms were freckled, both a plus in Damien's eyes. But he stayed professional and kept his eyes on the tent.

"I don't know how it got in," the biker said.

"They'll grab any opportunity you give them," Damien said. "Any food in there?"

"Yes, but it's all in a coolbox."

"They'll still sniff it out."

As he said this, the tent canvas moved suddenly as if it had been punched from inside. The girlfriend gave an involuntary yelp and there was a sound of claws scrambling across plastic groundsheet.

"Sorry," she said after a moment.

And the biker said, "If it just turns out to be a squirrel, I'll feel like an idiot."

"No," Damien said. "You did right to call me." He signalled for the biker to stop so that he could approach the tent alone. The man joined his girlfriend by the Goldwing.

Damien said, "You didn't get a good look at it, then?"

"It moved too fast."

Damien was now closing in on the tent, never taking his eyes off it and moving with care.

He said, "It's best to treat your wildlife with respect. You get a nip from just about anything in these woods, and you'll know about it. You might want to move a little further off."

The couple exchanged a glance, then moved together to the edge of their camp. Damien was around the far end of the tent now, with the valley and the view at his back. He crouched down before the half-unzipped flysheet.

The girlfriend called out, "Any danger of rabies?"

"Who knows," Damien said.

Their tent was one of the old Vango Force Tens, a ground-hugging tunnel of cotton-canvas over steel. The central zip on the inner tent was closed but the zipper across the bottom had been left open. Fine if you wanted to keep flies out, but an open invitation for anything bigger to shimmy under.

Holding the liner at the bottom, taking care not to startle whatever had made its way inside, Damien slowly opened up the zipper and then lifted back one of the flaps.

They weren't going to be happy campers. As seen in the stifling red-gold light of the tent's interior, their possessions had been trashed. The sleeping bags shredded, stuffing dragged out and scattered. Maps had been ripped up. Clothing thrown around.

At the far end, in a kind of low apse formed by the tent's extended shape, was their luggage and the coolbox. The coolbox was a dark blue plastic chest with two white clips to hold the lid down. The clips were thrown back and the lid was off.

And there, rummaging around in the contents, was the culprit.

It was greeny-brown and bug-eyed. About the size of a cat, but with rough skin like bark. It stood on two sturdy legs and rummaged with four racoon-like arms. Its skin was covered in sharp thorns, and it had a tail that was in constant motion. Damien couldn't see much of its face until it suddenly became aware of him, and looked up.

It had been stuffing bread or cake into its mouth. Its cheeks bulged even more than its eyes. It stared at him and its mouth moved a couple of times, in a cud-chewing motion.

Then it spat the whole mouthful in his direction, with a force and accuracy that would have drawn gasps of admiration in any Western saloon.

Damien dodged back just in time, and the mess spattered harmlessly on the inside of the canvas.

He ran the zip down again before rising to his feet and taking a step back.

"Yep," he said. "It's a squirrel. You couldn't do me a favour?"

"Sure," the biker said, eager to earn back some of his dignity. "What?"

"Go down to the truck and bring me those thick gloves out of the cab? And you'll find a canvas sack in the load bed."

The biker went hopping off down the hill, which left Damien with the girlfriend. He gave her a grin. She managed something like a smile in return.

The biker came back with the gloves in one hand and the canvas sack in the other, looking doubtfully between them. The gloves looked as if they'd been dragged through the cogwheels of some big machine a few times. The canvas sack wasn't in quite such good condition. It had leather straps on it, like the fastenings on a straitjacket.

"These?" he said.

"Those are the ones," Damien said.

With some low cunning and fast reactions and an unavoidable disregard for the campers' property, Damien managed to get the creature into his canvas sack without letting them see it. He got the sack into the iron cage on the back of the pickup and then he didn't wait around for their response to the mayhem inside their tent, or for the questions that would follow. Once his captive was secure, he was out of there.

Bouncing his way on the dirt track down to the valley's metalled access road, he unhooked the pickup's radio mike and raised his father at the lodge. Don Ryan responded right away. He'd been close to the radio and waiting for the call.

"I've got it," Damien said.

"Did they get a look at it?"

"No," Damien said. "And just as well. With those four arms I'd never be able to persuade them it was anything common. It's not a form I've seen before. And it's got a foul temper, I can tell you that much."

"Any other distinguishing features?" Don said, and Damien gave him a description... the thorny skin, the uncannily accurate and forceful spit-missile ability.

"Let me see if I can look it up," Don said. "I'll call you right back."

Damien tried to hang up the radio mike as he drove one-handed, fought with the curly cord a couple of times, and then gave up and left it hanging onto the floor like he always did.

He could imagine his father at this moment, pulling his dusty old books off the shelf in his study, looking through the indices and engravings for some clue as to what they had in the cage. Don Ryan had been the valley's Ranger before Damien, for more than thirty years. These days he was semi-retired, mostly due to his arthritis. He answered the phone, dealt with campsite bookings, and dispensed advice to his grown-up children whether it was wanted or not. He knew the valley better than anyone; theirs was a line that had forested and lived off this woodland since the time of the English Civil War.

Some of the volumes on his study shelves were unbelievably rare, and probably worth a fortune. No one since the Victorians had approached the taxonomy of the preternatural world with the meticulous rigour of scientific enquiry; but for Don Ryan, the books were no more than a working reference library. Some had been handed down from his grandfather's time. Others, he'd picked up as he'd gone along. He scoured library sales, and had contacts who kept an eye on country auctions for him. He'd been unbearable for a few weeks when he'd first discovered eBay.

But good information was essential. Every species was different. They misbehaved at the least opportunity, and the opportunities were many. Whenever one strayed, identification was always the first step in dealing with it.

As he was driving along the lakeshore, Damien's eye was caught by something out on a promontory overlooking the water. It looked as if someone had been dumping rubbish. He pulled off the road and got out of the pickup, leaving the windows open so that he'd be able to hear the radio if Don called him back.

Before leaving the vehicle, he checked the iron cage. The canvas sack moved a couple of times, and he could hear a muttering from inside it. A spell in darkness ought to calm the creature.

In theory.

Out on the promontory, it was as he'd suspected. He found the remnants of a burned-out campfire, and beercan litter all around it.

He took in a deep breath, and sighed it out. He'd seen this so many times before. Why come all the way out here for the beauty of the place, and leave a trail of shit like this?

Town kids, probably. Beauty seemed to make them angry. He'd never understood why.

He got a rubbish sack from the roll he kept in the cab, and went around picking up the discarded cans. All he could do with the fire was kick over the ashes and leave the land to heal the damage.

Now, here was something strange. Some of the opened cans were almost full. And here was a six-pack, completely untouched. Like the campout had been abandoned all at once, and in a tearing hurry.

He looked all around, but could see nothing else unusual.

Don was calling on the radio when he got back to the truck.

"Damien," his father said unnecessarily, "it's me. Looks like it's just a low-level wood sprite. Did you say four arms?"

"And a grip like the meanest monkey you ever saw."

"Can you look and see if there's a blue stripe under its belly?"

Damien cast a doubtful eye over the sack in the cage, just as the thing inside it seemed to be embarking on a new bout of restlessness.

"If you want to get that close and personal," he told his father, "you're on your own."

"It probably doesn't matter," Don said. "Meet me at Fiddler's Point."

Fiddler's Point was a relatively new planting on the valley slopes just above the dam. The slopes had been badly scarred when the dam was being built, and once the heavy machinery had gone away an extensive programme of replanting had begun.

That had been more than a century before. It had left a legacy of young woodland that was neat, ordered, and almost entirely without soul.

Wood sprites, Damien was thinking as he drove up to the Point. There are thousands of those. You could live your whole life in a place like this and never come across the same species twice.

Maybe those people down at the lakeside had disturbed something with their partying, and given themselves a scare. They'd be civilians, unaware of what lay in hiding all around them, assuming—when they thought about it at all—that the preternatural was no more than the stuff of dreams and stories.

Which suited Damien fine. The less people knew, the less likely they were to interfere. For him, the preternatural was something to be dealt with on a daily basis. A whole other stratum of wildlife with its own, very different set of rules. Don had taught him to see his trade as a combination of conservation and pest control, protecting the people from the wildlife and the wildlife from the people. For which a need-to-know arrangement was probably the best.

Don was there ahead of him. He could see his father's blue-grey Land Rover waiting in the parking area. The area was of gravelled earth, with ruts and low spots where rainwater collected. Damien made a mental note to send out a crew to level the ruts before the season got fully under way.

Don was out of the Land Rover. He was poking his walking stick into one of the puddles to test its depth.

He said, "You want to get a load of stones ordered and—"

"I'm on it, dad," Damien said.

Damien put on the gloves, and lifted the entire cage out of the back of the pickup. He remembered how lively the sprite had been when he'd struggled it into the sack, and didn't want to risk having it fight him through the bag while he was trying to carry it.

"You got it?"

"I've got it."

Don led the way. All the trees here were tall, straight, and evenly spaced. As woodland went, it was kind of boring. It could take a thousand years for a forest to grow a soul. There were many theories as to how it happened, all of them more speculation than science. One went that if a habitat was cleared, then its nature spirits were gone forever; slow migration was the natural way, as the creatures rarely bred. Throw a chainsaw into the equation, and it stopped adding up.

All the more reason to conserve what remained. They followed a straight path up through the trees, on ground that was covered in a spongy carpet of pine needles and dead bracken.

After a while Damien said, "How much further? This thing's heavy."

"Stop complaining," Don said. "At your age I could do one-armed press ups."

"Only because you never took your other hand off your wallet."

Don paused for a moment. He was getting his breath, but he pretended that he'd stopped to point through the trees with his stick.

"That one, I reckon," he said.

At first glance, it was a Scots Pine no different to all the others. But on closer inspection it seemed slightly less healthy. It had been marked with a red circle of spray paint.

When they reached it, Damien set the cage down with some relief. The thing in the sack was trying to flip itself around.

"Still pretty lively," he said.

"Well, let's put all that energy where it can do some good."

Don placed his walking stick on the cage to steady it while Damien slid back the door and reached inside. Damien deftly unbuckled the straitjacket straps and then withdrew his hand before the creature could work itself free. Which it did at the first whiff of fresh air, fighting its way out to the light and then rocking back on its haunches and looking around blearily.

As soon as it saw Damien, it bared its teeth and launched at him. It was a short-lived show of aggression because it instantly hit the bars with a bang and fell back, eyes rolling up in its spiny head.

"Idiot," Damien said.

Spotting an opportunity to make a tricky job easier, Don quickly slid open the door and reached into the cage. He took the sprite by the scruff of the neck and hauled it out, rising to his feet and turning to the tree. With one hand bracing his weight on his cane, he offered up the sprite to the waiting pine.

The sprite dangled in his grip like a slaughtered turkey. For a moment nothing happened, and then it began to rouse and open its eyes.

"Come on," Don said, seeing that he was about to be stuck with a fistful of one very lively and pissed-off entity. "What are you waiting for?"

What happened then happened with speed, and with no voluntary participation from the sprite at all. As its eyes began to open, it was as if some great force was already drawing it toward the ailing tree. The creature had no time to panic or resist; wham, bang, and it was gone. Sucked in as if by the backdraft of a Bullet Train.

Don showed his relief. "Thank God for that," he said.

Then he fumbled in the pocket of his outdoor coat and brought out a spray can. He shook it, and the metal ball inside it rattled around noisily.

Raising his voice over the noise, he said, "Any chance you could go and meet your sister for me?"

"I thought you wanted to do it."

"That was the plan. But something's come up. There's been a sighting."

"You get sightings all the time. What's so urgent about this one?"

Instead of replying, Don popped the cap from the can and sprayed a red X through the circle on the bark.

"See how that goes," he said. Then: "Well? Can you do it?"

"I suppose."

They started back down toward their vehicles. All had gone to plan. The errant sprite would settle in its new home and the woodland on Fiddler's Point would gain a little character, in more senses than one.

They walked side-by-side now. Don said nothing, and seemed preoccupied.

Damien wondered.

What could deter a father from rushing to meet the daughter that he hadn't seen in almost a year?

❧

Ariane's train was due to pass through their little rural halt at around four o'clock. When Damien's pickup arrived in the lane beside the station, the train was just leaving. It was a branch line Sprinter service. Two little carriages that always looked as if they ought to be carrying goats and milk churns from one village to another.

For someone who'd been travelling for at least the past thirty-six hours, his big sister was looking remarkably fresh.

"No dad?" she said.

"He's checking something out," Damien said. "How was Borneo?"

Ariane slung her backpack into the pickup's load bed and moved around to the passenger door.

"You know you're on a loser when the lost tribe you're studying wants to clear all your questions with its PR agent," she said. "I want a pint mug of real tea and a hot bath. Let's drive."

Damien drove. She sat with her feet up on the dash and her head tilted back against the rest.

Ariane Ryan was a leggy, low-maintenance beauty with all the social poise that Damien knew he lacked. As soon as she'd been old enough, she'd been out there into the world. And with a vengeance. Borneo! Damien had once grown homesick on a school trip to Scarborough.

Without opening her eyes, she said, "So how is he?"

"He doesn't get out so much now," Damien said, "but he keeps busy. He's making a database."

"For what?"

"Every woodsprite and nature spirit that goes AWOL. A kind of Nature's Most Wanted list. He's got his silver-surfer mates up and down the country emailing him sightings."

She turned her head and looked out of the window. She probably wanted to sleep but was too wound-up by her long journey to manage it. Damien glanced at her as they turned into the valley road.

Ariane was older than him, by a couple of years. Old enough to remember their mother. Damien had always been a little in awe of his sibling; while he went to the agricultural college, lived at home, and went out with local girls, she went away and got a degree and continued on to a doctorate, heading off to remote parts of the globe to study anthropology in the field.

Damien could barely imagine it. The valley had too much of a hold on him.

The valley was home. How do you turn your back on that?

Before the building of the dam and the flooding of part of the valley to make a reservoir, succeeding generations of the Ryan clan had lived scattered throughout the farmhouses and small villages on its lower slopes.

The reservoir had wiped out all the villages, and time had taken care of the clan. Now there was just the family and they were, as Damien sometimes put it, pretty much the Last Ryans Standing.

Back at the time of the big relocation, most of them had moved to a small barracks of newly-built wooden cabins in an upland clearing. It was only supposed to be temporary, and it stayed temporary for the next seventy-five years until the stormy night that a lightning-struck ash came down onto a roof and started a fire that had spread to the other buildings.

No one had been hurt because, by then, most of the buildings were no longer occupied. Uncle Wilf had gone to a nursing home and the cousins had gone to live in Canada, leaving Don Ryan and his new bride to continue the line. After looking over the damage, the forestry people had decided to replace it with a modern timber lodge that would double as a Visitor Centre and the Head Ranger's home.

Ariane got her pint of tea, and fell asleep in her hot bath. Damien had to bang on the door to rouse her for dinner.

They dined as they had in the old days whenever there was something to celebrate, in the rough and ready fashion of children who'd been brought up by their father alone; good food, with no finesse, and everybody mucking in to help. The meat sat on the table in the foil in which it had been cooked, and none of the crockery matched. A candle sat in a beer bottle. Don had iced some champagne, which they drank from school-style water glasses.

"Blame your brother for that one," Don told Ariane. "I gave him your mother's best crystal to wash, and he snapped every stem."

After dinner, they moved through into the sitting room. It was fairly spectacular, with a rustic stone fireplace and a high angled ceiling of wooden beams. The architect had been thinking big and hoping for an award.

"Is anything wrong, dad?" Ariane said as they went. "You seem a bit out of it tonight."

For a moment it looked as if Don was about to deny it and make some excuse.

But then he turned serious. "We have a problem to deal with," he admitted.

"I knew it," Damien said. "Ever since the break-in." He turned to Ariane. "Whenever *I* asked him, he said there was nothing."

"What break-in?" she said.

"It was about ten days ago," Don said.

He went on to explain. Someone had got into the lodge and disturbed a few things. Up here in the woods and miles from anywhere, he and Damien tended to be lax about domestic security until the season got under way. When there were more strangers around, they took more care.

No great damage had been done. Some old clothes had been thrown around and a few of Don's books had been pulled from the shelves, but the intruder couldn't have known their value because none of the books was missing.

"I wanted to think that was all there was to it," he said. "But this morning I got an email."

It had come from one of the people that Damien referred to as 'Don's silver-surfer mates'. There were several dozen of them in a loose online community; in all corners of the land, mostly retired, all party to the Well-Guarded Secret and forever telling each other the same old stories that they'd told each other a hundred times before. Some had worked on the land. Others just had an interest in the subject.

One had posted a forum entry on the sighting of a particular errant earth spirit, way down south of here.

"It had started the change to human form," Don said, picking up a book that he'd left out on the coffee table, "but the spotter picked up enough detail to identify it. Sylvanus Roscoe, of the genus Sylvani. That sounded familiar so I went to the shelves to look it up. When I came to the relevant entry, I found this."

He showed them the opened book. About four of its pages had gone; ripped out in a hurry, and without much care.

Don said, "I had to get a friend at the Bodleian to scan their copy and send the pages to me."

"Are you saying that this woodland spirit was behind your break-in?" Ariane said as he passed the scans of the missing pages over for them to see. The first showed a meticulous engraving of a puck-like creature. Not a piece of fantasy art, but a scientific illustration.

"This is not your usual woodland spirit," Don said, "but an Elemental. And not just any old Elemental, but a prince among his kind. Folklore traditionally associates him with... "

"The Blackwood Oak," Damien read aloud.

In the visitor centre's map room, Damien switched on all the lights so that they could look at the big display. The room's centrepiece was an enlarged then-and-now map of the valley, surrounded by historic photographs from a time before the building of the dam.

Don said, "In the eighteen-nineties, they flooded this valley to make the new reservoir. It meant losing three villages and a forest that had been there since well before the civil war."

He pushed one of the interactive buttons that had been set in a row along the bottom of the map, and a black-and-white photograph was spotlit. It showed people in old-time dress by the base of a magnificent tree, obviously a great tourist attraction of its day. Its trunk was the size of a small carousel and many of its roots were above-ground, as if it had tried to prise itself free of the earth. Iron props supported some of the longer branches.

"At the highest point of the forest stood the Blackwood Oak," Don said. "They couldn't dig it up, so they cut it down. The timber went to panel the staterooms on the Oceanic and the stump ended up at the bottom of the lake. And that's how it stayed until a couple of months ago."

Ariane said, "What changed?"

"Remember those earth tremors we had last October?"

"I wasn't here."

"So you weren't. The dam sprung a few leaks. They're draining the reservoir to repair them. You probably saw the machines on the drive from the station. Anybody want to tell me what that means?"

"If the water level drops far enough, we'll see all the old ghost villages again," Damien said.

"And the old forest," Ariane said.

Now Damien was beginning to understand.

"Uh-oh," he said.

"Any sprite, sylph or elemental that didn't get out of that woodland will have been trapped under the lake for close on a hundred years," Don said, at which point the timer on the interactive button cut out with a *thunk* and the photograph of the Blackwood Oak went back into shadow. He turned to them. "I'm not going to dress it up," he said. "An Elemental in its human form could be one hell of a loaded gun."

Later that evening, while Don was online and the dishwasher was dealing with the aftermath of dinner, Ariane joined Damien out on the deck. Moths danced below the outdoor light. Damien was leaning on the rail with a glass in his hand, looking out into the darkness of the forest.

Ariane had been studying the printout images of the stolen pages.

"What do you reckon?" she said.

Damien gave a little shrug of his shoulders. "Drive down, do the gig, bring Roscoe back," he said. "Piece of cake."

Ariane opened out the pages, and held them out under the light so that she could and read aloud from them.

"'The Elementals occupy a position between humans and pure spirits. Made of flesh and blood, they eat and sleep and procreate like humans do. But unlike mortals, they are long-lived, capable of superhuman speed and movement, and without immortal souls.'"

Damien tried not to seem too worried.

"Just another day on the ranch," he said. "Hunting fairies with pickup truck and cattle prod."

"Hey," she said, and punched his arm. "That's quite enough from you. Don't ever let dad hear you using the 'f' word."

Then she grew serious and leaned on the rail alongside him.

"So how is he?" she said, with a glance back into the lodge. "Really?"

"He gets lonely," Damien said. "He's got his mates online. And I'm here a lot of the time. But you know how it is. That can never be the same."

Damien was out behind the lodge at dawn the next morning, loading up ready for the long drive south. The little birdcage affair that he used for wood sprites would be of no use on this trip, so he put that into storage and brought out the big cage that, by tradition, one of his great-uncles had made for the great Undine hunt of '22. He was struggling to get it off the hand-trolley and up onto the load bed when Ariane appeared and helped with the lifting.

They heaved, and on it went. The pickup bounced on its springs and everything in the load bed jumped.

"You're up early," he said. "I thought you'd be ready to sleep for a week."

"No chance," she said. "I'm coming with you."

"Says who?"

"Says me. I thought we could make it like the old days."

"Okay," Damien said.

He fixed the cage in place and got the rest of the gear loaded. A tarpaulin to cover it. Ropes. His padded gloves. By the time they were ready to go, Don was up and about.

They shared some breakfast. Don gave them all the details and the contact information that he had, and then he walked out with them to the truck.

They stopped beside the cab and he said, "Look. I'm not going to insult you. You both know the score. Hunting these nature spirits can be a tough and dirty business. We try to use compassion, but there's no room in it for sentiment. That's why I want one of you to have this."

He produced a heavy-looking flashlight. When he held it out, Damien saw that it also had two short pins on either side of the lens.

"That's not just a flashlight, is it?" Damien said.

"It's a stun gun," Don said. "I bought it over the internet. So far I've never had to use it. You almost certainly won't need it. But I want you to have with you it just in case."

He handed it to Ariane. Then he turned to Damien.

"Look after your sister," he said, and then he turned to Ariane. "And you look after your idiot brother."

"Hey," she said, snapping the stun gun on and off and making it crackle. "Watch out, world. Armed feminist."

She stowed the stun gun under the passenger seat. Then they said their goodbyes and off they went.

When they reached the lakeside a few minutes later, Ariane turned to get a look at the water level. It was well down from the shore, and as it retreated had left a series of bands that resembled contour lines drawn directly onto the bed.

Somewhere out across the water, probably not even visible from here, the surface would be broken by a shallow island with the low stump of the Blackwood Oak.

They lost sight of the lake as the road descended by the dam. Here a mobile brew hut and some heavy machinery were marshalled in the shadow of the dam wall, looking like the world's most functional carnival. The Water Board crew had to be brought out from the town and taken back at the end of every day. Eight or nine men in hard hats and safety jerkins, ferried back and forth by minibus.

Damien stopped to fill the pickup's tank with diesel and then they were on their way, joining the A-road that would take them out of the region and onto the motorway network.

"I feel like some kind of hillbilly," Damien admitted. "Heading for the big city to bring back a runaway pig."

Ariane had her desert boots off and her feet back up on the dash, looking about as relaxed as it was possible to be under the circumstances.

"You need to get out more," she said, and that was all that was said for quite a while; for although their trip was nothing special and its purpose routine, the stun gun under Ariane's seat was Don's reminder to them not to take the job lightly. They'd made the joke about hunting earth spirits with a pickup truck and cattle prod; but now, with an Elemental in their sights, that seemed to be exactly what they were about.

Four hours later, after just one break for a sandwich and a stretch and a wrong turn at a junction where Damien misread the numbers on the sign, they left the motorway and stopped in a service area to locate their destination. Traffic whizzed by on the far side of the wire. Damien's head buzzed. All around them was asphalt, cars, and concrete.

"A do-it-yourself warehouse?" Ariane said.

"A superstore," Damien said. "With a timber yard."

"But of course."

It was no coincidence that most of these places ran a seniors hiring policy. They needed savvy people in the woodyard, when disoriented nature spirits regularly turned up in timber shipments like tarantulas on banana boats.

It was evening when they pulled into the parking lot of the trading estate where the DIY Superstore was located. There were other businesses on the estate—a shoe store, a sportswear barn, a multiplex cinema—so there were plenty of cars and people about. They could wait around in the pickup until closing time without seeming conspicuous.

As the sky grew dark, the parking lot grew brighter and somehow more sinister. Cars came and went all the time. Every now and again, a few people would drift over from the Burger King or Pizza Hut to catch the start of a movie. Minutes later, a few more would make the reverse journey as the previous show ended.

Damien was startled by a knock on his window.

He lowered the glass.

"You must be Don's kids," the man said.

He was somewhere over sixty with pale blue eyes, thinned-out hair, and a grey beard with some traces of his old colour in it. He was wearing the striped shirt and red apron of the DIY chain's staff uniform. It made him look like a refugee member of a barber shop quartet. According to a badge, his name was Edward and he was Happy to Help.

Damien said, "How did you spot us?"

"Ranger Service on the side of your truck and a big covered animal cage on the back," the man said. "It wasn't exactly rocket science. We're closing up in twenty minutes. I'm going to stay behind. It'll be easiest if you're already inside."

He told them where to hide themselves within the store, and then he went back in alone. They gave it a couple of minutes. Then Damien got his gloves and his sack, and Ariane the shock baton. Damien locked the pickup and they walked over.

As instructed, they hid themselves in a display conservatory when no one was watching; it was all glass, but there were bamboo blinds on all the windows. Once inside, Ariane slid the catch on the door.

The two of them sat in silence as the store closed down around them; the announcements, the music switching off, the final call, the last staff check and then the all-clear.

It was another half-hour or so before Edward came for them. Damien emerged first, feeling a little nervous.

"I'm the keyholder for tonight," Edward said to them. "I've switched off the internal alarms. As long as we keep away from the main windows, we'll have the place to ourselves."

He led them through the store. It felt strange. Still bright, but emptier than empty.

Ariane said, "Who made the sighting?"

"One of the girls on the paint counter," Edward said, looking back over his shoulder. "She's been telling everyone she saw a ghost. But as soon as I heard the description, I knew there was something going on. I poked around a bit, and that's how I found this."

"This" was in a corner of the section where hardboard, plywood and sawn timber were stored. A tall entranceway hung with heavy plastic flaps led to a staff-only area with a forklift and all the packing debris from the week's deliveries.

In amongst the debris, someone—something—had put togeth-er pallets and boards and cardboard to make a kind of den or a nest. They took turns peeking in through the entranceway. It was a strangely comfortable-looking bolthole, and it had been furnished with items from all over the store… a battery-powered lamp, a picnic set, a lightweight sleeping bag from the outdoor section. And, in the corner, opened packets and a lot of stale cake.

An Elemental in its native shape needed none of these. But the longer it was abroad, the closer it would grow to human form.

After he'd taken a look, Damien turned to Edward and said, "What makes you so sure this isn't just the work of some homeless kid who's found himself a warm place to hide?"

"Well," Edward said. "The girl said that she'd seen a green teenager. Said he walked right past her after closing time but when they checked the tape, you could see her looking at someone. But on the tape, she was alone."

"Is she still working here?"

"What do *you* think?"

"It's our boy, all right," Ariane said. She'd found some papers under the sleeping bag. Now she showed them to Damien.

They were the torn pages from their father's reference book. The first showed the early engraving of Sylvanus Roscoe that they'd already seen. Along with the text there were other illustrations; a crude carving, an aerial photograph of an earthwork figure, a black-and-white reproduction of one of the Victorian fairy paintings of Atkinson Grimshaw.

"So where is he now?" Damien said.

"He goes out and forages," Edward said. "Don't ask me what for. I haven't been able to work it out."

Their host led them up to the manager's office. In here were CCTV monitors with camera feeds from key areas of the store, and a cupboard with long-play VHS tapes covering the past thirty days.

"We can wait here and watch for him," Edward said.

"But we've already established that TV cameras won't pick up an Elemental," Ariane said. "They just won't see him."

"True," Edward said. "But I've looked at tapes for the past few nights, and they're starting to pick up *something*. As he approaches human, he's starting to register."

They kept the lights at a minimum in the manager's office, and when they spoke it was in the lowest of tones.

Edward looked on with some concern as Damien checked over the gloves and the extra-sized sack that he'd brought along.

"That seems kind of extreme," Edward said, "Why don't you try talking to him first?"

"My great-uncle Harry nearly made that mistake," Damien said. "He thought he was talking down a nature spirit, turned out that he'd cornered one of the Sluagh. That's the Host of the Unforgiven Dead. He was lucky to get out of it with his skin on." Damien looked at Ariane for support, only to see that something seemed to be troubling her.

"What?" he said.

"What does he want?" she said. "He's come all this way. He's made himself a base, here. He goes out every night and searches for something. What's he looking for?"

"Trust me," Damien said. "I've done this often enough. You don't waste time in conversation. What does it matter what he's looking for? You have to grab your chance as soon as you see it. With an Elemental, you might not get another."

It was Ariane who saw the first sign of movement on one of the screens; a ripple down one of the aisles that in a recording could easily have been taken for a crease in the tape. Moving in silence, Damien shifted to the window of the manager's office and looked down onto the sales floor.

There it was; just disappearing from view, heading into the timber section and, to Damien's dismay, wearing one of his old overcoats.

"The cheek of it!" he whispered, as the figure flitted away and out of sight.

They descended from the office to the sales floor. It was almost as bright down here now as at any time during the shopping day; lights were left on all night in order to deter intruders and thieves. Without darkness, they'd no cover. Something which didn't seem to trouble their quarry this evening.

The three of them reached the hanging plastic barrier. Edward held one of the heavy flaps aside and the others eased through the gap ahead of him. No one had spoken since they'd left the office. Damien noticed that, despite her reservations, his sister had the combined flashlight and shock baton ready in her hand.

Sylvanus Roscoe had gone to ground in his den. He'd switched on the electric lantern and they could hear the sound of cellophane wrapping being opened. He sounded busy.

Damien signalled to the others to spread out and stand ready. Silently, he opened up the mouth of the sack and laid it on the ground. Then he drew on the animal handling gloves.

Chopping the air silently with his hand, he counted. One, two, three. Then he heaved the wooden pallet away so that it fell forward with a crash, exposing the tableau within.

Roscoe was sitting on his unrolled sleeping-bag, knees up, overcoat cinched around him by its knotted belt, his bare legs rattling loose in a pair of the superstore's Wellington boots. He was unwrapping more cake. A knitted cap had been pulled over his head, covering the tips of his ears. At first glance he might pass for a boy. But his features were pointed. Nose, cheekbones, chin… unnaturally pointed, as if carved in hard angles.

And he was green. Not a vivid green; not even a green that you'd notice if the light wasn't good. More as if his skin had been dusted with it.

Damien hesitated. He was used to weaselly sprites, all kicking and teeth, that he could grab by the scruff of the neck and thrust into a bag. Sylvanus Roscoe was looking him right in the eye.

Then he moved.

Boy, did he move.

With a speed that seemed to cut through the air, he turned and reached around for something in the back of his den. He didn't find it. His hand moved here, there, almost too fast to follow. He spun back to face them again.

Ariane called out, "Is this what you're looking for?" And she held up the pages from Don's book.

Roscoe stared. And then he launched at her, so fast that he'd reached her before anyone else could even move; she hadn't even begun to raise the stun baton when he'd snatched the pages from her hand and, with a terrific bound, passed right over her.

She'd later say that she was aware of only a blur. Damien saw Roscoe switch his plane of movement entirely, running horizontally along the shelving before righting himself and dropping to the floor behind her.

Then he was off.

Damien pushed past Ariane and gave chase, out of the forklift area and into the main part of the store. He couldn't see Roscoe but he could hear those Wellingtons slapping on the vinyl floor. He was aware of Ariane somewhere behind him, moving on to take one of the other aisles. They'd already left Edward some way behind.

Damien ran along the ends of the aisles, looking down each in turn. He came out into an open area with lawnmowers and barbecues on display. He stopped and listened; he had to still his breathing, which was ragged and loud, to give himself a chance of hearing anything.

He couldn't hear Roscoe's running footsteps any more. Which meant that either the Elemental had outrun him and was gone, or had stopped and was listening for him in turn.

Damien took a step, keeping it silent and looking all around. Ahead of him was the gardening section, with bags of peat and garden tools. To his left, on the other side of a sliding glass door, the area where they sold outdoor plants and garden furniture.

He took another step and then suddenly the glass door began to open, unbidden, startling him; Damien realised that he'd moved within range of its motion sensor and triggered it off. In the silence of the huge building, it was like a tumbling stack of books in a library. He turned back to resume his search of the store...

And there was Roscoe, running straight at him.

The doors had begun to close. Damien realised that Roscoe was aiming for the opening. On the other side of the glass was open night air and a high security fence with razor wire along the top of it; enough to deter a normal intruder, but small beer to someone who could run sideways along a vertical wall as if it was just another floor.

Roscoe hurdled a patio set. He went by so close and so fast that Damien could feel the breeze of his passing. But he couldn't move quickly enough to grab him.

No matter. The glass doors had continued to close. Just as the Elemental went undetected by the store's CCTV, he was invisible to the door's sensors.

Roscoe mistimed and hit the glass so hard that Damien couldn't believe it didn't break.

The Elemental bounced, and landed flat on his back. The book pages, the ones that he'd snatched back from Ariane, were still clutched in his fist. Damien saw his chance. He ran over and threw himself onto the sprite, pinning him down. It wasn't very elegant and it wasn't dignified, but it got the job done.

There wasn't much to the creature. He tried to struggle. Damien realised that, fast as he was, he wasn't strong. He'd very little mass. But by the same token, like a spider surviving a fall, he hadn't suffered much in the collision.

Ariane came out of one of the aisles at a run, summoned by the racket.

"I've got him!" Damien called to her. "Find me something to tie him with!"

She looked around, and saw a shelf of baling twine. As she crossed toward it, the sensors were triggered and the doors began to open again.

It was then that Roscoe pulled a trick that Damien had never seen before; in a brief, big-effort and highly effective transformation, he inflated his face into something golden-eyed and horrific. Only inches from Damien's own, the effect was momentarily terrifying.

He lost his grip on the sprite. In a second the boy was out from under him, and racing for the opening.

Ariane sensed him as he passed behind her. By the time she was turning around, he was out and the doors were closing behind him. Damien scrambled to his feet and launched after. He and Ariane emerged into the sales yard just in time to look up and see Roscoe at the top of the fence.

He'd just cleared the razor wire and was starting to drop. His skinny legs were cycling in the air. The stolen coat had filled up and was flapping wide. He seemed to float down, and staggered only slightly when he hit the ground.

He looked back at them.

Then he recovered and was off across an empty stretch of the car park, passing from one pool of light to another.

"He stole my coat," was all Damien could say.

"He should have stolen some underwear while he was about it," Ariane said.

They trudged back into the store. Edward had caught up with them and had seen the last part of the escape through the glass.

He said, "Will you go after him?"

"There isn't much point," Damien said. "He's away by now. We'll need to wait for another sighting and then find him where he next goes to ground. I'd better call dad."

He took out his phone and moved a few steps away, leaving Ariane and Edward making small talk. There was an atmosphere of disappointment, and he felt that it was his fault. They'd come all this way, and then he'd messed up.

"Dad?" he said. "We lost him."

"What happened?"

So Damien explained. Don pushed him for more detail. His father didn't forgive him, exactly, but only because he seemed to share in the blame as well as the disappointment.

"I should have briefed you better," he said.

Damien said, "Shall we come home?"

"No," Don said. "Not yet. Is Ted there?"

Ted? Damien realised that he meant Edward. Damien waved to catch the older man's eye and then handed him the phone.

Edward listened to Don for a while. He didn't say much other than to agree with him a couple of times.

Then he said, "No problem. I've got plenty of room."

After the conversation with his son, Don Ryan rubbed his hand over his short-cropped hair and paced up and down in the lodge's kitchen where he'd taken the call. His footsteps echoed on the tiles. This place was too big all around. Sometimes he felt more like its caretaker than a person who could call it home. Sometimes he just yearned for the old ramshackle cabins that had stood on this spot, and in which he'd grown up. Those were simpler times. When Damien was away and he was left here alone, the feeling was ten times worse.

What to do.

He'd never had to deal with a problem quite like this one before. Elementals were usually fine as long as you respected them and let them be. But trapping an earth spirit under a lake for a century or more—who could say how that would affect its disposition? Don tried to imagine being confined in the dark for a hundred years, deprived of all senses and unable to move, but he couldn't. If such a thing were to happen to him, he'd probably go mad.

And if that proved to be the case with Sylvanus Roscoe, that was where the danger lay. Elementals were powerful. They were easily the most complex of the nature spirits. Some of their urges could be childish, their emotions overwhelming. Even their love could be terrifying; he tried to picture that same power channelled into a mass of negative feeling, and his imagination just wasn't up to it.

He felt responsible. He *was* responsible. Retired or not, this was still his valley. In a few days' time, Roscoe would be able to pass for human. There would be no more sightings then.

Don went into his study. He switched on his laptop and waited for it to boot and hook up with the wi-fi, wondering how many of his people were likely to be online at this hour. Quite a few, probably; the hard core of old men like himself, their lives filled and their memories vivid and their minds too active to be ready to let go. Talking about the old times, griping about the new, keeping alive names that the world had forgotten.

He found five of them online and active. They included Brownlow up in New York State and Toni over in Finland. When he joined the forum, they were trading off-topic messages about the film career of Agnes

Moorehead. Don wrote up a quick summary of his problem, hit *send*, and waited. Responses and suggestions started to arrive within minutes, but none of the gang had anything useful to offer; it quickly descended into a grousing session about civilians in water management all over the world.

He signed out and went into the visitor centre, where he stood with the lights off looking out of the big panorama window. Whenever there was a moon, it was possible to see its reflection in the lake. But the sky was cloudy and there was no moon, just an occasional pearly cloud-glow where the moon ought to be.

After fretting about it for a while, he went and got Damien's Ranger-issue night vision binoculars. He was halfway down the hill in the Land Rover before he remembered that yet again, he hadn't locked up the lodge.

He often didn't. It was an old habit from those less worrisome times. Well, he didn't plan to be out for long. He drove down to the lakeshore and along until he reached a wide strip of fine shale that made a kind of freshwater beach. By day this was probably the most popular picnic spot in the valley.

There he parked, killed the Rover's lights, and stepped out with the night glasses in his hand.

Thanks to the lowered water level, the shale beach was five or six times its usual width. Don raised the night glasses and looked out across the water; darkness that was impenetrable to the eye now sprang out in vivid green detail. Sky, shore and water were all clearly distinguishable. He hunted around at maximum magnification and eventually found it; the uncovered island on which the Blackwood Oak had once stood, no more than three or four feet of outcrop with a flattened top that had to be the stump.

Something obscured his vision for a moment. He reacted by lowering the glasses and looking, but of course that was of no help at all. So he decreased the magnification and looked through the glasses again.

Now the view was too wide and he couldn't see the island, or much of anything else; he was picking up all kinds of movement but most of that was reflections from the water.

He lowered the glasses, and waited for his eyes to adjust. Somewhere up above the cloud parted and let a little moonlight through, which helped.

As he became more attuned to the darkness, he began to make out a figure that was standing between him and the water.

He looked again with the night vision glasses, and saw nothing there. Which set his eyesight back and meant that he'd have to wait for it to adjust all over again. This time he switched off the power to the binoculars, in case he forgot himself a second time.

There was definitely a figure standing there. A figure that electronic glasses did not see.

"Miriam," he said in a low voice.

No more than a dim shape against the lake, the figure moved closer. As it moved, it made no sound. It stopped some distance from him, and waited.

"It's not for me," he said. "It's the kids. I think they're going to need some help."

The next morning, Edward was up and moving around before anyone else. Damien was aware of him tiptoeing past the sofa to get to the tiny house's kitchen. Crunched up on the sofa with pillows and a spare duvet, wondering if his sleeping posture was going to give him a case of DVT, Damien shifted his position a little to relieve the leg cramps but kept his head down and his eyes shut. At least until he began to smell real coffee, followed shortly afterward by the smell of frying bacon.

Ariane came down about fifteen minutes later, lured by the same airborne incentive and looking ready for the day. Edward had fixed her up with his spare room, after bringing the Ryans home to the two-bedroomed Victorian terraced house that he'd once shared with a wife named Enid and now shared with a cat called Skipper. The furniture and the décor were all Enid's taste. The widescreen TV and the multimedia PC were Edward's more recent additions.

"I always like to start the day with a cooked breakfast," Edward said.

"So do I," Damien said. "But it's very rare that I ever get one."

His phone rang.

"It's dad," he said, and everyone fell quiet as he answered the call.

Damien listened for a long time. Then he said, "Ted? Can you check your email?" and then went on listening as his father continued to speak. He could see Ariane watching him, trying to read something out of his changing expression.

When Don finished the call, Damien closed up his phone and looked at Ariane and said, "Apparently it's all in the painting."

"What painting?" Ariane said.

"I've got it right here," Edward called from the next room.

They went through. Edward was seated at the workstation in the corner. Don had mailed them a link. On Edward's screen was a picture that Damien thought he recognised, and which Ariane immediately identified.

"It's the Atkinson Grimshaw painting," she said. "It was on one of the pages from the book."

And so it was. On the torn page, it had been in black and white. Here it was in colour, and accompanied by different text.

Damien said, "Can you make it bigger?"

Edward clicked, and the thumbnail image was replaced by one that more than filled the screen.

John Atkinson Grimshaw. A Yorkshireman, and a self-taught late Victorian painter of townscapes and landscapes and middle-class women in gardens. Not the most prominent of the fairy painters, but one whose choice of subjects reflected the market of his day.

This one was called *The Fairy Bride's Abduction* and showed a canvas crowded with figures, most of them involved in the business of the title. An ugly horde of twisted creatures were carrying off a fairy—depicted as a barely-grown woman with dragonfly wings, her nubile form clad in little more than a veil—while others held back a struggling creature who was attempting to interfere. Over it all stood a great dark figure, one arm outflung in a pointing gesture, clearly in charge of the atrocity.

As a picture, it was hard to read. There was so much going on that the eye kept getting drawn off into some detail… this elf pulling the hat off another, that hobgoblin falling back into the brambles, something unnameable riding piggyback on the shoulders of something indescribable. In the background were some buildings, and in the few uncrowded inches of canvas beyond the buildings were a tiny patch of landscape and a moonlit sky.

"You could get a headache just looking at this," Damien said. "I wonder what dad expects us to make of it?"

"Look at that figure, there," Ariane said. "Don't you recognise him?"

She had Edward reposition the image on the screen so that the struggling male figure was central. Two evil creatures were holding his arms and another had him about the waist. Every line of his being suggested that he was straining to reach the abducted sylph; every line of hers indicated her inability to resist the forces that were carrying her off.

The struggling figure was green; his face a mask of fury, his eyes a raging gold.

"That's Roscoe," Damien said blankly.

And so it was. Sylvanus Roscoe, in his unaltered, natural, non-human form.

"You realise what this means," Ariane said. "If that's a recognisable likeness, then it must have been drawn from life. What's the date on it?"

Edward read it out.

"Just before the valley was flooded," Ariane said excitedly. "Look at those buildings in the background! Don't you recognise them? Dad's dug the albums out and showed them to us often enough!"

Damien probably wouldn't have spotted it without prompting. But now that he looked—yes, she was right. They very much resembled the wooden cabins in which the Ryan clan had been rehoused after the construction of the dam. Moonlight shone through the roof of one of them. In the painting, the buildings were unfinished.

Ariane said, "The artist saw Roscoe. He obviously went to the valley around the time when the cabins were built. What if the rest of it's true as well?"

"What? The whole kidnapping thing?"

"A historical record."

Damien was beginning to feel a little overwhelmed.

Edward said, "It would explain what's been driving him."

They looked at the older man. His was gazing at the screen. He moved the mouse, repositioning the image so that Sylvanus Roscoe and the Fairy Bride were both in frame. Even though most would assume the scene to be fanciful, the distress of the two separated creatures was evident and real.

"He's been in the dark all this time," Edward said. "So for him, this is like yesterday. Someone took her from him and he's set out to find her. He thinks he's on a rescue mission. This painting is the only clue that he has."

ᗯᚽᗢ

It was neither the most accomplished nor the most famous picture in the city gallery, but it was one of the most popular. When a new-broom curator had taken the decision to retire it to the basement stacks because she considered it second-rate art, the resulting local outcry ensured that the picture stayed in its place and the new curator didn't.

It was an enormous canvas. Postcards and textbook reproductions couldn't do it justice. It occupied almost the entire end wall of one wing of the building. There was a rope barrier to discourage touchers, and a low padded bench in the middle of the room for the weak and weary. In the soft light from a glass roof above, the woodland tableau was there to be observed from ten until six every day.

As Damien and Ariane entered the wing, they could see a solitary figure on the bench before the painting. It was mid-morning. They'd encountered no more than three or four people on their way through the gallery, and two of those had been members of staff.

Roscoe was a small figure before the enormous canvas. Much smaller than his painted self. He was still in the stolen overcoat, with the knitted hat pulled down to cover the pointed tips of his ears. He didn't move or react as Damien and Ariane approached the bench and sat, one to either side of him.

Ariane said, "Painted over a hundred years ago."

"From life," Roscoe said.

Damien said, "You know what we're here for."

Roscoe took in a deep breath, and finally looked down from the picture. His features had softened a little in the hours since they'd chased him.

"Whenever you're ready," he said.

"As simple as that?"

Without looking up, Roscoe nodded.

Ariane said, "Don't you want to tell someone the story?"

Outside the city gallery, there stood a city park. They walked out of the great doors, down stone steps flanked by white stone urns, and found a place to sit by a shallow pool with a fountain that looked as if it was never turned on.

Roscoe looked at the dead leaves floating and said, "We can only be as we are. My nature is to fly at any challenge that I face. I thought that if I seized my opportunity and moved with speed, I would surely prevail. Now I can see that it was a hopeless task and that whatever effort I might have made, it would have been in vain. Sometimes there are things that are lost, that we cannot hope to regain. Accepting that is hard."

He looked down. Damien was finding this strange. Here they were in a slightly run-down park in the middle of a city; not neglected, but frazzled at the edges as public spaces always are. Behind them was the public building that housed all the city's art treasures, such as they were. Roscoe looked like a scruffy modern boy. But he spoke like the ancient prince that he was. Ariane seemed unfazed by the oddity of it; but she'd travelled so much farther, and seen so much more.

Roscoe went on, "I'll tell you the tale. And when it's ended, you can take me back. I slept in the darkness while the world moved on. Now that I know what I know, I will welcome the chance to return.

"I lived in the valley, in the Blackwood Oak. Time meant nothing to us there. To leave is to become mortal, and to become mortal is to die.

"I was counted a prince among my kind. One of the duties of a prince is to marry, and to choose his bride with care. I was lucky. For me, love and duty were as one. I wooed a Dryad, from the willow circle on the hill. Her name was Elaby.

"On the night of our wedding, there was a remarkable appearance. A group of the most distant guests brought in a soul that they had found and at first taken for dead by the roadside. She had been making her way to the valley. Elaby recognised her as Eithna, one of her sisters, disappeared and long thought lost.

"We halted the celebrations and gathered to hear her story. Some had believed her captured, and this turned out to be the case. She told of being tricked and then trapped in a sack."

Here he looked pointedly at Damien, who had the decency to shrug and look embarrassed.

"Who trapped her?" Ariane said.

"She spoke of being taken to a camp in a meadow. She said there was a caravan, and there were horses. A ring of fire encircled the camp. Beyond the ring of fire there were presences that she could not see.

"She was confined in iron and interrogated. Her captor was a tall man. A dark man."

Damien thought of the shadowy figure in the painting, standing over all and giving orders to the horde.

"Eithna was defiant. She told him that she belonged to one of the oldest and the strongest groups of folk in the land. She believed that we would soon be arriving to rescue her. We are a gentle people. But in force we can be formidable.

"Her defiance was in vain. No one came for her because at that moment, none of us knew that she was gone. And by the time that she was missed and we started to search, the dark man and his accomplices had hitched up their horses and doused all the fires and the long journey south had begun.

"All along the way, she protested. And little did she realise it at the time... but the more she threatened him and boasted of our community, the more interested the dark man became.

"Eventually they reached their destination. She said they called it the Sunshine Farm. It was a place of horror.

"It was a place where our kind were confined and tortured and studied to find out what makes us as we are. The dark man exchanged his coat for a white one and Eithna found herself in the company of others like herself, who'd been captured in other parts of the land. All were subject to the same treatment. All were the objects of his research.

"Some were in a poor state. It was whispered that when their secrets were all known and their use was finally exhausted, they would be classified and then held in a preserved state that was like a living death.

"Eithna glimpsed such horrors in her time at the Sunshine Farm. Nature spirits in jars with their light dulled to a faint, eternal glow. Lesser forms dead and pinned to boards in case after case, as men do with butterflies.

"She'd abandoned her hopes of rescue, but resolved to escape before her strength waned. At every session she cursed her tormentor, and spat out threats about the anger of her people.

"Then, one day, she was taken from her storeroom to the dark man's laboratory, and there she was left alone. The dark man did not come, and the room was not secured. At first she could not believe her good fortune.

"She seized her opportunity and escaped from the Sunshine Farm. She was far from the ancient woodland and had seen nothing of the journey down, and her instincts were weakened. But in crossing the country she came upon the great iron way, and followed it North; and in time the countryside softened and became ever more familiar. As she drew closer to home, she could feel some of her strength returning. The damage that she had suffered was great.

"Her best chance of recovery was to be returned to the willow circle, to which she belonged. But it was not to be.

"As Eithna reached the part of her story that concerned her homecoming, those of us listening became aware of a dark and growing presence surrounding the wood. At first it had gone unnoticed, so caught up were we in the horrors of her tale.

"I was the first to realise that her escape had been no accident. We are an elusive people and until now her captor had been an opportunist collector, making forays into the countryside and gathering his specimens in ones and twos.

"He was not intimidated by her threats of our numbers, but intrigued by them. He had contrived her escape in order to follow her to us, and he had not come alone. We were about to discover the true and terrible nature of his accomplices.

"A baying went up all around. It was designed to cause panic and dismay, and it had its effect.

"Within moments, we were being overrun. We had no time to prepare ourselves or to flee. It was here that we learned how Eithna's captor, the owner of the Sunshine Farm, held command over the Sluagh, the Host of the Unforgiven Dead."

As the boy spoke the name, Damien flinched. He couldn't help it. The Sluagh were powerful, bitter, pitiless, and without any fear. The unforgiven dead were creatures with nothing to lose.

"We had no opportunity to resist, and no chance of escape," Roscoe said. "We were corralled into the willow circle and held there by the Sluagh, while men and women with lanterns dispersed themselves through the woods all around us. Wherever we looked, we saw a waiting light. It was an organised and well-planned attack.

"For a few moments, nothing happened. Then the circle opened and into it walked the dark man. Eithna had said little to describe him, but I knew him on sight.

"He moved slowly, taking his time. He carried a silver-tipped cane and as he passed among us, he used it to point; indicating some of us, passing others over.

"When he came to the spot where I was holding onto Elaby, my fairy bride, he stopped. We'd been forced to sit on the ground and one of the Sluagh was keeping a close watch over us, daring me to move.

"The dark man raised his cane and pointed to Elaby. He did not point at me. Then he moved on.

"The Sluagh who'd been watching me obviously knew that I'd give trouble, and now seized me around the waist. Two more caught my arms as Elaby was taken away. I realised later that the dark man had a special fascination for those of our kind who most resembled human women. .

"Much as I fought, and much as she struggled to hold on, Elaby and I were parted.

"I was overpowered, and she was borne away. Normally we make no sound. But I could hear her screams, and the screams of the others, from all the way down the valley.

"In the hours and the days that followed, I grew to understand the magnitude and the organisation of the dark man's design. This was no one-off raid. It was a campaign, planned for the long term and to serve as a model for others. He'd recruited the Sluagh for the purpose, and re-hearsed his forces in advance. He had even brought along an artist to record the event for the generations yet to come.

"The Sluagh had been left behind, posted in an impenetrable cordon. The dark man's aim was to contain our woodland as an exclusive preserve, to be quarried for new material whenever his researches required it.

"Not a day passed without me making some effort to follow and find Elaby. Others tried to leave the valley and were even less lucky than I. The Sluagh would terrify, damage, and ultimately destroy any being who tried to pass through their lines, dragging the horrifying remains of their vic-tims to the heart of the woods where they'd be left on display as a warning to the rest of us.

"Every now and again the dark man would return and make a new selection, his forces beating the woodland folk out of our refuges and taking certain ones away. But nothing ever equalled that first terrible purge.

"I hatched a plan. One time I managed to follow the raiding party with their captives, and to hang onto the underside of the dark man's carriage. Gone were the horses, and here instead was machinery; the sud-den noise of it startled me and I was thrown into the road, where I was discovered. The Sluagh gave me a mauling and threw me back into the woodland, where the others found me after a while.

"I was close to death. They placed me on a litter and carried me to the Blackwood Oak, so that I might return to it and be healed.

"The healing process took so long that by the time I was well enough to stir, the oak had been cut back and what remained was under water. I could not move. My home had become my prison.

"Time meant nothing. It was as if I dreamed. But the moment when I sensed that the waters had fallen and the oak was exposed, I leapt from my place.

"There was the first of my shocks. Instead of the valley that I knew, I found a lake. I dared not sink. I ran across its surface as if it were a piece of glass, until I reached the land.

"More uncertainty awaited me there. So much had changed. I called the names of those I knew, and none replied. I made my way up to the willow circle, but the circle was gone. In its place stood a great building of timber and glass."

"The lodge," Ariane said.

"I entered the building. I searched for some clue to what had been before. I found books."

"Are you telling me you can read?" Damien said.

"The pictures told me all that I needed to know. These were the books written by the dark man and his kind. These were the results of their studies. I found myself in there. I found a reference to the raid.

"I continued to believe that there was hope. I set out and followed the iron road south, using it to guide me toward the Sunshine Farm as Eithna had to find her way back to the valley.

"But the Sunshine Farm is gone. Eithna is gone. Elaby is gone. All have gone and only that painting and I remain. If you wish to be kind, then leave me out here. Then I can grow mortal. Then I can die."

"We can't do that," Damien said. "The land's been stripped of too much as it is."

"You're part of the valley," Ariane said. "It needs you. I'm sorry."

"Then put me back," Roscoe said. "The waters will rise and I'll sleep again, and perhaps this pain will stop."

He walked with them to the pickup, which Damien had left on a meter in a square a couple of streets away. Their time was expired but they'd missed getting a ticket. Roscoe climbed into the narrow seat in the back of the cab, and they set off for home.

Little was said on the journey. Roscoe lay across the back seat, curled up, eyes open, seeing nothing. When they stopped for diesel, Ariane took Damien's phone and walked away from the fuel court to call their father.

Damien was waiting with the engine running when she got back to the pickup. She reported that Don had heard the story through to the end and then told her to call again when they were closer to home.

"Time's getting short," she said. "He says they've finished the dam repairs and closed the sluices. The lake's already rising. There's no saying how long before the Blackwood Oak goes back under."

Roscoe had turned around, his back toward them. He stayed that way for the rest of the journey.

It was getting dark when they arrived. Ariane had made the second call as they'd left the motorway network, and they were met by Don waiting on the lakeshore with a boat. It was a small dinghy with an outboard. It belonged to the Ranger Service and was usually kept in a padlocked boat house.

Roscoe climbed in without a word. He sat alone at the front of the boat on the journey across the water, looking out toward his island in the fading light and evening mist. Damien felt a pang of sadness for him; he glanced at Ariane and was about to say as much, but saw that she was subdued to a point close to tears. Seeing the extent of her upset, he found that his own had suddenly become more intense. It seemed better not to risk speaking at all.

When they reached the oak, the islet was all but gone and the waves were beginning to wash across the sawn-off surface of the stump. It made an uneven platform, with the jagged planes and lines of the old saw-cuts still evident. The timber had been blackened by its long immersion, but hadn't rotted.

Damien wondered how his father had managed to navigate out to it in the gloom. It was at no more than fifteen feet across, although it probably widened out more under the water.

There was nowhere to tie up. Don had to keep them close with short bursts from the outboard motor every time the wind and the waves tried to carry them away.

He called forward, "Do you know what to do?"

Sylvanus Roscoe seemed not to hear him, but it was of no matter. He appeared to understand what was required. He rose in the boat and stepped up onto the side, his weight barely tipping it as he balanced with ease on the narrow rail. He was an incongruous figure, still wearing the wool cap and stolen overcoat and with his skinny legs rattling loose in the Wellington boots from the DIY store. He was looking down at the remnant of the once-great oak; then without warning he seemed to let himself fall toward it, toppling smoothly forward with his arms by his sides.

In a second it was over. Roscoe was gone and the coat and boots were floating.

Damien hauled in the sodden coat, Ariane grabbed one of the boots, and Don gave a few blips on the outboard to chase the other as it drifted away. The hat had already sunk and there was no sign of it at all.

"Well, that's that," Don said.

He engaged the outboard, took them around the Blackwood Oak in a broad circle, and headed back toward the shore.

For Ariane it was the second homecoming in just a few days, but this one was much more subdued than the last. This despite the fact that, as retrieval operations went, it had been one of their most difficult and successful ever.

All the same, there was no sense of celebration. Ariane curled up in a seat in a corner and leafed through some of the books in her father's library, while Damien put on a fleece and went out onto the deck.

When Don had finished composing a lengthy post to his forum, he came out to join him.

"All sent?" said Damien.

"Just the bones of it," said Don.

They sat on the deck furniture in silence for a while, looking out into the evening.

Then Damien said, "Why didn't we stop him?"

His father considered for a moment. Then he said, "I'm not sure I know what you mean."

"This dark man. Whatever his name was."

"Sir Norman Slingsby," Don said.

Damien looked at him in surprise.

"Professor Slingsby," Don said, "later Lord Slingsby. Author of *The Romance and Superstitions of the English Counties*. The book that Ariane's looking through right now."

"Look," Damien said. "I know I'm the stupid one in the family. But we've looked after this valley for ten generations. How could he come and go, and do all those things he did, without our people knowing or doing anything about it?"

"Because we were helping him," Don said quietly, looking out into the evening air and not at Damien.

"*What?*" Damien said. "What do you mean?"

"We were part of it. We, us, the family. He couldn't have managed any of it without the family's co-operation. Who do you think was carrying the lanterns?"

"But why would we—they—why would they do that?"

"Different days," Don said. "Different times. I wasn't there, and I'm not going to speak for anyone else. But everything we know today, it comes from what we learned back then. I'm not saying it wasn't cruel. I'm not saying it wasn't wrong. I'm just saying that's how it is."

"That makes me feel like crap," Damien said.

"Try not to think about it too much," Don said. "I don't."

And he went back inside.

The City Art Gallery and Museum, founded in part with the Slingsby Bequest, occupies a building that had once been a mid-sized country house with an extensive estate. Back then, it had stood outside the town by some way. But the town had grown, and the estate had been sold off one field at a time, until eventually a new city surrounded it and only a park remained.

In its heyday the estate was self-sufficient, with a large kitchen garden and a dairy herd. The dairy buildings were painted an ochrous yellow, inspiring local children to call it The Sunshine Farm. With some older people the name is in use to this day, even though the outbuildings in question are long gone.

By the time the house and land were gifted to the city, the Slingsbys had more or less abandoned it. It was a damp and draughty place then; grimy classical in style, but architecturally undistinguished. The upstairs rooms were taken over as offices for various departments of the council, and the reception rooms became exhibition space.

Aside from the occasional wet-weekender or school party, the permanent exhibition draws about as much attention as any other regional rag-tag cultural assortment of its kind.

No one has been in the basement for years. No member of the public, anyway. The basement is where they store all the inherited bric-a-brac of the museum; exhibits of little interest or academic value, that wouldn't look out of place in job lots at a country auction.

The only visitors ever to unlock the unmarked door and descend the stairway are maintenance people, following some pipe for leaks or looking for a junction box. On those rare occasions, doors are opened and lights are switched on in one room or another, throwing a few beams into areas that otherwise know only darkness.

Typical of the content of those rooms is the collection that can be found stored at the back of one of them. Right up against a wall, and inaccessible behind two broken pennyfarthings and an incomplete human skeleton. There are boxes of files and ledgers, case after case of specimen boards, and jars of a preserving fluid long grown too murky to see through.

The Slingsby Bequest. Forgotten, ignored... and left far behind by the science that it was created to serve.

Time moves on, fashions change. Yesterday's hot topic is today's academic dead end. So the collection stands in darkness, and silently gathers dust.

Mice shred the records to line their nests. Spiders throw webs between the boxes, like fine ships' rigging.

And every now and again, should a door open and some stray light briefly fall across one or another of the jars, something within it will stir. ❧

# Tailpiece: Nine Horrors and a Dream

§ FAIRYTALES apart, Joseph Payne Brennan's *Nine Horrors and a Dream* was the first honest-to-God horror book that I ever got my hands onto. I was about nine years old, certainly not much more. It scared me stiff, gave me nightmares that actually shaded into major-league hallucinations, probably warped me for life, and certainly set me on target for what would eventually become a career. I loved it, and still do. How much more can you ask of a book?

First let me tell you how I came to get hold of it. The collection had originally been published in an Arkham House edition with a number of the stories already having a *Weird Tales* pedigree, but the version that reached me was a luridly-covered Ballantine reprint... and when I say lurid I mean bright pinks, lime greens and purples, with the kind of lettering that they used in the opening credits of *The Invaders* on TV. A huge bulbous spider straddled the artwork from above, while down at the bottom of the cover a tiny naked woman stood amongst Easter Island statues watching the sun rise except that it wasn't the sun, but an immense and inhuman head with wide-staring eyes. Crude, but effective, as the villains used to say of their buzz-saws in the chapterplays.

I'm pretty sure it belonged to my uncle. He was an ex-Teddy Boy, ex-army conscript, ex-railway worker, then an employee on the Manchester docks. US paperback imports rarely made it into the shops in those days but a number of titles would make it over as ballast with other cargoes, as used to happen with comic books. Whether or not the Brennan was one of these, it's hard to be sure. It's only when I look back from here that I can appreciate how my uncle filled in some much-needed gaps in my early literary education; when they were making us read *Black Beauty* at school, he was the one who was telling me how the Frankenstein monster was put together. He provided my introduction to Edgar Rice Burroughs with a description of how the Leopard Men tenderized human flesh for consumption by breaking the limbs of their captives with clubs and then tethering them submerged up to their chins in a fast-flowing river. He told me who Doc Savage was.

And he lent me *Nine Horrors and a Dream*.

Ten stories don't exactly make for a doorstopper of a book. I read it quickly and in a state of awe. The one that I think impressed me most was *The Calamander Chest*.

It had many of the elements that I've come to think of as characteristic of the genre post-Lovecraft and pre-1970s, when tales of solitary young men and locked-up secrets gave way to a much broader sense of involvement that was more akin to soap opera. Each of the tales (with the possible exception of *Slime*, which at 32 pages was a more ambitious novella) was a similarly lean narrative built around a weird hook and calculated to leave the reader with that oddly satisfying sense of having taken a peek into forbidden territory from a place of safety.

Did I mention that I was staying the night at my grandmother's house when the book came into my hands? I'd better, because it has some bearing on what was to follow. My grandmother had a modest little place in a well-kept Salford backstreet (bulldozed, now, like everything of value in that city). It wasn't a spooky house at all, by any rational standard… but to a child of my age, the gulf of time and taste was enough to make me feel ill-at-ease and a stranger in the home of any elderly relative. I read the last couple of stories in an unfamiliar bed with flannel sheets and heavy blankets—my own blanket at home had pictures of parachutes and jeeps on it—and when I finally switched off the bedside lamp, there was still a weak illumination in the room from a streetlight just outside the window.

I could see the big, dark shapes of the furniture and, lit from the window like a little stage, I could see the top of the dressing-table.

On this dressing-table stood—or rather, knelt—two figurines. They were carved out of smooth black stone and they represented an African man and woman, both unclothed but tastefully featureless. Black naked-ness somehow seemed to be considered apart from the taboos of the age, which would explain why *National Geographic* was never kept under the counter with all the skin magazines. I must have been lying there for about half an hour before anything happened.

So, what *did* happen?

What happened was that the male figurine got to its feet, and walked to the edge of the dressing-table and looked down. He seemed to move at double speed, with a flicker like an overcranked film. As he turned away from the edge, the female was standing up with the obvious intention of repeating the action. I tried to close my eyes and look away, but I couldn't. As the woman came forward the male was pacing back and forth be-hind her, as if trying to get the measure of this surface on which he found himself trapped. Neither of them made any sound. Every now and again they would dash back to their carved plinths for a few moments of rest and recharge.

I don't remember anything that ever scared me more. Not then, not since. I know exactly what was happening, of course. My body was on the brink of sleep and my mind was still racing, and the barriers be-tween imagination and perception had dropped. I don't know how long I lay there, watching this bizarre show that my imagination was conjuring out of the available materials, but what I do know is that I believed in it without question.

I still do, in a way. You can add all of the later rationalizations that you want, but when you strip those away you're left with one simple certainty: you know what you saw.

I returned the book. Didn't see it again for twenty five years, when I moved some paperbacks while browsing a convention bookstall and found myself face-to-face with that same Ballantine edition, graced with what I could now recognize as a Richard Powers cover. There had been other landmark books for me in the intervening time—Wells, Bierce, Levin, Farris, King, Straub—but this had been the first.

I hesitated—there are few things more elusive and disappointing than past magic—and then I bought it. How could I do anything else? I felt as if I was welcoming it home.

The stories held up. Styles and fashions have changed, but for me the line back in time stays unbroken. There's only one difficulty that I find myself unable to resolve.

I still can't work out which nine stories are the horrors, and which one the dream... &